THE GIRL AT THE LION D'OR

Sebastian Faulks worked as a journalist for 14 years before taking up writing books full time in 1991. He is the author of *A Trick of Light*, *The Girl at the Lion D'Or*, *A Fool's Alphabet* and the celebrated *Birdsong*. He lives with his wife and their two children in London.

BY SEBASTIAN FAULKS

A Trick Of Light
The Girl At The Lion D'Or
A Fool's Alphabet
Birdsong

'*The Girl At The Lion D'Or*'s opening sequence in a small French railway station is so minutely, meticulously and vividly described it is as if the place were being viewed through a slowly tracking camera. This beginning points to the whole. It is a book which reads like French and at times his characters even speak as if they had been translated – not quite perfectly – from the French. The novel is not only a topographical achievement, refracting life through the eye of a middle-aged, middle-class Frenchman caught in adultery's torments. It has a greater concern – with Anne and the way that the end of her love affair is only one more devastation in a life already laid to waste. Abandonment, Faulks says persuasively in the novel, using a psychiatrist's phrase, is the one true originator and motor of grief. And Anne, who has been greatly abandoned in life, suffers one more abandonment. . . . Faulks suggests that while there are limits to what a country can collectively endure in terms of suffering, 'there is no limit to the endurance of individuals. And it never ceases to amaze me.' And at the end of this enthralling novel you gather the sense that Anne will indeed come through. A form of transcendence is exhilaratingly celebrated.'

Guardian

'In mid-Thirties France, seeking asylum from her past, a penniless orphan turns up as a waitress at a tatty hotel by the sea. Befriended by the local landowner, the girl entrusts him with the highly charged scandal that in the Great War left her parentless. Her longing to be loved seduces him into tackling his own problems – trauma at Verdun, decrepit estate, childless wife – with a courage matching hers. They redeem each other's past. But has their love a future? To convey their fraught affair in an era stiff with threat, Faulks bravely deploys not only the charms of romantic fiction, but also a crisper response to politics, landscape – and character. His icy concierge, bootboy with acne and lout of a chef are jewels. With his second novel Faulks has deepened into a soft-hearted analyst of both the differences between people and their raw humanity. This is a sentimental novel of rare intelligence and passion.'

Mail on Sunday

'*The Girl At The Lion D'Or* is not only a rare achievement, a supremely accomplished piece of work, but, it seems to me, a glorious justification of the traditional novel. It reminds one that novelists don't have to try to be clever. Instead, they have to look at life with respect and imagination, draw from it, and arrange their material in aesthetically satisfying shape. Here in this marvellous evocation of a particular society at a particular time, Sebastian Faulks has done just that. He has also reaffirmed the importance of character in the novel; his Anne and Hartmann are as real, as moving and convincing as Anna Karenina and Vronsky or Colette's Chéri and Léa. It is a novel to cherish and delight in.'
Scotsman

'Sebastian Faulks loves the cinema of Renoir and Carne and Bresson. *The Girl At The Lion D'Or* is a journey through time to pre-war France, the diary of a waitress at a provincial hotel. Her love affair with a married Jewish lawyer and political arranger allows the author to treat major themes of conscience and guilt, of anti-Semitism and the collapse of national morale . . . She believes what her guardian has told her, that courage is all – and she is enduring. She also comes to believe what her lover believes, that evil is continual rejection through death or desertion. This moving and profound novel is perfectly constructed, and admirable in its configurations of place and period.'
The Times

Sebastian Faulks

THE GIRL AT THE LION D'OR

VINTAGE

Published by Vintage 1990

13 15 16 14

© Sebastian Faulks 1989

The right of Sebastian Faulks to be identified as the author of this work
has been asserted by him in accordance with the Copyright, Designs
and Patents Act, 1988

First published in Great Britain by
Hutchinson 1989

Vintage
Random House, 20 Vauxhall Bridge Road,
London SW1V 2SA

Random House Australia (Pty) Limited
20 Alfred Street, Milsons Point, Sydney,
New South Wales 2061, Australia

Random House New Zealand Limited
18 Poland Road, Glenfield
Auckland 10, New Zealand

Random House South Africa (Pty) Limited
PO Box 337, Bergvlei, South Africa

Random House UK Limited Reg. No. 954009

A CIP catalogue record for this book
is available from the British Library

ISBN 0 09 977490 9

Papers used by Random House UK Limited
are natural, recyclable products made from wood grown in
sustainable forests. The manufacturing processes conform to
the environmental regulations of the country of origin

Printed and bound in Great Britain by
Cox & Wyman Ltd, Reading, Berkshire

FOR MY PARENTS

The French newspapers in the 1930s offered a mixture of rumour, spite and inaccuracy. There was usually plenty of scope for all three. One bright November morning a national daily on the streets of Paris offered three items on its front page. The first brought the latest news of the investigation into the death of a government minister, Roger Salengro, whose body had been discovered by his maid in his apartment in Lille. The second concerned some final ramifications of the Stavisky affair – a matter of bribery and high finance in which only the suspicious demise of the protagonist himself, two years earlier, had prevented the involvement of an even greater number of powerful people.

The third story rated no more than a paragraph at the bottom of the page. A female intruder had been surprised in the garden of the Prime Minister's official residence. A negligent security guard was being questioned, but the police were not hopeful of finding her.

'The girl, believed to be from Paris, is said by police to be approximately 20 years old. The Prime Minister, M. Léon Blum, was last night unavailable for comment.'

These were the formulations of a tired journalist on a wet Friday night, anxious to finish and go home. In an editorial comment, held over for three days owing to pressure on the space, the newspaper asked questions about security at the Prime Minister's house. Two or three readers wrote letters expressing their surprise at the incident.

The security guard was dismissed; nothing was ever heard of the girl again, and there the matter rested. Compared to the deaths of public men like Stavisky and Salengro, the fate of an unknown girl was not important. It had no significance.

PART ONE

I

IN THOSE DAYS the station in Janvilliers had an arched glass roof over the southbound platform as if in imitation of the big domes of St Lazare. When it rained, the impact of the water set up a nervy rattle as the glass echoed and shook against the fancy restraint of its iron framework. There was a more modest rumble emitted by the covered footbridge, while from the gutters there came an awful martyred gurgling as they sought out broken panes and unmended masonry down which to spit the water that was choking them. The thin sound of the locomotive's wheeze as it braced itself for its final three stops up the coast was thus barely audible to the two people who alighted from the train that damp but not untypical Monday night.

One was the driver, who was following the custom of years by climbing down from his cab, hat pulled over his ears, and racing to the side-door of the station buffet where his glass of brandy would be waiting for him. There was no time for conversation – just a quick gulp and he was gone, as usual, scuttling back up the platform, hoisting himself aboard with a word to the fireman and a reinvigorated haul on the levers as the engine hissed and the train set off to arrive, as usual, a minute and a half late at its next stop.

The other was a slight, dark-haired girl with two heavy suitcases, frowning into the rain and trying not to feel frightened. She stood in the doorway of the ticket hall, hoping someone would have been sent to fetch her. 'Be brave, little Anne, be brave,' old Louvet, her guardian, would have said to her if he had been sober, or there, or – for all Anne knew – alive. After a time she did see the long bending approach of headlights, but the car circled the fountains in the middle of the square and disappeared in a spray of water.

Louvet, who thought himself a philosopher, had a theory

11

that all unhappiness was a version of the same feeling. As Anne felt a tremor of abandonment, gazing over the rainy square, she pictured him explaining to her: 'When the good Lord made this world from the infinite number of possibilities open to him and selected – from another limitless pool – the kind of misery that his creatures should be subject to, he selected only one model. The moment of bereavement. Death, desertion, betrayal – all the same thing. The child sent from its parents, the widow, the lover abandoned – they all feel the same emotion which, in its most extreme form, finds expression in a cry.' Practice had given an almost religious eloquence to Louvet's blasphemous conclusion: 'One cannot, my dear Anne, escape the conviction that the good Lord was, if not unimaginative, then at least rather simple.'

Anne, who was not a philosopher, saw a dripping form, male by the look of it and wrapped in a cape, approach her from the darkness. His voice was rough and grudging. 'Are you the waitress? For the Hotel du Lion d'Or?' His face now appeared in what light spilled over from the yellow lamp in the ticket hall. He was a youth of about nineteen with thick black eyebrows and dark curls stuck against his forehead under a leather cap. He had an extinguished cigarette between his teeth and his cheeks were traumatised by spots.

'Yes, that's right. Who are you?'

'I work there. My name's Roland. I've got the van. The boss said to come and pick you up. It's over here.'

He led the way, shambling in a mixture of embarrassment and an attempt to keep dry by wrapping his cape around him, which caused his knees to come too close together. Anne followed, struggling to keep up under the handicap of the heavy suitcases. Roland took her round the back of the station yard and gestured to a small van. He unlashed the canvas from the open back and gestured to her to throw in her suitcases. With considerable swearing and violence towards the tinny machine, he succeeded in making it creep, then jerk, then rush across the darkened square as he fought to locate the gears. Nervous at what might be waiting for her, Anne began to talk.

'What do you do at the hotel?'

'Stuff no one else wants to do. Boots. Washing up. Waiter on Sundays.'

'Do you come from here?'

'Yes. Never been away. Don't really want to. I went to Paris once.'

'Did you like it?'

'No.'

'Why not?'

'Don't know.'

'I've come from Paris.'

Roland made no reply but pulled back the window on his side of the van and pushed at the little windscreen-wiper. The rubber had almost worn away on the fragile stick, and its small motor functioned properly only in dry weather. Roland peered forward in an attempt to see through the misty swathe that the wiper cut intermittently across the glass. Anne couldn't think what to say to him; it seemed rude not to make conversation, but she didn't want to distract him.

'Do you often drive this van?'

'No. Well, yes, it's not that I'm not used to it, of course. I drive it just as much as anyone else. But petrol, you know.'

'Is the boss very mean then?'

'No, it's Madame. *He* couldn't care less.'

'Madame his wife?'

'No. Madame Bouin, the manageress. The Cow. She thinks we should only go to the market once a week and load up. You know, the big market down the road. The rest of the time we have to get the stuff from here. She sends us on foot.'

'If you only go to the big market once a week, doesn't the food get stale?'

Roland's nose emitted a snort of what might have been laughter. 'Makes no difference to Bruno. It all tastes like pig-shit, what he does with it.'

They negotiated the perimeter of another square, with the town hall, a curious building beneath a black slate roof in the grand eighteenth-century manner, in one corner. They drove on in silence down a street called the rue des Ecoles,

13

swung sharply left and found themselves face to face with the Hotel du Lion d'Or.

'I hadn't realised it was so near. I could have walked,' said Anne.

'Easily,' Roland agreed, getting out of the van. 'It was the old man, apparently. The Patron. Said I should come. I was playing cards.'

'I'm sorry, I – '

But Roland had gone, shuffling down a small alley by the hotel and vanishing into the night. Perhaps the other card players had waited for him, their hands concealed face down on some kitchen table. Perhaps they had cut the pack to see who should have the chore of picking up the wretched girl. Anne breathed in deeply.

The hotel was secluded from the square by a courtyard and a grey wall with a pair of rusting iron gates. Anne heaved her cases up to the front doors through whose glass panels she could make out a broad lobby, leading up to a staircase in the crook of which was the concierge's desk. She was aware of a woman behind it watching her as the suitcases dripped gently on to the parquet floor. She put them down on a threadbare mat in front of the counter.

'Mademoiselle?' It was the woman behind the desk who spoke, her voice not so much interrogative as menacing. Mme Bouin, Anne supposed. Her eyes had a calm quality despite the fact that one of them was monstrously enlarged by the thick lens of her spectacles. Her bearing managed to combine world-weariness with a feline state of readiness. Anne had a sense that anything she herself might say would have been anticipated by this woman, and nothing she could devise would please her. Presumably she behaved in the same way with the guests.

'I've come to take the waitress job.'

'Have you now? Then why have you come through the front door? I understood from Monsieur the Patron that you had had previous experience of hotel work. Is this what you were told is normal?'

The woman's voice remained as level as her eyes.

'I'm sorry, I – I didn't know the way in. The young man

who brought me, Roland, he – ' Anne checked herself, fearing to bring Mme Bouin's displeasure on to Roland, who had only been anxious to finish his game of cards.

'Where did he go?'

'I'm not sure. It was kind of him to come and pick me up on a night like this.'

Mme Bouin said nothing. Instead, she took a card from among a sheaf of papers in front of her. 'Details. Insurance and so on,' she said, handing the card across the desk.

'Do I have to do it now?'

Again the woman said nothing but swivelled on her chair and took the handset from a telephone switchboard which she cranked vigorously by hand. She spoke fast and indistinctly. Anne noticed a pile of needlework on the table beneath the board from which hung the numbered bedroom keys. She took the forms and a pen from the desk.

Surname: Louvet. She had grown used to this lie. The local lawyer had advised her as a child to abandon her family name when it was appearing daily in the newspapers. Forenames: Anne Marie Thérèse. These at least, and the date of her birth, she could give truthfully. Her handwriting was determined and precise. By the space for 'Previous Place of Employment' she put the name of a café near the Gare Montparnasse. Next of kin: she wrote down the name of Louvet, her assumed father, blurring with skilled certainty, though not without a qualm, the lines of her identity.

She handed back the completed card to Mme Bouin. 'When will I meet Monsieur the Patron?'

'Monsieur the Patron? How should I know? He has the hotel to run and his other duties to attend to. Monsieur the Patron is an extremely busy man. Here now, you had better follow me.' Mme Bouin stood up and circled the counter. She was much taller than Anne had expected. Her grey dress was inflated by a large bosom on which rested a gold chain and a handful of keys; she walked with an agile bustling movement, pulling a black cardigan about her shoulders as she led Anne to the foot of the stairs.

'You may use the front stairs tonight. At all other times you will use the back stairs.'

15

She went ahead up the thinning carpet. Anne watched the black-stockinged legs in their plain black shoes recede before her, briskly mounting the main sweep of the staircase and turning up another narrower set of stairs, then down a corridor lined with wardrobes and out on to a landing with a bare wooden floor.

Mme Bouin indicated a further, twisting and carpetless flight of stairs. 'Your room is at the top. There is a staff bathroom at the end of this passage on the left, though you must ask in advance if you wish to take a bath. Hot water is restricted and staff are not expected to bathe more than twice a week. You will find a jug and bowl in your room which are adequate for daily washing. You will be required in the kitchen at six-thirty tomorrow morning.'

Anne heard the rattle of keys on Mme Bouin's bosom as she returned the way they had come. Alone again, Anne looked around her.

The bedroom she had been allotted was under the eaves of the Hotel du Lion d'Or and its single window overlooked a back yard where she could see only filmy rain tumbling into the dark. There was an iron bedstead, a plain wooden chair, a small writing table and a chest of drawers with, as Mme Bouin had promised, a jug and bowl. A curtain in the corner concealed a hanging area for clothes which contained a black uniform. Although the room was plain and small, the rafters that slanted diagonally from above the window gave it a secure rather than imprisoning feeling; the agonised Christ above the bed could be moved somewhere he would be less visibly tormented; the bed linen, though rough and thinning, was clean; the bare floor, even if it was made only from boards, not parquet, had been scrubbed; and above the writing table hung a picture of a medieval knight.

Everything Anne owned was in her two suitcases. Her favourite possession, a second-hand gramophone with a cracked but sonorous horn attachment, she had had to sell, since it was too heavy to carry and she didn't think the Patron would approve of the sound of dance music coming from a servant's room. The records themselves she had been unable to part with – half a dozen heavy black plates in brown paper covers which she stowed in the bottom drawer of the chest.

Anne had left her door a few inches ajar so anyone on the landing below could see her light and might then be tempted to come and talk to her. Apart from Roland, Mme Bouin and the Patron, she had no idea who else the staff might comprise, but she hoped there would be at least someone who would be a friend for her – a girl of her own age, perhaps, with a big family in the town where she would be taken at weekends. When alone, Anne constructed fantasies of a kind in which the events were all conceivable but in which the crucial element of luck ran well for her. She didn't want to live in a grand manor with cavernous rooms and wooded lands, but in one of those simple houses behind gates where children could be seen playing on the sandy paths and a dog padded silently across the grass. If once she saw such a place, her fantasy was unstoppable and she would bare its inner rooms to her scanning eye, and reshape, recolour and repeople them until they contained what she wanted.

With her clothes unpacked, she arranged her half dozen books along the top of the writing table and propped her picture – a view of Paris roofs, layered and rainswept – on the chest of drawers. On the writing table, next to the books, she placed a photograph of her mother, taken fifteen years before. She wore a formal, posed expression which did not quite conceal a look of timid puzzlement about the eyes.

The rain had stopped when Anne closed the shutters on the small window, though from outside she could hear the water that had gathered as it dripped from the eaves and rang on the paved courtyard below. She pushed her door a little further open and listened. She could hear the sound of crockery, distantly, and of a door banging, but otherwise nothing. Most people, she guessed, would now be in bed, so it was too late to ask Mme Bouin or anyone else whether it was permissible for her to have a bath. She took her dressing-gown from behind the curtain and went quietly down the twisting staircase and along the corridor to the bathroom. She went in and locked the door, a simple action which caused an eruption of furtive activity backstairs.

*

17

Roland's scabrous face was boiling with a mixture of anguish and excitement as he bent down and took off his shoes. He tiptoed out of the back pantry and down the corridor. He passed a vast sink which was awash with cold water and the hotel's feebly crested crockery ('Leave it for the new girl in the morning,' Bruno, the chef, had said) and a wall full of unused culinary implements of the more sophisticated kind – peculiar fish-kettles and elaborate double-steamers – which Bruno regarded with robust contempt.

The room next to the servants' bathroom was a linen store, and it had been Roland's aim, planned over many months, to steal the key from Mme Bouin's bunch, copy it and return the original before she should notice. Since the keys seldom left her bosom this operation had not been without problems. The copied key didn't fit very well, but it did turn the lock into the little windowless box whose slatted shelves were heated by the long pipes that ran down the wall. Roland breathed heavily, smelling timber, mice and mothballs, as he lifted the linen from one of the shelves, noting how it had been stored, before he put it to one side.

High on the other side in the bathroom he had removed a tile, and twice a week on bath-nights he had worked away at the plaster, taking away the débris in his washbag at the end of the operation. Once the connection was made, he had concealed the hole in the linen closet with old bedspreads and curtains he knew were unlikely to be required. He ended up standing on one leg on the support of a lower shelf, craning diagonally upwards and drawing the rogue tile through to the linen room on a piece of string.

The reward for his hard work had been the sight of Sophie, Anne's predecessor, taking her twice-weekly bath. She was a sturdy girl from Lyon and not one who had previously attracted much attention from men, but Roland was loyal to her charms. Although the steam sometimes made it hard for him to see as clearly as he would have liked, he never missed an opportunity.

He had waited anxiously for his first view of Sophie's replacement and, when he had first glimpsed her at the station, he had not been disappointed. Now in his hurry he pulled the tile through with more than the usual noise. He waited for a moment, holding his breath, listening for a sound of protest from the bathroom. He heard nothing, and when he could wait no longer he jammed his bursting face against the opening.

The first thing he saw was a girlish undergarment of whose exact name or purpose he was unaware. It had lace trimmings and hung over a wooden towel horse, irritatingly close to his line of vision. Through the equally frustrating steam that rose from the bath tub he saw the girl's hair pulled up from her neck by a ribbon and saw where the stray wisps hung dark against the whiteness of her shoulders. There were perhaps some freckles there too, but Roland's eye scorned such detail.

She leant forward to turn on more water and he saw the fall of her breasts, a movement of surprising weight given the slightness of her frame. Then she raised her knee and he could make out the line that traced the distance from calf to mid-thigh; it ran like the outline of the fashion drawings he sometimes saw in newspapers – just a casual sweep that seemed to hint, by slenderness, at unforetold curves. He remembered the sturdy legs of Sophie which, until then, had seemed quite adequate.

Anne herself had little vanity about her body, though sometimes she felt a vague gratitude towards it for what it had taken her through. When she looked at her ankles and feet, so soft they seemed almost unused, or gazed in the mirror at her dark eyes, which were unlined and full of light, she wondered where she carried her experiences. Perhaps they lay stored in microscopic cells in her blood, or perhaps they lay waiting to ambush her in her mind. The body itself seemed full of health and latent energy; the physical contrasts of girl and woman, still not quite resolved, gave it charm.

When she stood up with her back to him, Roland almost made the mistake of closing his eyes in ecstasy. She let the water out of the bath and went to the wash basin where she cleared the steam from the mirror and leaned forward, her feet apart, to look closely at her face. She moved then with a youthful swiftness, her body visible only momentarily as she dried it out of the line of Roland's questing eye.

*

19

Anne climbed the stairs after her bath, glad that she had not been interrupted by Mme Bouin hammering on the door. She pulled out the bolster from under the sheets and up-ended it behind the hanging curtain. She lay down in bed and found the ache of carrying heavy baggage, the noise of the train and the fear of newness were all forgotten as she clutched herself tight beneath the eiderdown, sailing out into sleep.

Frequently she dreamed, strange unpleasant dreams relating to the events of her childhood. She never told people about them. She had read in a magazine that it was bad manners to tell others what you dreamed at night. Things which seemed so real to you meant nothing to them. It was hard enough to show an interest in the actual events of other people's lives without being bored by their night-time imaginings.

The trouble was that Anne's dreams weren't really fantasies or exotic figurations. They were prosaic, repetitive and based on fact. Her dream on that first night at the Lion d'Or held all the usual elements, though with the puzzling variation that much of it took place in an old-fashioned inn with straw on the floor, perhaps because Anne had fantasies about rustic inns which the Lion d'Or had not fulfilled.

The end came in what old Louvet termed the only misery, abandonment. She ran into a field and called out some word, some mysterious sound.

Then, that night anyway, she fell away into calmness.

2

ON HER FIRST evening Anne was sent to work in the town bar, which was on the other side of the hall from the main dining-room and had a door opening straight out on to the street behind. The position of the hotel made the bar a meeting place for people passing through and sometimes this gave it an agreeable air of bustle and change.

Two men stood with their feet on the rail of the bar and their elbows on the zinc counter, talking in voices which, although conspiratorial, were not in any way muted, so that as she went about her work Anne could hear everything they said.

'Hartmann. Yes, I've known him since we were children,' said one, a man in his middle thirties with unusually curly hair and a mellow speaking voice. There was something angelic about his head, but his hands were small and restless. He reminded Anne of a man she had seen in a film magazine.

The other man grinned. 'I never thought he'd take on that leaky old manor when his father died. He'll be needing a lot of work doing on it, I shouldn't wonder. All good news for the workers.'

He was small and dark with a chirpy note in his voice that seemed to place him lower down the social scale than his companion. His name, it transpired, was Roussel.

'If he can be persuaded to part with his money, of course.'

'Is he mean, then?'

The film star rolled his eyes. 'When we lived in Paris, Hartmann used to walk round to my apartment every night, though it was a long way away, so he could use my telephone because he was too tight-fisted to use his own.'

'But I thought M. Hartmann was a friend of yours?' said Roussel.

'Yes, he is. My best friend.'

Roussel glanced down at the bar and moved his drink from hand to hand. 'I suppose it's the Jewish blood in him. Have you known him for a long time?'

'We were at school together. I remember another time. Hartmann invited me to bring a girl – a young woman I had met at the opera – and come round to his apartment so we could all go on to the theatre. He was to bring his floosie of the moment. Then we went out to dinner afterwards, a place he said he knew off the rue Saint Denis – all of this was to be a treat on him, you understand. And then suddenly at the end of dinner he says he's left his money behind and has no means of paying. He presents me with the bill from the theatre and from the restaurant. He said he'd pay me back, but of course he never did.'

'But that's terrible,' said Roussel, standing up on tip-toe in agitation. 'Why didn't you ask him for the money back? I mean, if he had agreed to it?'

'There are certain things one cannot do. As a gentleman, you understand. I reminded him once, politely. That's really all one can do.'

Roussel looked shame-faced, and swirled his cloudy drink round in his glass. Then his manner lightened as an idea seemed to strike him. 'I suppose he'll want a builder at the Manor, won't he? You know my company has diversified. We do all sorts of different kinds of work now, it's not just earth-shifting and that sort of thing.'

'Yes, he may need someone. If you don't mind a few delays with the payments.'

'Well . . . things could be better in business at the moment. I mean, we're doing well, but it's the general feel of the times, isn't it? And I thought that since you know him, you might be able to . . . put in a word. We could do it ever so cheap. Though I wouldn't want to put you in a tricky position – you know, having to talk business with him, something that might damage your friendship.'

Covertly, Roussel motioned Anne to refill the film star's drink, which she did, earning a conspiratorial wink from Roussel as he slipped some coins across the counter.

'I'm rather tired of fixing things for Hartmann,' said his

friend. 'I've just arranged some work for him. You know, the big negligence case when three men died last year in the accident at the marsh reclamation works. It's coming on in Paris and Hartmann is acting for the company.'

'You fixed that for him?'

'I put in a word here and there. He told me he was looking for work and he hasn't been in these parts for such a long time I think most people have forgotten who he is.'

Anne watched Roussel's eyes widen. She was surprised at the way they talked so openly in front of her, as though she didn't really exist, or as though being a waitress made her deaf or wholly discreet.

'Have I shown you our new business cards?' said Roussel. He took one from his pocket. 'We're the first people to have them in this area. Here. Building, construction, decoration. We do anything really.'

'Very nice.'

Roussel tried several more times to bring the conversation back to Hartmann and any work he might need doing, but the other man seemed to have lost interest. Eventually Roussel took his coat from behind the door and said goodnight.

When he had gone, the man with the curly hair turned slowly to face the bar. 'It's obvious from your accent,' he said to Anne, 'you're not from anywhere round here.'

'No, that's right. I'm from Paris. I arrived yesterday.'

He silently appraised her face and she looked back at him. His eyes were narrow and his nose was hooked, but his face was boldly shaped and the overall effect was handsome in a striking if unusual way.

'So you've replaced the girl – what was her name, Sophie?'

'Yes. Her mother was ill and she had to go back to Lyon.'

'Do you know anyone here?'

'No one at all.'

'Now you do. André Mattlin.' He held his hand out over the bar for her to shake. 'Would you like a drink?'

'I'm not allowed to, monsieur.'

'Not now. I meant when you'd finished here. What time is that?'

'I think we close at eleven-thirty, but – '

23

'That's fine. I have my car outside and there's a place I know near the station that stays open till quite late. I could take you there and show you something of the town.'

Knowing that she should say no, Anne agreed.

3

IT WAS FIVE days later, on her first afternoon off, that Anne walked up the boulevard and took the bending road to the left that led down to the public gardens on the river bank. Some people called it the main boulevard, which was misleading in that it implied there were others. Its claim to the title was in any case dubious since it didn't offer the broad leafy sweep that people associate with the word. It did, admittedly, have trees on either side of it – plane trees chiefly, with one or two unaccountable cypresses – though their effect was less than majestic. The mayor at this time was a forester, a man bloated with civic pride as well as by the numberless municipal meals he ordered to be served in the formal dining-room of the town hall. The best way he could bring his woodland skill to the town, he thought, was by taking a special interest in the trees. The planes along the boulevard were thus, on his instructions, pollarded with a proud frequency. Their branches, naked against the grand houses behind, took on a pained, over-tended look, when the thin sandy pavements on either side and the slatted wooden benches needed something denser in the way of foliage if the road were really to aspire to the name of boulevard.

It had been built originally on top of an old wall that had marked the edge of a small village fortification and the houses set back on either side were the oldest and certainly the grandest – to those who liked that solid provincial architecture – that Janvilliers contained. Most had four storeys, wrought-iron balconies overlooking the boulevard and shady gardens behind them. Those on the west were considered slightly smarter, and it was not unknown for socially ambitious families to cross the street into an identical house on the other side when they felt they could afford it. There was no good reason for this preference unless it was that the gardens on the east side backed on to the rue des Ecoles, which could be noisy. Both rows of houses presented a monumental face with their double iron gates and frequent notices warning of hostile dogs.

The afternoon was freakishly hot for early spring and there was a game of tennis in progress at the far end of the public gardens. The court belonged to the town's richest family who, in a dubious deal with the mayor, had bought a site for it in the park where they allowed selected friends to borrow it, at a price. Thus Janvilliers, so backward in most respects, could boast a touch of Deauville in its public gardens.

If the mayor had been over-zealous in his pruning of the plane trees along the boulevard he had gone for the opposite effect in this part of the otherwise trim park. When Anne spotted the court by chance through the small gate that broke the iron fence along the river bank, she felt as though she had found a clearing in a jungle.

Four men were playing vigorously, with the sound of their rubber-soled shoes pounding the dry, sandy surface and the gut ringing in the wooden ovals of their rackets. One of them was Mattlin who, catching her eye, waved and motioned her to a green bench beneath the tendrils of a willow.

Anne's evening with him had passed off without difficulty. She found it strange that, having asked her to go with him, he then showed little interest in her, but talked of the people he knew in Paris. He smoked a good deal and glanced around the café; it seemed as if he were expecting a friend, or rather as if he were afraid of missing someone. This wasn't flattering to Anne; but, she thought, if he has used me merely for display then so, in a way, have I used him to escape from the confines of the hotel and the presence of Mme Bouin, so I am in no position to complain. And nor did she, but drank her coffee and talked to Mattlin when his attention was on her.

Now, as the men paused to change ends he spoke briefly to her from the tennis court and called out inaudibly the names of his friends in introduction. With the social moment past, Anne settled into her solitary watching. It was hard to know how seriously they took themselves, panting and running after each ball, yet teasing each other between points. Mattlin, the tips of his curls dampened and stuck to his face and neck by sweat, played with great energy, his thin legs never resting as he scampered over the court. On the other side were two men referred to as Jacques, Jean-Jacques, J-P, and sometimes Gilbert. It was impossible to say which name applied to which; both were shortish, rather stocky, and starting to go bald. This, and their rapid familiarity with each other, dispensing with half sentences and whole words at a time, made Anne think they must be brothers.

When, from beneath the shade of the willow, she had watched them all and watched the ball fly, she found it was to the fourth man, Mattlin's partner, that her eyes returned. She noticed at first his hands, which were curious. They were of great size, the right hand engulfing the handle of the tennis racket, but of startling articulation, with each joint visible under the skin and the knuckles thus slightly bent, as if over-assembled. At the tips, however, the fingers tapered into something like elegance, so that the hand attained a brutal delicacy. The wrist was inconsequently small, with a sharp little bone sticking out and a big blue vein pumping visibly, even from where Anne sat. His arm thickened from this point to the extent that it might have been called broad or muscular, though neither word was right because his arms, when not clenched by action, looked quite slender. Anne watched him as the players ran and hit the arcing ball and this man, though he sweated as much as the others and seemed to Anne no more skilled than they, appeared by turns angry and amused. He spoke less than the other three – perhaps, she thought, because he was unfamiliar with them. But his quietness was broken between games, when the players periodically changed ends. The atmosphere for a moment became awkward, neither ritual game nor ordinary social meeting, and it was he who filled the spaces until, with a louder jollity, the game was restarted by someone banging the ball over the tarred and shredding net.

Anne no longer made her eyes desist, but scanned the man's body, from the white shoes and flannel trousers to the bare arms and neck, where the long sinew from collarbone to jawline also seemed to join opposite things – the thick base of neck and shoulder with, at its tautest stretch, the soft and vague underline of his face. Once, when he hurried back behind Mattlin after a ball that one of the brothers had sent looping high up towards the sun, he overran it and plunged into the back netting of the court, which he leant against, breathless, as the brothers taunted him. Anne watched his diaphragm contract beneath the shirt and puff out again, as he gasped for breath, the material of the shirt seeking out the sweat-dampened parts of him that had marked it with skeletal patterns like pale symmetrical ink-blots. He lowered the head of the racket to the court and leaned forward to rest on the up-ended handle before giving way to a squat, so that his hair flopped down on to his forehead. In a moment Anne could see in his large hands and the strength of his movements all the other ages of his life, as if his body were a palimpsest on which had successively been inscribed the stories of his childhood, adolescence and youth, none of them entirely effacing its forerunner, so that suddenly the contradictions of his bigness and delicacy became understandable and she found herself seeing through his manly self-possession to the ghost of his vulnerable boyhood.

In a dream of sympathy and excitement, she stared at him. She was convinced with a certainty that was both delightful and frustrating that she already knew him; that she knew him in fact better than these friends of his did, and that any slow acquaintance they might go through would be a waste of time because she had already seen into the heart of him. He stood up again and threw the ball back across the net, pantomiming exhaustion to Mattlin and indicating that it was he who should have run for the ball.

The game ended. Anne stood up as the players made their way to the gate in the corner of the court and round under the overhanging branches to her bench. Mattlin shook hands but seemed uncomfortable as he formally introduced the brothers, Jacques and Jean-Philippe Gilbert, and his partner, Charles Hartmann. Anne remembered the name from Mattlin's tales of Hartmann's meanness.

Jacques, the portlier of the two brothers, said, 'What a welcome addition to the poor old Lion d'Or. We must all come and see you.'

Hartmann and the other brother, Jean-Philippe, murmured polite agreement.

'Did you enjoy watching the game?' said Jacques.

'Yes, thank you. But you seemed to go on for such a long time.'

'These brothers will never give up,' said Hartmann. 'They never know when they're beaten.'

'But, mademoiselle, I expect you play yourself,' said Jacques. 'You must join in.'

'No, I'm afraid not,' said Anne, blushing. 'We never saw a tennis court where we lived. It's very expensive, isn't it?'

Jacques tried to press her, but it was clearly pointless.

Mattlin threw his sweater over his shoulders and glanced at his watch. 'Can you give me a lift back?' he said to Hartmann.

In a rush Anne said, 'But I could come along and pick up the balls. Or watch.'

She was aware of the four men looking at her – Mattlin with some embarrassment, Hartmann and Jean-Philippe with blank politeness. Then Hartmann said, 'That would be delightful. Alfonse or I will let you know when we're next going to play. We can make it coincide with your afternoon off.'

'Come on,' said Mattlin, still apparently restive. 'I've got to get back.'

'Why don't we all go and have tea somewhere?' said Jacques, looking towards Anne.

Oh yes, why not? she thought, not daring to look up. Hartmann and Jean-Philippe were impassive, but Mattlin said, 'I'm sorry. I really have to get back.'

'Well, come with the two of us anyway,' said Jacques. 'Eh, J-P?'

'But of course.'

Anne smiled. 'All right. Thank you.' And Jacques took the opportunity of putting an apparently paternal hand on her arm to guide her through the dense undergrowth out on to the sandy paths and ordered flowerbeds of the main part of the gardens.

Here Mattlin and Hartmann said goodbye, Mattlin adding to Anne, 'I'll call in later, probably.' The two men walked off, sweaters over their shoulders, rackets swinging by their sides as they made their way to where Hartmann's old black tourer was parked.

When they were out of earshot, Hartmann said, 'Was that the girl you were talking about the other day?'

'Yes. Don't you think she's charming?'

Hartmann shrugged.

'Well, I certainly think so.'

'What are you going to do about it?'

'Lay siege. She'll come round before long.'

'The Mattlin charm. Persistence.'

'It has a good record.'

Hartmann opened the gate from the park and stood back to let Mattlin pass.

4

IT WAS A pleasant day with only a whisper of wind coming off the headland when Hartmann stood in front of his house and explained to Roussel what he wanted done. He made large, suggestive movements with his hands, but found that Roussel kept asking awkward technical questions.

The Manor was an isolated house, some five kilometres from Janvilliers, surrounded by acres of woodland. In his last ten years Hartmann's father had quarrelled with most of his staff and had sacked both groundsman and gardener. The appearance of wildness had increased. The house was dominated by two towers with conical grey slate roofs. The rectangular section which joined them formed the main part of the Manor, though at its junction with the towers it extended backwards, away from them, as well as forwards, into them.

'Now have you got that?' said Hartmann.

'Ye-es. I think so.'

'I can't think why there wasn't a cellar built in the first place.'

'Yes, it's unusual in a house like this, Monsieur.'

Hartmann senior had had a hole driven sideways into the bank at the rear of the house and had stored his wine in the resulting damp burrow whose roof was held up by shaky-looking planks. One day it had caved in when a storm caused a displacement of the earth in the woods behind it. Later, when the rain had eased, the bottles were dug out like the victims of a mining disaster. The rain had washed off or defaced many of the labels so that dinner at the Manor often had an air of suspense; to his irritation the old man frequently found he had treated his guests to a rare burgundy he had been meaning to save.

The house was built from pale stone, and the windows and shutters were painted grey. In the middle of the long

31

slate roof was a triangular protuberance, also slate-covered, into which was let a brick-surrounded dormer window. This had been boarded up with wood and now looked rather like the door half way up a barn through which bales are loaded. On either side of it reared two thin rectangular chimneys in what appeared to be an unwise defiance of gravity. Some of the building was covered with dense ivy, spangled green and red, which helped to counteract the bleakness of the pale stone and the house's isolated position on the headland. Theoretically it was sheltered from the sea winds by the finger of land that stuck out and by the dense pine forests on the far side of the lake it overlooked. In fact, on bad days the wind seemed to accelerate off the bend of the land and funnel itself through the woods before sucking and tearing at the shutters and shaking the windows in their frames.

'You think you'll be able to manage a cellar, then?'

'Oh, I think so, M. Hartmann. I'll let you have an estimate.'

'That's wonderful. My father would have been pleased to think of someone bringing the old place back to life. We'll have a party when you've finished. We could have it out here in front of the house, and people could go swimming in the lake.'

Hartmann saw in his mind a covered walkway, hung with candles, leading from the house to a marquee with tables at the water's edge. He would have all his own wine installed in the new cellar and begin to do something with the upstairs rooms as well. Perhaps they could have another party at the end of the year when all the redecoration would be complete. It would be better than Paris, better than Montparnasse or the Opera.

'I could begin on Thursday,' Roussel was saying.

'Yes, yes.'

'Here, monsieur, take one of our cards. We're the first people in the town to have them.'

He pressed into Hartmann's palm an outsize card with a poorly printed drawing of a house with scaffolding. Hartmann looked at it and then at Roussel's eager face.

For reasons he could not explain, he felt a disabling surge of pity for Roussel. He looked at the small, dark-haired

32

builder weighing up his job and felt for a moment as though he had lost his own identity in the other man. It was not a conscious act of sympathy, but an involuntary and unpleasant loss of control. Nevertheless, the feeling was so strong that he felt he could have cried.

'Why on earth are you sitting there like that?' said Hartmann's wife Christine when she came downstairs ten minutes later with a bunch of dried flowers in her hands.

'I was just thinking.'

'What about?'

'A strange thing happened. I was standing out there with Roussel, the builder, talking about the house, when a peculiar feeling came over me. I felt this desperate sense of pity for him.'

'Why?'

'I've no idea. I've no reason to think he's in trouble. It just came from nowhere.'

'Charles, you are ridiculous. Is he going to do the job or not?'

'Oh yes. There's no problem about that.'

'Well, you've got no reason to feel sorry for him. Marie-Thérèse said he was very good with the work he did for them and not all that expensive either. Even so, this is going to be quite a big job, and I don't suppose our M. Roussel will undercharge for it.'

'No, I don't suppose he will. It wasn't anything specific, this feeling, you understand. Just a general . . .' Hartmann trailed off, with a gesture of his hand.

They crossed the hall to the small morning-room at the foot of the northern tower where Christine rang the bell for the maid. She was a small woman with fair wavy hair cut in the fashion of the times, parted and held by combs. There was a heaviness about her that was unbecoming; her features seemed to have been moulded roughly, leaving her lips full and set in a permanent pout. To her admirers, they were her most attractive feature; others thought them simply a part of her generally unrefined appearance. Her eyes were blue and knowing.

'So, Charles, soon you'll have all your father's beloved wine stored up beneath your feet. A little Aladdin's cave for you to wander round.'

'Yes, there should be quite a choice. All those strange wines from Alsace and Austria he collected when he was old. I'm told his house in Vienna has crates of Italian wine too.'

'Italian! I couldn't drink *Italian* wine. Sometimes, Charles, I wonder about your taste. And your father's. You know perfectly well what I like.' She stood up and made as if to leave the room. 'I'm going to carry on with my work. We're having lunch promptly because I've given Marie the afternoon off.'

'I shan't stray far.'

I wonder, thought Christine, as she strode across the hall; I wonder. She watched her husband with a caution that bordered on jealousy and was aware that slow changes were taking place in him. Her hope was that by not making too much of them she could turn them to her advantage. He seemed to have reached a new threshold in his life and she wanted to be on the right side of any door that might be closing. Hartmann's ease of manner and attention to social form had at first appeared to her merely the polished exterior of a man who had spent much of his life in polite society. Patiently she waited for them to evaporate and for the man inside to be revealed to her. She knew him to be passionate and thought his punctiliousness therefore only a mask; but it was one that he had never lowered.

As well as a ready sense of the absurd, he seemed to have a reserve of anger inside him which he hardly ever turned on the world, almost, it sometimes seemed, out of politeness. Although he was quite willing to offer his opinions on any topic, he would never test his feelings on anyone except himself, and this perplexed Christine.

They had married when she discovered herself to be pregnant, but she had miscarried and, as a result, was unable to have children. Hartmann was adamant that it made no difference and that he loved her for herself alone; Christine, however, sometimes feared that he stayed with her only from an innate sense of duty.

I shan't stray far, she repeated to herself as she went out into the garden with her secateurs.

5

THE NEXT MORNING Roussel began building a cellar beneath the Manor. He had discovered a trap-door in the kitchen which led down some steps into what had once been used as a store for wood and coal. His plan was to enlarge the area, install stone steps and an electric light and line the walls with bottle racks. He assured Hartmann that this would involve no major structural alteration to the house and could be finished in less than a month.

What it did involve was a large amount of dust. Roussel's workforce consisted of a very fat man in blue overalls and a youth in a beret with a bad cough. The fat man was of the opinion that the whole project was a mistake. Although he had two pickaxes and a number of spades and sledgehammers, which he carried nonchalantly under one arm, he spent much of his time smoking maize-coloured cigarettes and issuing doleful orders to the young man, such as: 'You might as well give it a try, son.' The youth would then wheezily aim his pickaxe at a partition in the store beneath the kitchen, causing puffs of old and evil-smelling dust to rise up on to the kitchen floor above. Roussel himself exercised a nervous supervision, occasionally removing his jacket to help, but more often taking the chance to bicycle back to town to pick up some vital tool that had been left behind.

Christine made no effort to hide her distaste for the workmen, whom she regarded as idle, dirty and inefficient. She had had to set up a temporary kitchen in the small scullery at the foot of the south tower where she had had a small cooker installed. It was not quite the same as the big range in the proper kitchen, she pointed out, and Hartmann must expect a decline in the standard of his meals. The maid Marie, meanwhile, showed an alarming disregard for the properties of escaped gas, frequently leaving the taps open for hours on end, so that even Hartmann, who had taken refuge from the sounds of Roussel's workmen in the attic, would occasionally look up from his papers and sniff suspiciously.

While Hartmann took to the attic, Christine sewed, read, embroidered and knitted, muttering to anyone who could hear, usually Marie, about the wretchedness of the peasantry. Roussel bicycled ineffectually round and round the house, trying to decide where best to place his sign – a large coloured board with the words 'Roussel Engineering'. He finally selected the top of the driveway where it joined the road into town.

Hartmann soon discovered he was unable to concentrate on work and so decided to sort through the three tin trunks of papers he had brought with him from his flat in Paris. He enlisted the help of the fat workman in carrying them up to the attic where he took a hammer and prised the nails from the boards that blocked the window, so the light fell on to the great empty space. He thought it unlikely that he would be needing many of the papers that were in the trunks; the attic was as far as most of them would go.

The most curious of the papers he came across was an ornithological notebook, begun when he was thirteen and the family had been living briefly in the countryside outside Vienna. He suspected himself of having copied it from a textbook, but the style was childish and full of mis-spellings and there were convincingly vivid journal entries. It seemed scarcely credible that the city man he thought himself to be could once have known all this country lore. Then he came to a trunk which contained letters, postcards and photographs that for varying reasons he had been unable to throw away. He took out one of the bundles of letters and began to read. They all seemed to be from women. There was one postcard from a male friend in Monte Carlo, but it was a rarity. More typical was a note from Françoise, a girl he had taken to dinner when she was hoping to find work in a lawyer's office in Paris. It was a pretty card with flowers that thanked him for the dinner and hoped to see him very soon.

There was a fragile determination in the word 'very' he had not noticed at the time.

Each letter or card he pulled from its envelope seemed similarly to rebuke him. He wondered how he could have failed to see what they were really saying. Admittedly, their terms were restrained, but that only made their delicacy and his unfeeling response seem more bleakly contrasted.

It had been an unreal world in Paris after the war. There seemed to be a conspiracy among those who had fought to forget what they had endured, perhaps because it was too large for them to understand. Hartmann had gone to the front at the beginning of 1917, having previously been too young to serve. What he saw there was not on the giant scale of Verdun the previous year, but its elements were the same – the ceaseless noise, the trenches built up from useless limbs as well as from sandbags, the sleeping and the eating with the week-long dead. Back in Paris no one spoke of these things. Hartmann often watched veterans of all four years to see if they would talk when the subject was raised, but they merely brushed it aside.

In the fretful joy of peace they had thought about nothing. Looking now at the letters, cards and written mementoes of the time, Hartmann felt no connection with them. He had obviously not paused to consider the thoughts or feelings of those who wrote to him. Perhaps, he thought, his heart had not merely been hardened for the necessary duration of the war but universally brutalised, his imagination cauterised and closed.

He didn't have long to ponder these things before he heard Christine's voice calling him down to lunch.

'Roussel has been on to me again today asking for more money,' she said as she ladled out the soup.

'I think he's due some more now,' said Hartmann.

'You know perfectly well he's supposed to have completed the first stage of the work before he gets any more. You already agreed to give him far more in advance than he should have had.'

To curtail a spiritless argument, Hartmann said, 'Take the

money from my desk this afternoon. Perhaps it'll encourage him.'

Christine waited till Marie had cleared the soup plates and brought the main course before saying, 'And another thing. I need some more domestic help. Marie's rushed off her feet with all this extra mess the workmen make.'

'We still have Mme Monnier, don't we?'

'Yes, of course we do. But we need someone younger who can do all the rough work.'

'Of course you can have some more help if you need it. I'll ask Roussel if he knows of anyone.'

'Thank you, my dear.' Christine wiped the corners of her mouth on her napkin. 'One day a week would be fine.'

After lunch they went for a walk by the lake, over the dyke and out on to the beach beyond. Hartmann was still a stranger in the countryside. He couldn't get used to the long, dense silence that was broken only by the sound of some wild animal in a way that was far more disturbing than the continuous rumble of city life in Paris or Rome. Nevertheless, he was beginning to feel at home in the rough tweed jacket he had bought in the town, even if it would take time for his boots to lose their rue de Rivoli gloss.

Looking back through the woods, he could just see the Manor with its bold towers and he felt a vigorous affection for it. He turned to Christine.

'I came across a strange thing this morning when I was going through my papers,' he said. 'A bird-watching note-book. I don't even remember being interested in birds.'

'I adore birds,' said Christine. 'That's why I like this house. I hear some wonderful songs and cries from across in the forest. And sometimes I've seen them when it's getting dark – the wild duck that come in from behind the trees. Do you remember your father said that one winter some swans which had flown in all the way from the Arctic came to nest here?'

'Yes, I do remember. He was very excited. They had some special name, but I've forgotten what it was.'

'Arctic swans is what *he* called them.'

'Yes, that's right. But they were the real thing – whatever

the real thing is actually called. I know, because he had an expert down from Paris to authenticate them.'

They walked on for a while until Hartmann said, 'I thought I might go into town tonight. Would you like to come?'

'No, thank you.'

'Mattlin's asked me if I want to go to one of the cinemas with him. Then we may go on somewhere afterwards.'

'With Mattlin?'

'Yes.'

'I don't know how you can bear it.'

'Oh, he's all right. And I've known him for a long time.'

'You know you've got nothing whatever in common with him.'

'I wouldn't say that,' said Hartmann, as he bent to pick up a stick, which he threw in a high looping arc over the lake.

That night Anne was on duty in the bar with Pierre, the head waiter. He was the only person at the hotel who seemed to have some sense of detachment from his surroundings. While Mme Bouin appeared to think only of enforcing discipline and Roland of how to avoid it, Pierre went about his work with a slow, self-sufficient smile and careful movements. When he trod the narrow corridor between the dining-room and the bar, the gathered air seemed barely disturbed by his passage. Between the agitation of Bruno's kitchen and the varying demands of the clients, Pierre spread tranquillity; without him, Anne thought, it was hard to see how the hotel would have reached even the level of service it offered. Pierre had thinning hair and sunken eyes with specks of black pigment beneath them. Although his manner was one of resignation he also enjoyed making small, polite jokes and he had taken a liking to Anne because she laughed at them.

Hartmann pushed open the door from the street at about ten o'clock and took a place at the table towards the back of the bar. He had forgotten about his meeting with Anne at the tennis court and for a moment could not remember where he had seen her before. He watched her leaning against the bar, her dark hair tied carelessly back, swinging her foot in its flat black shoe slowly back and forth as she waited for the next order. He made a rapid and almost unconscious inventory of her physical features, ticking off each one as his eyes moved casually up and down. Only then did he begin to wonder what she might be thinking and whether this menial job could be interesting; probably not, to judge from her distracted figure and her partly shaded face with its air of suppressed vitality. He tried to imagine what such a girl might aspire to, apart from a worthy marriage, and in what aspects of life she took her pleasure. Unlike the involuntary spasm of sympathy he had felt for Roussel, this deliberate attempt to imagine the life of another left him with no firm impression or shared feeling; he remained uncertain, though not uninterested.

Finally he caught her eye and she, at once recognising him, found herself blushing. She turned to the barman and made earnest conversation with him. Of course, thought Hartmann: the girl at the tennis court.

Anne gathered up some empty plates from a table near the bar and scraped off the uneaten food. Bruno's dish of the day was a kidney stew in a vigorous mustard sauce. It was of the same family as the previous day's lunchtime speciality in the main restaurant, though the powerful juice went some way to concealing the closeness of the relationship. Many of the locals were taking it manfully with the help of baskets of bread and frequent pitchers of soothing red wine that Anne had brought to their tables.

In the glass she watched her colour return to normal before she swivelled round to face the main room again. She moved between the tables with a measured neutrality. She was wearing her waitress's black dress and her waitress's smile through which, Hartmann thought as he watched, little bubbles of the private girl kept breaking. He found it easier now that he saw her at work to imagine what she might be thinking. The aura some people carry with them can deter others from approaching, but the uniform of a servant is so clearly artificial that it invites speculation.

At last he signalled to her from his table. She flattened the skirt over her hips and moved across the room, between the tables, holding a little round tray to give her hands some work to do.

'We met the other day at the tennis court,' he said as she reached his table.

'Yes, I remember, monsieur.'

He asked her about the hotel and if she was happy there. He thought that since they had been introduced away from her place of work it was polite – or permissible – for him to talk to her on a level of social equality. But as he continued his questions, Anne looked down, confused by his apparent interest. She didn't know if the gentleness of his manner was prompted by politeness or whether he really cared about her. Hartmann glanced up at her averted face, the dark hair pulled back by a piece of ribbon. He thought she seemed a forthright girl who would be well able to look after herself. This view was confirmed when, after a pause, she looked up brightly and said, 'Haven't you just moved into a new home?'

'That's right. How did you know?'

'I overheard two people talking about it at the bar. I suppose I shouldn't have listened, but I couldn't help it. People don't lower their voices when I'm there. It sounds a wonderful house.'

Her eyes were big with enthusiasm. Hartmann smiled. 'I'm afraid it needs a lot of work.'

'And have you got that builder, Monsieur Roussel, coming to help?'

'You seem to know as much about it as I do! Yes, my wife was told by her cousin that he was the best man for the job, so we've hired him.'

'Your . . . your wife recommended him?'

'My wife's cousin, to be precise.'

Anne didn't care about his precision. She felt as though she had been caught by a sudden blow behind the knees. All her life she had been cursed with a face on which her thoughts were boldly printed, and she knew that Hartmann must now be reading them.

A wife . . . It had never crossed her mind in the heat of her silly fantasy by the tennis court. But of *course* he would be

42

married. She was annoyed at her own stupidity and shamed by the way Hartmann rode her discomfort, lobbing her harmless questions and then talking of his house in a gentle, neutral way when all the time he must be thinking what a fool she was.

A loud call came from the barman.

'Excuse me,' said Anne.

'Of course.'

Surely he couldn't leave it at that? Perhaps he would speak to her again before he left.

'Anne!' The call was louder than before.

'I must go.'

'Yes, I think you must.'

She turned quickly. The two notes in his voice – one of concern, one of gentle irony – combined in a perfect yet noncommittal civility.

Pierre, the head waiter, slid up to her as she loaded her tray with glasses of beer. He held her elbow for a moment and spoke softly.

'It would be better, my dear, if you were not to spend such a long time at each table.' He lowered his head and raised his eyebrows. By his standards this was a rebuke. 'Especially,' he added, 'when the gentleman still has a full glass.'

He had gone before she could think of a reply.

Anne was polishing glasses when the door from the street opened and Mattlin's curly head was revealed from beneath his trilby. Hartmann went to join him at the bar and, as she ferried drinks to and from the tables, she heard only parts of their conversation. It concerned Mattlin's reason for leaving his job in Paris and returning to live in Janvilliers. He seemed evasive.

Anne was installed again behind the bar when the jaunty figure of Roussel came in and made his way over to join them.

'My benefactors!' he said. 'Let me buy you a drink.'

'Benefactors?' said Hartmann.

'Anyone who gives me work these days is a benefactor. I appreciate it, gentlemen.'

'Has Mattlin given you work too?'

Roussel looked puzzled. 'But I thought – '

Mattlin interrupted. 'Have a drink.'

'Ah, I see,' said Roussel, tapping the side of his nose. 'Shan't say another word. Not the done thing, eh?'

'Quite.'

Hartmann looked quizzically at both men, wondering what they meant. He knew Mattlin well enough to be aware that his versions of events were, to put it kindly, individual, and his curiosity was therefore aroused. Both men, however, seemed to want the conversation closed and Hartmann thought it would seem churlish to press them. Mattlin quickly raised the topic of the German intrusion into the Rhineland, a subject of which the newspapers were full.

'They have broken their promise!' Roussel exclaimed. 'Did all our men die for nothing at Verdun?'

Mattlin fuelled his indignation with deft promptings and Hartmann turned once more to the bar.

Anne, meanwhile, had had some moments to regain her composure. All she really wanted now was to limit her embarrassment by doing her job unobtrusively and not making a fool of herself again. But a more powerful desire impelled her to engage Hartmann once more in conversation, forcing her to adopt a brittle enthusiasm and an insouciance she didn't feel.

As Mattlin and Roussel moved further down the bar, she said to Hartmann, 'Is the work going well on your house?'

'I think so. It's hard to tell. The men make a lot of noise and dust, so I suppose they must be doing something down there.'

'And how does Madame your wife enjoy it?' said Anne, this time confronting the name early in the proceedings.

'She's driven half mad by it, I'm afraid. She doesn't like mess and noise. But she's very long-suffering, and she keeps them on their toes. I think.' He looked suddenly guilty. 'I don't know. I've not been very good about it, I've left it all

44

to her. I play records on the gramophone to try to distract her.'

'Do you? How lovely! I used to have a gramophone, but I had to leave it in Paris when I came down here. I love music, don't you? And dancing.'

'I can hardly dance at all, I'm afraid. But I like music.'

'And what do you play for her?'

'Oh, anything. She likes Chopin. And Brahms, I think. And sometimes I try to make her listen to Mozart, but she hates that.'

'She doesn't like . . . well, dance music?'

'You mean jazz?'

'That sort of thing . . .'

'Christine? Oh, I wouldn't imagine so. Too raucous for her, I think. But is that what you like? Jazz?'

'Yes, I adore it. I've got some records upstairs in my room. It's silly, isn't it? I sold the gramophone but I couldn't bear to part with my records. And now they just sit in my drawer.'

Anne laughed, then looked down to the glasses in her hands as a small silence came between them. Hartmann watched as her hair fell forward over her cheek.

'Cheerio, then, M. Hartmann.' It was Roussel from the door of the bar. 'I must be going now. Got to make an early start tomorrow. Important job, don't you know?' He laughed.

'Oh, I've just remembered,' said Hartmann. 'Before you go. My wife wanted me to find out if you knew of anyone who would come in and do some extra cleaning for us. Just one day a week while the work's going on.'

'Yes, I understand, M. Hartmann. I'll have a think about it. I can't think of anyone at the moment, but I'll let you know, shall I? Perhaps little Jacqueline, you know, the postman's daughter, she might be interested.'

'Yes, as long as she's strong enough. Poor old Mme Monnier isn't up to much more than dusting the ornaments these days.'

'You'll be wanting a sturdy woman, then. A young one. Always plenty of those in a town like Janvilliers.' Roussel laughed. 'Good night, gentlemen.'

Anne moved out from behind the bar, clearing plates from the tables and taking further orders for coffee and more drinks. There were always centimes left in the saucers on the bar when people had paid for their drinks, and sometimes whole francs left on the tables for her. It was a rule that at closing time all such tips were pooled; half the total went straight to the hotel's petty cash box, and of what remained Pierre and Bruno were entitled to a quarter each, while the rest was shared out between the barman and the waiters. 'Monsieur the Patron is very strict on this point,' Mme Bouin assured the truculent Roland, when he had once questioned the system. Diners who thought they were doing Anne a favour by leaving a larger tip than normal thus found their generosity registered only by the marbled ledger of Mme Bouin.

Anne, however, was not thinking about centimes as she leaned across the tables to gather up the dirty plates. An idea had occurred to her. The more she thought about it, the more she wanted to dance with excitement. The only difficulty lay in finding the courage to propose it. Before she could begin to form a plan the street door opened again, this time revealing the stocky figure of Jean-Philippe, the quieter of the Gilbert brothers. Hartmann bought more drinks and at once he and Jean-Philippe fell into agitated conversation with Mattlin.

Like Roussel earlier in the evening, like most men in bars and cafés up and down France that night, they were concerned by news that two days earlier the German army had reoccupied the Rhineland, a zone demilitarised by treaty at the end of the war. All three had at some time been in the army, Jean-Philippe from the first battle of the Marne until the Armistice, during which time he had twice been wounded. Although they talked robustly, each man knew with a low certainty that such supreme effort of resistance could never be made again, and they looked to their political leaders to ensure that it should not be necessary. In this they were constantly let down and their sacrifice, as they saw it, betrayed.

'But I suppose Mandel is at least aware of the threat,' said Mattlin.

'I agree,' said Jean-Philippe, who was the most passionate of the three. 'He is aware of the threat, but there is nothing he can do about it. Sarraut will do nothing. Did you hear him on the wireless last night? He will *insist* on doing nothing – that's why he was chosen in the first place.'

'And because he was not Laval,' said Hartmann.

It was not as if the three of them were arguing, Anne thought, as she passed by; it was more that each wanted to make the same point more loudly than the others.

'But Flandin,' said Jean-Philippe, 'at least he's an anglophile.'

'The best thing you can say for Flandin,' said Hartmann as he drained his glass, 'is that he's an extremely tall man.'

Anne left them talking until a few minutes before closing time. It would have been better for her to wait until another day to propose her scheme, but by then it might have been too late.

When she saw Jean-Philippe put his hand on Mattlin's shoulder the better to emphasise a point, thus momentarily excluding Hartmann from the circle at the bar, she moved over with her tin tray full of empty beer glasses, touched the sleeve of Hartmann's jacket and murmured, 'Monsieur . . .'

He turned and looked down to where she stood.

'Monsieur,' she began again, her voice very soft because she was frightened and she didn't want the others to hear, 'I overheard you say you wanted someone to come and do some work in your house while the builders are there. I could come and do it for you if you liked.' She lifted her gaze from the floor and looked into Hartmann's face.

He was surprised by the pleading he saw in her brown eyes. 'What a kind offer, mademoiselle. I didn't think I would find someone so soon. But how would you manage it?'

'I have Wednesday afternoon off every week.'

Hartmann knew this because she had said so at the tennis court, but he wanted to give himself time to think. What would Christine say when she saw this girl? She was expecting a sturdy peasant, brought up to carry milk churns and chicken feed, well-muscled from baling straw. She would be suspicious when she saw this slender young woman with her tight black skirt and the hair escaping from the scarlet ribbon. Yet he wanted to help her. Something in him stirred; perhaps, he thought, it was a flicker of the same feeling he had felt so unaccountably for Roussel that day when they were gazing at the Manor. Perhaps, on the other hand, it was something a good deal simpler.

'It's very hard work, mademoiselle. We have a maid already to help my wife. What we wanted was someone to do the heaviest cleaning. I'm not sure you'd like it.'

'I'm sure I could manage,' said Anne, whose hands gripped the edge of the tray. If he didn't decide quickly, Mattlin would butt in and ask what they were talking about, or the barman would shout at her with another order.

'Wouldn't you be tired after all your work at the hotel? Surely you *need* your afternoon off?'

'Oh no, monsieur, I'm not tired. It's all right, it's not that hard, the work I do here. And I need a little extra money, for my father, you see.' She looked at him again. 'Please let me do it.'

'All right. Come next Wednesday at two, and we'll discuss it with my wife.'

'Thank you, monsieur.'

She rounded the bar as calmly as she could, though inside she felt the bump and swell of elation.

When the barman asked everyone to leave, Mattlin and Jean-Philippe paused to interrupt their anxious questioning of the Government only to say goodnight to Anne. It was easy for them, she thought; their lives were both more elevated and more placid than hers.

Hartmann stopped gesticulating with the others and turned to smile at her. She thought there was a trace of uncertainty in his expression; he almost missed his step in the doorway as he turned. When he disappeared into the darkness she felt both the sudden pang of desertion and a surging tenderness.

Up in her room beneath the rafters Anne lay on her bed and

gazed up at the ceiling, hugging the bolster to her in delight, as she thought of the prospect of working for Hartmann. Such joy as she now felt was possible, and it was all in the world that was worth pursuing.

Later, when she went downstairs to the bathroom, it was with such a lightness of tread that her feet seemed barely to touch the boards.

The sound was loud enough, however, to be heard by one whose ear for such things was sharper even than that of Mme Bouin. And so it was, a few minutes later, as Anne lay in the steaming quietness, that a tense face pressed itself against an open space high in the opposite wall. She would probably not have noticed had Roland demolished the entire partition in his frenzy, such was her preoccupation with her thoughts. For Roland, the urge that drove him to his uncomfortable and dangerous balancing act on top of thin wooden slats and mothballed curtains was so strong that he would willingly have taken apart each tile and brick in the Hotel du Lion d'Or for the sake of half a minute alone there. To his surprise, there was a sound from the bath: the new maid appeared to be singing to herself.

Despite her elation, Anne's sleep that night was again disturbed. When she awoke from her dream, she lay for some time having an imaginary conversation with Hartmann in which she explained to him the thoughts that troubled her. If all your life you endure the consequences of a single deed, then you cannot imagine life before it; it is almost as if the consequences precede the action. The deed itself meanwhile becomes harder to imagine as some isolated event which, by some easy twist of human will, might not have happened at all. It becomes the subject of faint memory, conjecture, insufficient detail.

All this was very hard to explain, however, and in her mind Anne saw Hartmann merely smile his well-mannered smile and tell her not to worry. When at last she fell asleep again she dreamed that she had known him as a child and had enlisted his help to stop her life from changing.

6

ANNE AWOKE THE next day with what looked like tiny blisters on the palms of her hands. Her fingers were swollen and coloured white in blotches. They throbbed and itched intensely. She went down to the bathroom and held them under the tap. At first the water was cold, but gradually it grew warmer and finally reached a temperature at which it became too hot for the skin to bear. She kept her hands there for a moment longer until a shudder went through her body, causing her neck and spine to tingle. Although this eased the itching for a time it was not enough, and she had to take her towel and scrape her hands on its rough pile until all the little blisters of the palms were raw and the white blotches bleeding.

Then she ran a basin of cold water and plunged both hands into it. By the time she returned to the bedroom the itching had gone, but there was a good deal of healing to be done. She took a blue glass jar from the chest of drawers and dipped her fingers into the whitish greasy ointment it contained. It had been given to her by a doctor in Paris, and although it never seemed to do much good at least it stopped the wounds from cracking as they dried out.

She had been half expecting an attack of eczema ever since she had been at the Lion d'Or. The man who had given her the ointment said it would come on if she was nervous or unhappy; she maintained it was caused by certain things she touched, like raw potatoes. He had merely shrugged, and said it was not impossible. Her life over the past two or three weeks could have supported either theory, and Anne was convinced that she had not been helped by the excessive amount of washing up Mme Bouin gave her to do in cold water with stinging powder. She dressed gingerly, to avoid transferring ointment to her clothes, and wondered if the condition of her hands might now give her some respite.

She was not very hopeful, but after breakfast went anyway to search out Mme Bouin in her nook beneath the hotel stairs.

'Madame . . .'

'What is it?'

'Madame, I have this problem. My hands are very sore. I think perhaps it may be the powder for the pans. Or the potatoes, possibly.'

She held out her hands for inspection, the bleeding palms upward. The old woman lowered her face over them and peered; the widening of her left eye was magnified by the thickness of her spectacle lens. 'I hope,' she said, returning to an upright position, 'that you haven't been touching any food with those.'

'No, I don't think so. It only happened this morning and all I've touched was the crockery.'

'I see.'

'I'm not supposed to touch food anyway. It isn't my job to –'

'I am perfectly aware what your job is, mademoiselle. The first part of your job is to do what you are told by me and the second part is to do what is required of you by the head waiter and the chef, in that order.'

'Yes, madame.'

'Clearly we cannot have you waiting at table with hands in that condition. It might put the clients off their food.'

'But madame, I like waiting. I like meeting people.'

'I am not interested in your social aspirations. You will have to do cleaning work only for the time being.'

'I'm sorry, madame, I didn't mean – '

'That's all. I will give the chef instructions about what your duties are to be.'

'Thank you, madame.'

Anne knew she must be sounding too proud for a waitress, but there was something false in her relation with the old woman that irritated her. Why shouldn't she talk to clients? What was a client but someone who had paid to eat? Hadn't

51

she herself been a client in restaurants too? She searched out Pierre, who was going through the stocks in the cellar, checking the bottles in their racks against a long inventory he held clipped to a board.

'You're looking nice this morning,' he said, holding up a bottle of wine under the light and running a duster over it.

She showed him her hands and told him what Mme Bouin had said. He swore with genteel violence.

'You understand, don't you, Pierre? I don't want to be any different from anyone else. I like taking the plates and things through, and I thought I was doing it all right.'

'Of course I understand. I'll see if I can do something about it. Now you just sit and talk to me for a bit while I do this.'

'Would you let me serve in the bar tonight? I know Mme Bouin says I'm not to wait at table, but it would be all right in the bar, wouldn't it?'

Pierre put down the bottle and glanced at her briefly before taking another one from the rack. She could see his face clearly now. 'Anyone in particular you hoped to see?'

'No. Why?' Anne looked down at her feet.

'Who was the man you were talking to for such a long time last night? I thought he must be ordering a banquet, but then it turned out he didn't even want another drink!'

'I can't think who that was. M. Mattlin, perhaps?'

'I think not. A friend of Mattlin's, though.'

'Oh, that man. Yes, what's his name? I forget.'

'Hartmann.'

'Yes, that's it. I remember now. Why? Do you know him?'

'Oh well, one hears things.'

'What sort of things?'

Pierre put the bottle he was holding down on the table and peered at her over the rim of his spectacles. 'He used to live here as a child, but went away when his father travelled abroad. After the war he lived in Paris for a long time and then, when his father died, he came to live in the Manor. He's a lawyer by profession, but I think he did other things in Paris as well. They're a well-off family – Jewish blood, you know. The grandfather came from Austria. He made his money in some sort of business.'

'But what about him? I mean, what do you know of him as a person?'

'Anne?'

'Yes?'

'Is this wise?'

'What do you mean?'

'You know what I mean.'

Anne blushed. 'I don't – I – I only asked.'

'All right,' said Pierre. 'We'll say no more about it. Tell me about your family, then. What did your father do?'

'He was a shopkeeper before the war. But we – there was difficulty in the family, and now we haven't any money. Not that we were rich anyway.'

'And what about your mother?'

'What? Oh, Pierre, don't ask me any more, please. I'm sorry, but it's difficult, you see.'

'Not if it's upsetting you. I'm sorry.'

There was an embarrassed silence. Anne was familiar with the sequence of events. Often with someone she liked and wanted to befriend she had to repel intimacy at the moment it appeared to be offered. She watched Pierre who, for all his gentleness, looked a little affronted, and tried to win his trust again with unsuccessful small-talk.

She was glad for once to hear herself summoned from upstairs. 'Goodbye, Pierre,' she said, dashing up the steps to answer Mme Bouin's call.

On Wednesday afternoon Anne borrowed Roland's bicycle and made off on the south-west road out of town. She hadn't told anyone at the hotel where she was going. If the job became hers and the visits regular, then she might tell Pierre, but she feared that if Mme Bouin knew about the work she would find a reason to forbid it. She told Roland she wanted to explore the coast and go for a walk along the beaches. He agreed readily enough, though he gave her, she thought, a strange, hungry look as he loosened the nut beneath the saddle to lower the seat for her.

The road bent between dense pine forests for a while, then

opened up into a sparse and sandy-looking plain, in the middle of which was a small cluster of houses. As Anne cycled along, two or three men in fishermen's overalls looked up from a table beneath a clump of trees and stared at her. The walls of the dozen or so houses were draped with drying nets, and a widow with a face that seemed to have been turned inside out like a dried fruit was splitting oysters over a metal bucket.

Anne pedalled on up the hill where the road once more entered the pines. She was wearing her plainest dress with thick stockings and had her hair pulled back beneath a scarf. She knew she must look businesslike if she was to impress Mme Hartmann, and for the moment would have to sacrifice any hints at femininity which, for other reasons, she might have preferred. She wore some lace-up walking shoes, bought specially from a barrow in the market.

The entrance to the Manor came abruptly and unsigned between a clump of budding rhododendrons and the interminable conifers. Anne braked and rose from the saddle as the bicycle juddered over the stony, pot-holed drive. Suddenly the dense trees on her right came to an end and she glimpsed a terrace with crumbling stone pots; soon she was passing the side wall of the house before the drive smoothed out a little and turned to the right, bringing her round to the front of the twin-towered house.

Anne leaned over, almost toppling, as she lowered her foot to the ground. She felt an acute nervousness as she stood in front of the old house. There was so much grey in it, so many rooms and big forbidding spaces foretold by the giant shutters and that long, voluminous roof. It was grander than any house she had entered – although its dilapidation was faintly reassuring. She wheeled her bicycle round to the side of the north tower to find a servants' entrance and was met by a fat man in blue overalls pushing a wheelbarrow full of rubble. He muttered a greeting which was impeded by the cigarette between his lips.

'Where can I find Mme Hartmann?'

The man gestured over his shoulder to Christine's morning-room. Anne leaned her bicycle against the wall and went in through the kitchen door. The cracked tile floor was covered, in places, by sheets, and everywhere else by dust. From beneath her feet she could hear a dull banging, a pause, and then a long, parched cough.

She ventured through the kitchen and out into the small morning-room, calling, 'Madame?' There was no answer, so she glanced around her. The window in the front looked over the lake on which she could distantly see a rowing-boat crawl like a slow insect. There was some half-finished embroidery left in an armchair, down the side of which was stuffed a woman's handkerchief.

She went through into the hall, a vast square area flagged with black and white marble, that separated the two parts of the house. Around its edge were assembled a number of unrelated objects – a fine walnut grandfather clock, a low piano with two ivory elephants and some photographs on top, an assortment of chairs, some obviously valuable and refined, others with torn rush seating. The walls were painted in blue rococo scrolls on a faded beige background. Anne peered in amazement at the chaotic elegance of the huge open area. There was enough in it to stare at for an hour or more, but she was frightened that Mme Hartmann might materialise at any moment. She called out again, but with the same result.

Near the front door in a pedestal was an iron vase filled with dried bulrushes and next to it a large terracotta pot, from which protruded fishing rods and nets and what looked to Anne like a hunting spear. The dominant feature of the hall, however, was an oak staircase that rose broadly from the marbled floor and zigzagged visibly back on itself before disappearing to a higher landing. Propped against the under-side of the stairs was an old green bicycle.

Anne looked at the clock: five past two. She found that without meaning to she had set one foot on the big staircase. The spring of the wood beneath her foot and the broad sweep of the stairs in front of her made her feel like the lady of the manor, and with a sudden imperious movement she began to climb. It was satisfying to reach the half-landing and look down on the grandfather clock in the hall; and then to climb up to the first floor, feeling the carved banister beneath her hand. The landing was like an image from a dream: it had no logic or cohesion, and seemed half-finished. Corridors led off in all directions, through narrow doors with rattling handles. The main window was blocked by old, unpainted wooden shutters, while a smaller window gave a view of the terrace and the woods beyond. The polished oak wardrobe that stood grandly at the head of the stairs might have been rescued from a regal bedroom, but the dried pine chest and battered pewter jug seemed to have come from a village sale. There were thread-bare mats over the polished floorboards, and everywhere Anne looked there was neglect, with uncleaned oil pictures set against half-distempered walls. And as in dreams it was not the detail that was important, but the lingering impression of something real but unspecifiable that has come momentarily within one's grasp.

Anne gazed around her, entranced at the thought of the people whose lives had been played out in these surroundings. It was only an ill-tended aggregation of wood and mineral, of uncertainly commanded space and broken furniture, but something in her heart was moved by it.

Reluctantly she went downstairs to look again for Mme Hartmann. She found her at last cutting some flowers in the woods beyond the terrace. Mme Hartmann seemed surprised when Anne explained who she was.

'My husband said nothing about anyone coming today.'

'I'm sorry. I was sure he said today.'

'It doesn't matter. It's quite hard work. I don't just want the ornaments dusted, you know. I already have Mme Monnier to do that. This way.'

The two women walked through the rooms that Anne had just gazed at alone, and Mme Hartmann explained what she wanted done. She watched Anne quizzically as she nodded her head in silent assent.

'Of course this cellar is just a start. We'll be doing up the rest of the house later.'

'You won't change it too much, will you?' said Anne. 'I mean, it's so . . . unusual, so pretty as it is.'

'It's a mess. My father-in-law gave up caring towards the

56

end of his life. Half the bedrooms are full of things that belonged to the previous owners, and *their* family was here for a hundred years.'

Anne was taken aback at the frank way Hartmann's wife addressed her, a mere servant. She had expected her to be more distant and also, if she was strictly honest, more beautiful. She was rather forbidding, too, with small eyes that hardly seemed to blink as they travelled up and down Anne's body, from the headscarf to the stout shoes.

'Has my husband asked you about references?'

'No. He didn't mention anything.'

'Oh well, it's probably all right if you work at the hotel. I'll give you a trial period of four weeks to see how you get on, and then if we're both happy you can stay.'

'Thank you, madame. Thank you very much indeed.'

Mme Hartmann led the way through the morning-room and out through the dusty kichen. 'Wretched workmen,' she said, as she showed Anne where the cleaning things were kept. 'They don't do a stroke of work. And that silly little man Roussel, he's always drawing up charts in coloured ink, but how he expects those oafs down there to understand I just don't know. Anyway, mademoiselle, you can start now if you like. There's no shortage of things to do.'

Mme Hartmann took up a wicker basket and returned to her gardening, leaving Anne to make her own choice of where to start work. After she had swept the scullery and scrubbed the steps, she moved into a small room which turned out to be Hartmann's study. The floor was piled with books, and next to a desk was an open trunk of half-sorted documents. She allowed her eyes to linger on some papers on the desk. Some of the writing was angular and strong, some seemed rounder and less formed, but she recognised at once that they were different ages of the same hand. She forced herself to begin her work, though she longed to read what he had written.

She heard the back door slam and the sound of boots on the scullery floor. Instinctively she rose from her knees and made as if to be tidying a bookshelf. Hartmann had taken off his jacket, which he carried over his shoulder. For a moment he stood in the doorway, as if surprised by her presence.

She set about dusting, but found herself chattering nervously. 'Madame made me promise not to touch any of the papers. I've been very careful.'

'That's all right.' He picked up a book and sat down. She was working only a few feet from where he sat and for some minutes there was a silence which Anne didn't feel it was her prerogative to break. However, when he put down his book, sighed, and stared out of the window she took the chance to ask him what all the papers signified. From there it was quite easy to move on to the subject of his work. She thought he might tell her to be quiet and get on with her cleaning, but he sat back in the chair and told her about being a lawyer in Paris. It seemed he had had to advise various newspapers on what the laws permitted them to print. 'I don't have a very high opinion of our press at the moment,' he said.

He told her about the scandal involving a financier called Stavisky. Anne remembered reading about it, but couldn't recall why so many important people had been worried when the man killed himself.

'The government was very weak,' said Hartmann. 'It was frightened of what he might have revealed. That's why some people say the police were involved in his death.'

Although Anne had been living in Paris at the time, the events had seemed remote to a waitress in a small café. 'My boss, at the place where I used to work in Paris, he said we should have Marshal Pétain back.'

'Did he? Isn't Pétain a bit old?'

'But he's a hero, isn't he? The people like him. Wouldn't he be better than all these men we have now?'

Anne, who cared very little about politics, was relieved when Hartmann didn't laugh at her, but merely said, 'You may be right.'

Although he was gentle when he talked to her Anne was tense all the time with the fear that she would say something ignorant or foolish that would make him laugh. Against this fear she had to weigh the desire to know more about him.

'Do you miss Paris?' she said at last.

'A little.' Hartmann sighed again and stretched out his arms. 'My father was a traveller who lived all his life in cities. As soon as I was old enough I went abroad, and then to Paris.'

'Is that where your father came from?'

'Yes, but his parents were from Vienna. His father was a banker. I went to stay with them once as a child and the thing I remember most vividly is the amount they ate. Every day they used to have at mid-morning what they called "second breakfast", which my grandmother insisted everyone attend. There were plates of different meats – venison and cold pheasant, and eggs and dishes of sweetbreads with port and madeira. And they were expecting lunch two hours later. But the funny thing was that none of them seemed fat.'

'But your father, he didn't stay there?'

'No, he was a great disappointment to my grandfather because he wasn't religious. My grandfather was Jewish, you see, but my father was an atheist and rather proud of it.'

'What about your mother?'

'She was a good Catholic. She came from the Jura. They met at someone's house in Reims. They lived in Paris for a while, but my mother had a hankering for the country and wanted to be near some water. It was she who found this house. She was a nervous woman and she liked to look out over the lake. She found it reassuring.'

'Did she bring you up a Catholic?'

'Oh yes, though I wasn't very good at it.'

'They say the Jewish people are persecuted in Germany, just because of their religion.'

'I know,' said Hartmann. 'I've read that we're already taking refugees. But it's happening everywhere, throughout Europe, even in this country. The young men and the war veterans in their leagues, they seem insane to me.'

Anne thought she had taxed Hartmann's patience enough with her questions. She picked up a brush and began to sweep the grate.

It was he who eventually broke the silence. 'I don't know what I'm going to do with all these books. I'm going to have to get rid of half of them unless I want the house to look like a library.'

'There's room in the hall.'

'I suppose so. Do you like reading, Anne?'

'Oh yes. It's a wonderful way of escaping, isn't it?'

'Escaping? Yes . . . I've always thought of it as more of a means of coming to grips with things.'

'I suppose so,' said Anne uncertainly. 'You do learn things from books, I'm sure. I just like . . . stories, I think.'

Hartmann picked up some papers and put them down in a different place which Anne assumed had some significance in his private sorting system. Then he sat down again.

He looked her straight in the eye and said, 'You're a very self-confident girl, Anne, aren't you?'

His voice held such gentleness that Anne found herself calm. 'Not really, monsieur. I'm frightened most of the time, just like anyone else. There's so much in one's life over which one has no control – whether people will be kind to you, and so on.' She paused. 'I never know what's going to happen to me.'

Hartmann looked sceptical, which pleased her. 'Robust,' he said. 'Perhaps that's the word.'

'Do you mean because I can do this heavy work?' She glanced down at her body, whose lightness was concealed by her white apron, and laughed. Hartmann's eyes followed hers. She looked up and met his gaze, feeling now a slight confusion.

'Not physically,' he said. 'I meant you seemed to be a person who is naturally happy and who wouldn't be easily upset.'

'Oh, I hope so.' She smiled. 'I'd like very much to be like that.'

Hartmann frowned and looked away. 'I'm sorry,' he said, 'it's really none of my business. Sometimes I forget I'm no longer in Paris.'

'What do you mean?'

'Oh, nothing. A different place, old habits . . . Here in the country people are more formal, don't you think?'

'Yes,' said Anne, then added boldly, 'Don't you hate it?'

Hartmann laughed. 'Yes! I can't bear it!'

'So why come?'

'Lots of reasons. But first I want to hear about your life.'

'Oh, monsieur, there's nothing to hear. It's not interesting like yours. No government scandals or meeting famous people.'

'But everyone's life is interesting. Did your parents come from Paris? Were you born there?'

'I – no, we came from the south. But then we moved.'

His questions, about her family and her home, were simple and polite enough, but Anne's answers were oblique.

As she heard herself going through the quick formulations that had saved her so many times before from having to talk too frankly about herself, she felt the intimacy she had created with Hartmann begin to evaporate. Where he had been so honest with her about his life, she was giving him nothing but evasions. No bond, she miserably told herself, can grow between two people when only one is telling the truth.

More than anything she would have liked to trust him and tell him the secrets and fears of her life, but it was impossible. It was a double burden for her; not only did she live with a history forcibly closed to other people, but the keeping of the secret made it far harder to make the sort of contact that would enable her to reveal it.

Now Hartmann was laughing. 'Really, Anne, you make the simplest question sound impertinent. I was only asking where you went to school!'

Anne went quiet and bent down over the grate.

Hartmann stood up. 'I'm sorry. I didn't mean to make fun of you. It's none of my business. Listen, come over to the window. Isn't that a lovely view there, over the lake? Now *that*, since you were asking, is one of the reasons I came to live here; the countryside, the lake, the wild birds and of course the house itself.'

'Oh yes,' said Anne brightly. 'I love this house, it's like a house you dream about, where nothing quite makes sense.'

'I know what you mean. Have you been up to the attic yet? That's mysterious too.'

'Could I go and see it?'

'What, now?'

'Not if it's inconvenient. Some other time. I . . .'

'Come on.'

He led the way across the hall and up the big staircase. On the landing he turned one of the rattling door-handles and led Anne down a dark corridor in which the floorboards creaked. They passed several doors, through some of which she glimpsed marble-topped tables or wooden bedsteads, piles of dusty linen and opened suitcases. She wanted to grab Hartmann's arm and pull him back so he would show her round these cavernous rooms with their old closed shutters, garish crucifixes and spectacular jumble of family history. But equally she was thrilled by the momentum of the expedition, which brought them finally to the foot of a tiny staircase which rose more or less vertically into the roof.

Hartmann went up first and held out his hand to Anne, who felt the grasp of his fingers enclose her wrist and pull her up. Here there were more boxes and papers, as well as an old rocking horse. The attic stretched away down the whole length of the house.

'It was dark as hell in here,' said Hartmann. 'My father's eyesight was going and I don't think it occurred to him that he could unblock the window. It only needed a hammer to take the nails out of the boards – though I admit I did have the help of one of the builders.'

'The fat one?'

'Yes, with the blue overalls. He seemed quite relieved to get out of the cellar for a change. It's not very nice down there. I hate to think what it's doing to that young man's chest. He hasn't stopped coughing since he's been here.'

'And is this all your father's wine?' said Anne, pointing to a long row of dusty bottles.

'It's all that's here, yes. But there's more in Vienna. He had a small house there, too. And I've still got some in Paris. It's quite a hoard altogether. That's why I need a proper cellar.'

Anne wandered round the attic, not really noticing what she looked at. Hartmann knelt down to examine a box full of papers beneath the recently unblocked window. The light fell across his body, illuminating the dark, springy hair and the grave, flat expanse of his cheek. The longing Anne felt was so powerful that she had to turn away from him for fear that she might throw herself into his arms and beg for his protection. It was difficult now to say whether this was happiness or not; she was intoxicated by frustration. She walked to the other end of the attic so she should no longer be too close to him.

Hartmann raised his head from the papers and began to speak again, though in some ways Anne wished he wouldn't. She could not believe he did not now feel the same thing that she had felt by the tennis court. She was sure that he too must sense that their polite conversations weren't really necessary because they could more easily communicate on a different level. What she couldn't say for sure was whether he had deliberately chosen to exclude these feelings because he was afraid of what they might lead to, or whether all men were incapable of recognising what they felt until it was pointed out to them.

He walked down the attic and stood beside her, so they were both looking out of the window, to the south over the woods. He was so close to her that she could smell his clothes – a mixture of tweed and new cotton. His leather boots creaked as he leaned forwards.

He said, 'Would you be happier if you lived in a room in town rather than in the hotel?'

'I . . . I don't know. I couldn't afford to.'

'But if you could?'

'I suppose if I could afford to then I would, yes. But it's not possible on what I'm paid.'

Hartmann nodded. He seemed to be almost touching her. She could hear him breathing. For the first time she felt in herself the sudden intake of desire, which had previously been inseparable from other vague and more powerful feelings. Shocked a little by the simplicity of it, she turned away and looked down to the dusty floor.

'Books!' he said, walking past her and throwing half a dozen violently into a different trunk. 'Books and more wretched books.'

Anne picked one of them up and said, 'Is this one good?'

'What is it?'

'*Essays by . . .*' She turned the book on its side to read the name on the spine. 'Montaigne.'

'Yes.'

He seemed to want to say no more. To fill the silence Anne picked up another. 'And this one? *The Story of Troilus and Cressida*. What's it about?'

'About the lives of two people.'

'A love story?'

'Yes, a love story.'

'Will you tell it to me?'

'Not now. It's too long. One day, perhaps.'

'Do you promise?'

He looked up, surprised by her vehemence. She blushed. 'I just – '

'I promise.'

Anne felt no more desire, no more happiness, but only the gradual loosening of control on her emotions which she dreaded because it meant she was going to cry.

Robust, she thought: that's what he thinks I am. Perhaps, then, I had better be.

So she said, 'I think I must be going back to work now, monsieur.'

'All right, Anne. If you like.'

She moved to the top of the steps. He said, 'Do you mind finding your own way back? I want to stay here for a few minutes.'

She was hurt by his coldness. 'No,' she said. 'That's all right.' She quickly descended the steps before he should see the hot swell and flow of her tears.

7

ON SUNDAY EVENING Hartmann went to play chess with Jean-Philippe. Since his father had spent so much of his life travelling, Hartmann had seldom spent time at what was supposed to be his home. He had scarcely seen Jean-Philippe since they had been at school together, though that shared experience was enough to form the basis of a renewed friendship.

He left shortly before midnight, and on the way home the headlights of the car picked out the sandy paths that led away into the pines; through the open window came the smell of the trees and the black onrushing loneliness of the night. Such troubles as Hartmann had were barely yet stirring in his head and were not enough to prevent his taking pleasure in the scented darkness and the approach of home.

He climbed the broad wooden stairs on tip-toe, seeing the lights were out, then undressed in the bathroom and quietly opened the bedroom door in his nightshirt. There was no movement from the bed. Gently he pulled the shutters open and stood, barefooted in front of the big window watching the woods on the other side of the lake and the grey moon apparently charging upstream against the current of the clouds. He heard a rustle of bedclothes, then a hand touched his shoulder. Christine murmured in his ear as she ran her fingers over his chest and kissed his neck.

'Why are you so late?'

'It's not late, is it? I went to play chess with Jean-Philippe.'

'I was tired, I went to bed early.' She ran her hands through his hair. 'Come to bed now.'

Hartmann stood where he was, disinclined to move. Christine circled round in front of him, placing herself between him and the window. She kissed him on the lips, then let her head fall to his chest. She murmured to him as she knelt, and let her lips travel over his body. Hartmann felt a complete absence of desire — a condition that was so unusual in him that for a moment he couldn't recognise it. Then he quickly turned away. He could barely believe what he had felt, or rather failed to feel, as he climbed into bed.

During her subsequent weekly visits to the Manor Anne found herself devising little tricks to try to be alone with Hartmann. She disliked having to be so cunning but she couldn't bring herself to disapprove of the feeling itself: there seemed nothing in it that was mean or calculated to do harm; and, this being the case, there was surely no reason why she shouldn't act on the impetus of such a natural and friendly emotion. She felt some slight misgivings towards Mme Hartmann, but it would have been presumptuous to elevate them to the status of guilt.

Her chief problem lay in breaking down Hartmann's reserve. Although he was pleasant to her and talked to her as she worked, both at the Manor and the hotel, he never overstepped the limits of propriety. His relations with her were those that a married man of once bohemian habits, confident in his position, might have with a waitress of slightly unusual qualities. If he was occasionally more intimate or more indiscreet than one might expect, that merely proved his disregard for bourgeois prescriptions of behaviour. The spirit of that prescription, however, was one he followed faithfully. Anne thought that if she could once cajole him into something rash, it would perhaps unlock the feeling she felt sure he must be harbouring unknown, perhaps, even to himself. So when he ordered brandy in the town bar of the hotel she half-filled a tumbler with it; when he asked for red wine she placed the bottle on the counter and constantly refilled his glass. On one occasion she even fortified a dark beer with a covert shot of eau de vie. But his constitution or his self-control were stronger than anything she could concoct.

Mattlin, on the other hand, needed no encouragement to continue his campaign of attrition. He was philosophical in his pursuit of women. At this time he was carrying on an affair with a doctor's widow who lived on the Boulevard. Her husband had been twenty years her senior and had lived for only five years after their marriage. Mattlin's affair with her had begun before she met the doctor, had continued after his death and, as far as anyone knew, had not stopped at any point in between. He went to her house each Wednesday and Sunday for lunch. The visits were not without their disagreeable sides – chiefly the small but sharp-toothed dog that seemed to suspect Mattlin's motives, and the widow's own vague resentment of his behaviour. She was, however, a formidable cook who specialised in fish bathed in cream and brandy sauces and in elaborate puddings of her own devising built with egg yolks, spun sugar and yet more cream. As he hiccupped gently into his *digestif*, Mattlin sometimes felt too bloated to follow the widow through the double doors of her bedroom to fulfil the function of his visit, but the thought of losing her incomparable lunches proved a potent aphrodisiac.

And then there was Jacqueline, the postman's daughter, whom Roussel had suggested might be willing to take on the extra work at Hartmann's house. She was certainly an energetic girl. Mattlin had first encountered her when she arrived at his house one morning on a man's bicycle in the course of distributing some letters in place of her sick father. She had only recently left school but it took little persuasion from Mattlin to allow him to deflower her one evening on the sofa of his sitting-room after she had come round to deliver a telegram. She had developed a sentimental attachment to him which he had done little to discourage in view of the physical rewards she offered by way of her willing, freckled body.

There was also his sister-in-law, though she lived far enough away for their couplings to be both irregular and taken at full speed in the brief interludes of his brother's excursions into the garden.

Finally, there was also, technically speaking, Mattlin's fiancée, Isabelle, a timid creature with irregular teeth and a passion for collecting porcelain. After two years of postponed wedding plans both she and her father, a local magistrate, were beginning to suspect that Mattlin's heart was not in it.

With the doctor's widow, however, growing more rapacious and his own waistline thickening, with Jacqueline nearing twenty and starting to lose her allure, with his sister-in-law so far away and with Isabelle starting to grow restive, it was clearly time for Mattlin to strengthen his flagging love life with a vigorous new affair. So, the following Saturday, he sipped his pastis patiently till Anne had finished her shift in the dining-room.

But all was not well there. Bruno had decided that it was to be one of his gastronomic evenings and had prepared a fixed menu which was more adventurous than his usual leg of lamb and beans with thin gravy. To begin with he offered a sideboard full of hors d'oeuvre from which the diners were invited to help themselves. Anne explained that there were too many dishes for her to bring on a trolley or to enumerate for each of the clients. What awaited them was certainly varied, comprising a large number of pâtés and salads, but presented in a way that characterised Bruno's cooking. A wooden-handled knife, which he had intended as an invitation to a healthy portion, extruded from a trough of terrine; but the effect, in the mangled and undercooked meat, was of a murder weapon. There was a shoal of sardines arranged across three dishes without even a leaf of parsley to relieve their multiplied cyclopean stare. A flagon of wine vinegar with an inch-wide neck was difficult to control with any precision and the small, slippery drum of olive oil rebuffed all attempts to pick it up.

The centrepiece of the dinner was a saddle of venison stuffed with kidneys and other indeterminate offal. Bruno left Roland in charge of the kitchen and went to see how his hors d'oeuvre was progressing in the dining-room. He came from the Vaucluse and saw it as his mission to bring some southern warmth to the grey-fronted, shuttered town of Janvilliers. When he noticed that his food was hardly touched he imagined that it was because of a natural reluctance on the part of the guests.

'Don't be shy, my friends,' he said to a table of six. 'Take your plates back and fill them again.'

'You are very kind, monsieur,' replied the head of the family, Clissard, a clerk who worked at the town hall. 'I am sure we will in due course.'

Bruno's idea of charm was an unusual one. He was a man of enormous size with a squinting eye set like a bloated pearl slightly lower than the good one in a red expanse of flesh. He held his left arm limply from the elbow as though it had been mangled in a piece of farm machinery or deformed by the constriction of an unnatural birth. In fact it seemed to function perfectly well when he used it in the kitchen, and the dangling was just a mannerism he had cultivated in the belief that it added refinement to his appearance.

Mme Bouin disapproved of his excursions into the dining-room and had told him so on several occasions, but when the mood was on him Bruno could not easily be gainsaid.

In the kitchen Roland was prodding at the venison with a long fork. 'Stupid pig,' he said to Anne. 'He thinks they don't eat his dog-shit because they're too shy to go to the sideboard.'

Bruno came through the swing doors. 'Girl, where are those cheeses? Have you laid them out?'

Anne started and put down the pan she was holding. 'Yes, I put them on a vine leaf I took from the courtyard and then I put them on their board in the larder.'

'Larder! Jesus Christ, it's like a tomb in there. Go and bring them into the warmth where they can breathe. And you, boy, what are you poking at that meat for?'

'To see if it was ready. I suppose you'll want it carving.'

'Not yet, idiot. I'm going to take it in and show them next door before I carve it. You know nothing about food. All you think about is girls. Oh yes, I know your tricks. Don't think I don't know what you're up to, you perverted little bastard!'

Bruno's voice rang round the stone-flagged kitchen and echoed off the walls; it soared over the single beam with its throttled string of onions and round over the big stone sink, across the slatted rows of hotel crockery with its bogus crest acquired at auction in a bankrupt château; it boomed around the small back courtyard with its vines and cracked tiles in which the grey drizzle was seething; it travelled down the tight, dark corridor to the echoing hall and the bend beneath the stairs where a steel-nibbed pen rendered the costed hours into columns of black debit; and it pierced the gap between the swing doors to the dining-room in which it obliterated the polite formalities of the diners to ring with the kind of passion and authority that Bruno imagined were the identifying features of his cooking.

Clissard the clerk coughed and poured a glass of wine for his wife and some water for his sister-in-law.

Bruno carved the venison at the sideboard among the remnants of the hors d'oeuvre and handed the plates to Anne, who distributed them among the reluctant diners. One of them, a dentist with a thin moustache who was said to beat his wife, called out to her.

'Mademoiselle, I distinctly asked you for half a bottle of Bordeaux when I sat down. This is not Bordeaux. Even if you cannot read, you ought to know that this is not Bordeaux. The bottle is the wrong shape.'

Anne fetched him the wine-list and the dentist fussed over his spectacles before complaining that now the wine would not have time to breathe. 'And the meat is getting cold,' he added when he had finally found the vintage he had ordered.

Anne went to ask Mme Bouin for the key to the cellar. 'I'm afraid you gave me the wrong bottle last time,' she said.

Mme Bouin raised her head from the ledger. 'Are you suggesting that I am incompetent, mademoiselle?'

'What? No, no, of course not.'

Mme Bouin stood up and wrapped her cardigan around her. 'I will fetch it myself,' she said, and set off down the corridor. Anne stood by the counter and hummed to herself, swinging her left leg gently so the shoe grazed the floor in time to an imaginary beat.

'You are a disgrace, mademoiselle,' the dentist said to her when she returned to his table.

'I'm sorry, monsieur?'

'Your service is appalling. And as for the food. What is this muck? This "gastronomic" menu?'

'Venison, monsieur. It's one of the chef's specialities.'

'Specialities my foot! And those disgusting sardines. Has the man no idea of how to make even a simple hors d'oeuvre?'

'Monsieur, if you want to complain I can ask the chef to – '

'Don't interrupt me, young woman. You're new here, aren't you? You'll soon learn how I like things. I shall have to make a complaint, you know.'

'If Monsieur would like to speak to the chef about the food – '

'It's the service I'm complaining about. I don't come out to dinner to be told by the waitress she can't be bothered to bring me my first course because there's too much for her to carry. And then to be given the wrong wine. After all the years I've been coming here.'

'I'm very sorry, monsieur, I – '

'I don't want to hear your excuses. Just get back to the kitchen.'

'Yes, monsieur.'

Although she was taken aback by the dentist's ferocity, Anne felt pleased with the way she had remained calm. She hoped that now the dentist had given her a telling-off he would feel satisfied and would not complain to Mme Bouin or even the Patron.

When she pushed open the doors of the kitchen she found Bruno drinking deeply from the dentist's returned half-bottle which had somehow found its way onto the draining board. He put it down with a thump as she came in.

'Mademoiselle,' he said with unusual delicacy, 'will you take wine with me?'

'I shouldn't.'

'But you will. To please me.'

She laughed, her spirits quickly restored by Bruno's theatrical courtesy. 'To please you.'

'Allow me,' he said, taking a small glass from the top of the dresser and filling it. She raised it to him. He lifted the

71

half-bottle, drained what was left and threw it into the rubbish bin in the corner of the room.

'Your good health, mademoiselle.' He belched, as the air rushed back up his gullet.

'And yours, monsieur,' she said, quickly draining her glass.

'And now for some cheese,' said Bruno. 'Go and get the plates first.'

It was a melancholy job, thought Anne, collecting the almost untouched plates of food from the dining-room. It had gone quiet again in there and on every plate that she lifted the knife and fork seemed to clink more loudly. She dreaded the dentist's table where she tried not to catch his eye as she calmly lifted his plate.

'A disgrace,' he muttered again, 'a disgrace.'

She put the plates on a trolley in the corner, and, instead of taking them through the swing doors to the kitchen, wheeled them out through the side door into the corridor and along to the back yard. She quickly scraped as much of the rejected food as she could into a dustbin, covered it with some newspaper, wiped her hands and returned to the kitchen via the dining-room where she braved the inquisitive glances of the diners.

Bruno was too busy with the cheese to notice.

'They liked it, Bruno.'

'Yes, yes, of course. It never fails. Where's that boy taken the bread? Here, scab-face. Yes, yes, the secret is to get a great deal of garlic into the sauce.'

Bruno took the cheeses through himself and toured the tables with them, explaining the provenance of each. The last table was that of Clissard and his family. Bruno brandished his knife in the air and fixed Mme Clissard with his good eye. He stood behind her sister who arched her back away from his blood-spattered apron.

When Bruno returned to the kitchen, Anne described the woman's face as she had tried to keep her black dress and bare shoulders away from his belly. Anne clasped her hand over her mouth so the sound of her laughter would not be audible in the dining-room. She didn't hear the door from the corridor swing open and it wasn't until she heard a familiar voice that she realised she and Bruno were not alone.

'Mademoiselle.'

She turned to see the tall figure of Mme Bouin lit from the dingy light behind, her lips turned downwards in angular furrows.

'Please come with me.'

Anne wiped her eyes with the back of her hand and straightened her skirt. She followed Mme Bouin to the foot of the stairs.

'Mademoiselle, I don't know quite what you think your function in this hotel is, but I think it is time we cleared up one or two things. I have tonight received a detailed complaint from one of the guests about your slapdash service. It seems you failed to take down his order correctly – '

'I'm sorry, madame, it was because Pierre wasn't here. I – '

'Don't interrupt me.' Mme Bouin rapped the top of the desk with her knuckle, causing the keys to clank against her bosom. Anne noticed that her left eye seemed almost sightless now; perhaps she had a cataract. Then both eyes seemed to ignite as she leaned forward. 'It is not only the wine, mademoiselle. I understand you wheeled the trolley full of plates backwards and forwards like a – like a gardener with a wheelbarrow. And then, with this same guest, you make impolite remarks when he addresses a civil question to you – '

'But, madame, that's completely – '

'I wouldn't have believed it myself, but, when I come to the kitchen to see you, I find you in a state of collapse against the wall and I believe, mademoiselle, you have been drinking.'

The final word was cut off with the force of a slammed door. Anne felt the tears she dreaded beginning to prick her eyes. She told herself her only chance was to keep calm.

Mme Bouin breathed in deeply. 'Mademoiselle, from the day you arrived here you have clearly considered yourself too good for the job which was offered to you. You arrived here by the front door and strolled up to the desk as if you had booked a room. You then inform me that you are above doing kitchen tasks because of a rash on your hands. Don't interrupt me! Tonight I hear from a client who has dined in this hotel weekly for many years that you are not only incompetent but that your pertness verges on what is . . . what is quite intolerable. I then find you in a state of collapse in the kitchen. It is not good enough. Tomorrow morning I shall go to see Monsieur the Patron and – '

'Go to him, go to him! I don't care. That man – the dentist – he's a liar. He was rude to me, then he lied about it.'

'Calm yourself, mademoiselle.'

'I'm sorry, madame, but it isn't fair.'

Before Mme Bouin could reply Anne ran from the stairs, down the corridor and back into the kitchen. Bruno stuck out a pudgy arm and grasped her wrist as she went through. She paused for a moment, wanting to tell him what had happened, but found the feeling of indignation so strong that she couldn't speak. She tore herself from Bruno's grasp and ran across the courtyard, out into the narrow street by the side of the hotel. She thought of the thwarted desire of her life, which was to be loved, and sadness mingled with the speechless anger to press her throat in a grief that was a version – old Louvet would no doubt have contended – of the same and only emotion: abandonment. She leaned against the wall of the hotel, feeling the damp, grizzled stone against her cheek. The trapped air seethed in her lungs until at last it found expression in a cry that almost bent her in half.

It was heard by a tall man, water dripping from his hat and on to his new rue de Rivoli boots, who was about to enter the bar. With one foot on the step he saw her shape from the corner of his eyes. He moved towards her.

'Anne?' His voice held a deep certainty beneath its note of puzzled enquiry. 'Anne, is that you?'

She looked up and peeled her hands away from her face.

'Oh God,' she said, and threw herself against his chest, almost knocking him backwards.

He put his arms around her and wondered what sadness could have provoked that awful sound.

PART TWO

I

AS ANNE TOLD him the story of the evening, she could feel Hartmann's body grow tense with indignation. He appeared to be on the point of rushing off into action, but even in her distress she knew better than to let him go. As she laid her head on his shoulder and clung to his waist, she seemed to feel the force of his anger strengthen her.

'All right,' said Hartmann. 'Listen. I will telephone this wretched dentist and put the fear of God into him. I will then ring the Patron and explain what's happening before the old woman gets to him. I'll have to go to another telephone, though. I can't do it from the bar.'

'Can I come with you? I don't want to go back to my room. It's so lonely.' Anne was surprised at what she heard herself saying.

'Yes, come on.' Hartmann disengaged himself from her embrace but pulled her by the arm as they hurried through the rain to where his car was parked. Anne watched from the passenger seat as he negotiated the narrow back streets before joining the Boulevard.

'We'll go to the Café Gare. The telephone's quite secluded there.'

'But, monsieur, is it safe to ring Monsieur the Patron, do you think? Mme Bouin always says he's so busy and it might do me more harm than good if he thought someone was — you know, speaking up for me.'

'Leave it to me.' Hartmann seemed to have a faint smile on his face.

He sat her down at a table in the café with some brandy and went to the telephone which was in a passageway leading to the lavatories. Anne gripped the edge of the table. She could hear Hartmann's voice raised in anger; then the doors swung shut as someone passed through and she could no longer make out the words. The doors opened again and she heard what sounded like threats of violence. She thought back to what she had told Hartmann; perhaps in her sobbing she had exaggerated. Through the glass swing door she saw him ring off and then make another call. This one lasted a little longer but was conducted more quietly.

Hartmann returned and sat down opposite her and beckoned the waiter over. 'It'll be all right. He's going to telephone the Patron and withdraw his complaint – and he's going to apologise to you. I told the Patron he'd be losing a client, but he didn't seem to mind. He understands the situation.'

'Do you know the man in the restaurant? The dentist?'

'Yes, I let him take a tooth out once. Not a pleasant experience. I was glad of the chance to give him a piece of my mind.'

'It's very kind of you.'

'Nonsense. People like him mustn't be allowed to get away with these things.'

'If it wasn't for you I'd probably be packing my suitcase now.'

'Would you have minded that?'

'Not really. It's very difficult for me there. I like Pierre, the head waiter, and Bruno, and even Roland, but the work's very hard. And I think . . . they pick on me a bit.'

'Who does?'

'Mme Bouin, you know, the – the manageress. And Bruno, though I don't really mind. He's funny in his way.'

'Why don't you complain to the Patron?'

'Because he'd sack me. If you're in a junior position, you can't make a fuss or people think you're getting above yourself.'

'And do they think that already?'

'Mme Bouin does. She told me so.'

Hartmann lit a cigarette and rested his chin on his fist as he lowered his head and looked at her. 'I suppose you do rather ask for it.'

'What?'

'It's something about you. You don't conform to their

78

ideas of what a junior waitress should be like. It's not that you're haughty or impolite, it's just that you seem too self-possessed. You don't seem to understand how simple most girls in your position are. They may be very charming, but they're simple. You're never going to be like that, however hard you try.'

Anne pulled the comb from her hair as she looked down at the table and pushed it back and forth two or three times before resettling it. When she looked up again Hartmann's eyes were still fixed on her, his expression one of quizzical gentleness, as if he expected her to explain herself. Anne, however, was quite practised at changing the subject when it suited her, and said rather abruptly, 'Another thing I don't like about the hotel is that almost every time I have a bath I feel that someone's watching me.'

'What?' Hartmann laughed, incredulously. It was not the response she had wanted.

'Yes,' she said, feeling herself colour a little. 'There's a noise from high up on the wall and, although I can't actually see anything, I'm sure someone's looking at me. I can feel their eyes.'

'Who is it, do you think?'

'I don't know.'

'Perhaps it's the Patron himself.'

'Oh, really!'

'No, I don't suppose so. He's too busy. On the other hand, he is a widower. His wife was a beautiful woman. Perhaps he misses her.'

'Monsieur – '

'I'm sorry. I was being facetious. It's probably that boy who looks like a medieval villain with the fringe and those angry boils.'

'Roland? I don't think he'd be interested. He's too young.'

'I don't think so.'

Hartmann ordered two more drinks, overriding Anne's objection. Slowly the brandy trickled down inside her and soothed the feeling of injustice she had felt as she leaned against the hotel wall. She was aware that her eyes must be swollen, but there was little she could do about it. If she went to look at herself in the mirror, it might only destroy what little self-confidence she felt.

He said, 'You're a resilient girl, aren't you?'

'I was lucky to run into someone who took my part.'

'It wasn't only luck, was it? If you hadn't offered to come and work for me, I wouldn't have known who you were. If I'd just recognised you from the hotel, I would have thought it was none of my business.'

Anne shrugged and said nothing. The delicacy of her situation was beginning to embarrass her. There was nothing scandalous, of course, in having a glass of brandy with a married man, but she imagined everyone in the room could guess that it meant much more than that to her. Now that the tears had gone, it was difficult to find a level on which to communicate with him. He seemed to talk to her exactly as he talked to Mattlin or to anyone else, but her response was complicated by the nervous emotion she felt and by her fear of saying something stupid.

'What are you going to do now?' he said.

'I don't know. I haven't anywhere else to go, so I suppose I'll have to go back. Mme Bouin isn't going to be pleased, you know. She'll make me suffer for this.'

'Perhaps if you stay there for a little while you can find a better job somewhere else in the town.'

'What, in another hotel?'

'You don't have to be a waitress, surely. You must have other skills.'

'Not really. I can sew a little, and draw. But I left school too young to learn much there.'

Hartmann, who had obviously not often put his mind to the employment prospects of young women, frowned. 'Perhaps you could go somewhere as a receptionist, or a manageress. To a doctor's, perhaps.'

Anne found herself laughing. 'Monsieur, do I seem to you a typical doctor's receptionist?'

Hartmann smiled and ran his big hand back through his hair. 'No, I suppose not. Never mind. By the time you come on Wednesday, I'll have thought of something. You are coming on Wednesday, aren't you?'

'Yes.'

'Good. Now I'll drive you back to the hotel.'

He took his hat and ushered her out into the street. The engine fired into life and the short journey was over, it seemed to Anne, almost before it had begun. Hartmann pulled up at the end of the street at the side of the Lion d'Or. 'Are you sure you'll be all right?' he said, as Anne moved to get out of the car.

'Yes, I'll be fine. Thank you very much.'

'I'll see you on Wednesday.'

'Yes. Wednesday.'

Anne watched the black car reverse and stop, then pull away, the headlights catching little drops of rain in their beam. She stood at the side entrance of the hotel until it was out of sight.

2

THE DENTIST'S APOLOGY was not a thing of any grace. After breakfast duty in the dining-room, Anne was summoned to Mme Bouin's niche and there told that the matter of the previous night would not be referred to again.

'Monsieur the Patron has decided to keep you on the staff. No doubt, like the rest of us, he greatly regrets what took place, but he is a generous man as well as an extremely busy one and he will take no further action.'

She warned Anne that any further lapses would not be viewed so tolerantly. 'And before you go, mademoiselle, there is one further thing. If it had not been for the intervention of certain persons you would now be waiting at the station with your suitcase packed. What's done is done, but it is not permitted for the staff of this hotel to fraternise with the clients. Is that understood?'

'Yes, thank you, madame.'

'You will now return to the kitchen where I have given the chef instructions on your duties for the day.'

'Thank you, madame.'

In the kitchen Bruno was sitting at the big wooden table, dipping some bread into a bowl of coffee.

'Floors,' he said. 'Then the vegetables. And then if there's time before lunch, the windows.'

'But that's Roland's job.'

'Shut up, woman. And don't come whining to me this morning. My head's made of wood.'

'I see.' It seemed the dentist's half-bottle of wine was not all the alcohol Bruno had consumed. 'Did you drink a lot?'

Bruno grunted and waved a fat wrist at Anne, who laughed.

'Why do you do it, Bruno? You know it only makes you feel ill.'

'Don't ask me questions, you wretched girl, or I shall put you over my knee and spank you. Good and hard. I think that's what you need – you and your Parisian manners.'

'All right, not another word, I promise. Two bottles, was it?'

'Good and hard, I tell you. I'd have that tight skirt off your bottom and your knickers down and – '

'Bruno! You're still drunk! I'm going, I'm going.'

She went quickly to the store cupboard by the back door where the mops and pails were kept. It was boring work and the constant jar of the wooden handle on the palm of her hand began to irritate the dormant eczema. This morning, however, she didn't mind. She opened the back door and let through a thin breeze which was clear and cool after the previous night's rain. She felt protected. It was as if Hartmann's intervention had not only saved her job but had also insulated her from some of the tedium involved in performing it.

That night Christine Hartmann went to bed with a book she had taken from among the many that lay strewn around the Manor. From an early age she had developed the art of being alone and generally preferred her own company to anyone else's. She read books at enormous speed and judged them entirely on their ability to remove her from her material surroundings. In almost all the unhappiest days of her life she had been able to escape from her own inner world by living temporarily in someone else's, and on the two or three occasions that she had been too upset to concentrate she had been desolate.

Her husband had said he would be up late preparing some papers. He seemed to work late with increasing frequency these days. Christine registered the change but said nothing.

Hartmann sat at the desk in his study and stared blankly ahead of him, his pen abandoned on the papers.

All his life he had felt the implacable nagging of desire.

83

The feeling was more of a frustration than a pleasure, because the relief was only ever momentary. Sometimes, in fact, the length of time between the relief and the first intimations of the next frustration seemed so brief as hardly to constitute an interruption in the continuous longing. He had been affected by a mood of frivolity that had been widespread in people of his class after the war. The sustained feeling of euphoria – even if it was shadowed by a suspicion that such a climate couldn't last long – coincided with the period of his own greatest youthful vigour. After the sight of the wall of dead men in the mud, of severed limbs, of blown muscle and sinew; after the stench of decomposing flesh and field latrines, the landscape of blackened trees and gaping shell-holes; after the constant sense of fear and of life valued only by the day, and then the return to decimated villages, there had seemed no reason for self-restraint. The free embrace of womanhood, the touch and scent of femininity, were tokens of the peace.

For Hartmann and his friends in Paris there was serious work to be done in offices and banks and galleries, but there was also a parallel life of passion and sexual encounter. Hartmann and Mattlin, though they barely knew each other, were alike in one respect, that they each spent many hours wondering how to stave off the battering of desire. For Mattlin the solution lay in numbers: by increasing the aggregate of women he slept with he felt he could eliminate the potential sources of frustration. For Hartmann the answer always seemed to lie in the next encounter. He did not accumulate in the same way as Mattlin but saw each lover as potentially definitive. The next woman, he was sure, would prove so complete, so satisfying, that she would at last extinguish the tormenting itch that made it hard to concentrate for so much of the working day. Mattlin valued the difference in each woman he made love to because, by isolating each new trait, he hoped to inoculate himself against the frustration it might otherwise have caused; Hartmann found in individual differences only varying and sometimes tantalising degrees of incompleteness. Each went forward in the hope of relief from the force that drove him and each was unsuccessful.

The recognition of his failure had been one of the factors

that had reconciled Hartmann to marrying Christine. He knew he would never find a woman to end all desire, but there was much in his relationship with Christine, leaving aside the problem of her pregnancy, which disposed him to think they might be happy. There had been various outcomes and problems in his dealings with women, but the presence of sexual desire was something he had always taken as axiomatic. Yet now, with Christine, it had gone. Where once this feeling had been the most dependable presence in his life, now there was nothing.

Hartmann got up from the desk and turned out the lights. He went through to the hall, pulled the bolt across the front door and climbed the stairs to bed. Christine was still awake and smiled to him as he came in. He stood barefoot on the boards and gazed out across the lake to the swell of the woods on the other side. He was conscious of deferring an action, and knew that Christine would be aware of it too. When he climbed into bed he saw that she was naked – a sight which on countless previous occasions had caused a simple response in him. When he looked at her now, he felt something not unlike compassion. He saw her legs and arms, her heavy breasts and her face, eager and friendly, and he thought of all the difficulties of her life and of the way she had overcome them.

It occurred to him that really this was the normal way to view a naked woman. It was the way one would look upon a mother or a sister, or a work of art: with affection, with understanding, with an appreciation, even, of their elegance, but not through the filter of desire. It seemed that the way in which he had previously seen women was false. Here was this aggregation of flesh and skin and hair, not repulsive, but merely human, like his own body. No doubt its owner could view it with detachment, wishing it were different in some respects, but also with kindliness and respect. Why, then, shouldn't he also see it in this way? Was this not the most civilised approach? It was not absence of sexual desire that was strange, he thought; on the contrary, the strangeness was in the leap of imagination and sustained belief, against all the evidence, that allowed men to see women through a veil of make-believe allure.

Christine wanted him to make love to her, and he felt baffled by his disinclination. It was as though he had cut himself and not bled, or opened his eyes and not seen. In his mind he thought of all the other women he knew, and in this mood he viewed them all in the same way. None was arousing. It didn't occur to him to think of Anne or of what he had felt so strongly in the attic only a few days earlier.

3

THE NEXT DAY Hartmann had a letter from Etienne Beauvais, a former colleague in Paris he had not seen for some years. Etienne had married and moved with his wife to a house near where her family had a large farm. He invited Hartmann to come for a weekend of shooting and 'other country pursuits'. He concluded: 'Bring yourself a companion. All is discretion here! Do come, Charles; it will be a jolly party and we haven't seen you for a long time.' Such a long time, in fact, that he clearly hadn't heard that Hartmann was married. He would ask Christine if she wanted to go.

He stuffed the letter inside his jacket pocket and went to look for her. As he crossed the hall he was accosted by Roussel, his hair white with dust.

'Ah, M. Hartmann, I'm so glad to have caught you. A little matter I wanted to discuss.'

'You look as though you've been working.'

'Ah yes, indeed. I thought I'd lend a hand today. We're making such good progress. I wanted to show you what we've done and then perhaps you might think it's time for another instalment.'

'All right. What do you want me to look at?'

'This way, monsieur. The cellar.'

Roussel led the way over the dust-sheets and into the kitchen, where they discovered the fat workman leaning against the range smoking a cigarette. The man grunted and held out his hand to be shaken. Hartmann took it with a nod before following Roussel down the steps.

There followed half an hour's pleading from Roussel in which he argued that he had almost finished the job and was thus due to be paid the third of the four instalments. However, it was clear to Hartmann that Roussel had barely completed the first part of the job. The builder was also insistent that there should be an extra payment for the floor.

'But you haven't put in a floor,' said Hartmann.

'Not as such, I admit,' said Roussel. 'But I think it must be considered a separate item from the decoration and the main structural work.'

Hartmann looked at two huge struts that stuck up into the roof of the cellar.

'Temporary supports, M. Hartmann. Just until the new joist settles.'

Roussel was a tenacious arguer. When it was obvious that Hartmann was unconvinced by his progress with the schedule, he suggested that the requirements had been changed. Next he said that his youngest daughter was sick, and needed care. Hartmann, bored with the arguments, agreed to pay him some more money. Perhaps, he thought, that's how Mattlin wears down his girlfriends: he bores them into submission.

His presence no longer required, Hartmann picked his way over the dust-sheets and out into the hall. He had felt no recurrence of the pity he had experienced on the first day that he and Roussel surveyed the house, though neither had he found an explanation for it.

He went to his study to do some work, but found to his irritation that he couldn't concentrate. He was thinking about Anne. She had reminded him of feelings he thought he had put behind him.

He sighed and looked back at the desk. The negligence case needed work. He pulled out a bundle of papers giving details of the motor systems used in mechanical dredgers and bent his mind to them.

He kept seeing her face and the movement of her body. She was always demurely dressed, but it couldn't quite conceal a rather womanly heaviness about the bust which was charmingly at odds with the girlish quality of her face.

Good heavens, he told himself, three men died in this accident. Fiercely he studied the movement of the engine and tried to imagine the sound it made.

But he heard only the sound of Anne's voice and felt the

88

tugging of her hand on his sleeve. That look of pleading when she had whispered, 'Monsieur . . .'

He looked back at the papers. He had once met one of the victims of the accident. He tried to remember what he was like.

Only one presence took shape in his mind. My God, he thought, throwing down the pen. He held his head in his hands, then rubbed his eyes fiercely.

He stood up and remembered that before Roussel had accosted him he had been going to find his wife. It was her birthday and she had invited some friends to come to the house for dinner.

She was still in bed, reading.

'What time are the people coming this evening?'

'About seven o'clock. But Marie-Thérèse is always late.'

'Would you like your birthday present now?'

'Oh, Charles, how delightful. Yes, please.'

Hartmann took out a package from the cupboard in the corner and handed it to Christine, who pulled eagerly at the strings and ribbon that held it together. The shop girl had done up the package with care, and it was some time before Christine's impatient fingers were able to disinter a pair of binoculars.

'For watching the birds,' said Hartmann.

'They're beautiful. Such a lovely finish.' She climbed out of bed and walked to the window with them. 'They're very powerful, aren't they? There's a moorhen out there, a long way out, and I can see it quite clearly with these. Do have a look, Charles.'

Hartmann took the binoculars and aimed in the direction Christine pointed. He saw the little bird paddling along across the lake, its diminutive body dwarfed by the expanse of water and the stretch of trees beyond. He handed the glasses back to her.

'If you walk up to the dyke,' he said, 'you should be able to see a lot of birds in those trees on the way up. The water birds nest in the weeds there.'

Christine smiled and kissed him on the cheek. 'It's a lovely present.'

*

It was not at dinner that night that Hartmann made what in retrospect he could see was a decisive move in his affairs. He merely sat, tilting his head politely to Marie-Thérèse's chatter and pouring more wine for Christine's guests. Nor was it in the long hours of the night when he lay marooned in the giant bed his father had acquired at auction in Alsace, with the sound of his wife asleep beside him. Then he merely reflected on his father and on his pride in his assumed identification with the region of Alsace (Hartmann, he pointed out, was an established name in the district). He also thought about Poincaré, the fiddling Prime Minister who had retired to the neighbouring Lorraine, and about more mundane matters, such as his next game of tennis with Jean-Philippe Gilbert.

At no point did he relent and decide that the only way he could find relief from the tormenting presence of Anne in his thoughts was by doing something. Even violent acts, he later told himself, cannot be seen clearly by the perpetrator until they are finished. And as for his own gently willed inertia, which might occasionally spill over into innocent gestures of kindness, it would take a philosopher of iron sternness to spot the moment at which an unformulated wish became, almost by inaction, a completed act.

Nevertheless, perhaps the thought of his father recalled to him the old man's former secretary and her sister, Mlle Calmette, who was still living in Janvilliers.

It was her name, in any case, he mentioned to Christine the next morning when he told her he had to go into town on business.

'There are some little details of a trust fund for her sister which need clearing up,' he said, as he laid down his newspaper in the morning-room.

'Shall I expect you back for lunch?'

'Certainly. It won't take more than half an hour at the most. I feel rather guilty about her really. I ought to have done something before.'

It was not until this final claim, which was partially true, that he felt any unease about his expedition.

Christine was looking down at her needlework. Hartmann

tried, but failed, to catch her eye in order to give her an insouciant smile. He cleared his throat and ran his hand quickly back through his hair. She looked up and smiled vaguely. He nodded, coughed again, and turned, the metal caps on the heels of his glossy boots ringing on the flagged hall.

4

AT ABOUT FIVE o'clock the same day a note was delivered for Anne by Jacqueline, the postman's daughter. It was in an angular but firm hand that she at once recognised from the papers in the study at the Manor. It said, 'Call as soon as possible at the address below and ring the bell bearing the name Mlle Calmette. You will, I hope, learn something that pleases you.' It was signed in an illegible scrawl. Anne read the note through several times, tracing the hurried movement of the spluttering black ink.

She found Pierre in the cellar and asked him where the street was. He told her it was on the north-west side of town, not far from the church; she estimated she just had time to go before her evening shift began. She hurried up the rue des Ecoles and into the Place de la Victoire from which she could see the spire of the church. In the Place de l'Eglise she asked the way from a widow with bandy legs and a headscarf who looked at her with toothless disapproval, as if she had asked for directions to a house of ill-repute. Anne barely knew what to expect, but was prepared to rush to any destination prescribed by that handwriting.

The street was narrow and quiet; some of the houses had dried wooden gables, and some had huge double doors that would lead into paved courtyards beyond. It was one of these doors, painted a dark green, that bore the number in the note. She found Mlle Calmette's bell and rang it. There was a remote, disconnected jangling. A thin bark rose from behind the wall and was abruptly silenced.

At last she heard slow footsteps from behind the door and then a lock being turned. A small woman of about seventy with a crinkled face opened the door and peered nervously round it. Anne introduced herself.

'Ah yes, mademoiselle.' Anne noticed that the old woman's

hair seemed unnaturally brown for the age of her face. 'Please come this way.'

A cat was sleeping against one of the side walls of the courtyard where a flowerbed held half a dozen wintry shrubs and under-watered plants. The woman paused at a narrow, black-painted door and fumbled in her cardigan. She pulled out a single key on a piece of string, then turned to Anne and smiled. 'You are just as he said.'

Anne felt a moment of panic, as though she were a counter in a game being played by two other people.

The door opened on to a small square hallway and a flight of scrubbed stairs. Anne followed the old woman, tense with a mixture of fear and excitement. On the landing was a rug and a pair of glass-panelled doors.

'This is your sitting-room.'

'My . . . ?'

She looked around a small neat room on whose polished wooden floor and circular table the sun shone gently. She felt a thin hand grip her forearm.

'This is your bedroom.'

A door opened on a broad wooden bed with lacework and broderie anglaise covers and a mahogany dressing-table with a vase of freesias. The wrinkled hand waved again. 'Bathroom. And behind the curtain on the landing is a little space for cooking, if you can get the gas to work. Don't forget to open the window.'

'For me?'

'There's a note for you on the dressing-table. From M. Hartmann. My apartment is next door if you should want anything. My sister used to live here, but since she died I've let it go on short lets. Here's your key, and here's one to the street door. I hope you like it.'

Anne was too confused to take in what the old woman was saying, but then it was too late and she had gone down the stairs, her heavy black shoes ringing on the bare wood.

Anne went back into the bedroom and tore open the letter on the dressing-table. 'Dear Anne,' she read, 'I have rented these rooms for you because I thought you might like them better than your attic at the Lion d'Or, and I am sure you will have no problems with voyeurs. You don't have to take them if you don't want to. I won't be hurt if you prefer to stay at the hotel, nor does taking them confer any obligation on you. Mlle Calmette is an old friend of our family (her sister worked once as my father's secretary) and our financial arrangement is easy-going – by which I mean you shouldn't feel uneasy about any expense you might think I'm incurring. It's not much and, in any case, it is money I would like her to have.

'I hope you'll like it here. I suppose it will mean getting up ten minutes earlier each morning to get to work on time but perhaps it's worth it. I have to go to dinner in town tonight and I will look in around eleven to see that you're settled. If this is inconvenient, you must telephone me at the Manor early this evening. I will make sure I answer the telephone. My wife doesn't know of this arrangement and if she did she might draw the wrong conclusions. I'm sure you understand.'

Hartmann arrived shortly before midnight, full of apologies. 'It was impossible to get away earlier, it would have been rude. I left just as soon as I could. And now you'll be tired in the morning, while I can lie in bed till eight o'clock. I wouldn't have come at all, but then I thought you might wait up and that would be even worse.'

He was wearing a dark suit and a formal white collar. His eyes seemed sunk a little deeper than usual into his face – an illusion produced by a shadow of fatigue beneath them. In the shaded light that hung from the centre of the small sitting-room his face seemed all contours and hollows, defined by the sharp expression of apology that had replaced his more customary one of just-suppressed humour.

'My dear Monsieur, that you should apologise when, when . . .' Anne threw her arm wide to indicate the room. 'Do you like it?'

'Like it. Oh, my God, it's wonderful, wonderful.'

Hartmann saw her eyes brim with tears and the look of worry left his face. He turned away for a moment. 'It was a dreadful dinner,' he said. 'From the moment we sat down my heart sank. It became a test of endurance. The old woman who brought the food in took an age between each course and then, when we'd finished, our hostess insisted that we listen while one of the other guests played the piano.'

'But wasn't that nice?'

'I'm afraid not. I'm no musician, but even my ears were offended.'

Anne smiled. 'I've bought some brandy. I thought perhaps you might like some. I'm afraid it's not very good, but it was all I – all they had in the local shop.'

She handed him a glass from the cupboard and filled it. 'It's fine,' said Hartmann as the liquid seared his throat. 'But won't you have any?'

'I don't know, I hadn't thought about it. I don't normally drink brandy.'

'Go on.'

'Well, I can't see why not.' She poured herself some and sipped at it suspiciously. It made her eyes water.

'Here's to your new home,' said Hartmann, raising his glass.

Anne smiled and raised hers. 'To you, monsieur.'

'You'd better not tell anyone at the hotel about this arrangement. If they want to know how you can manage to live in your own rooms you'd better tell them that an aunt left you some money in her will or something like that. It's not that there's anything wrong in the arrangement, it's just that in a small town people talk. If they knew I paid for you to be here they'd jump to only one conclusion. So you must tell no one.'

Anne turned her head. 'Very well, monsieur.' She felt uneasy, as though she really were his mistress. In the excitement of the afternoon she hadn't thought properly about these things; now she felt the sense of panic returning.

'What's the matter, Anne?'

She looked up and smiled, though without much spirit. 'Nothing, monsieur, nothing. It's wonderful, these rooms, this little courtyard . . . But I don't like the feeling of secrecy.

I don't like to be furtive. I've kept too many secrets in my life. I would like things to be more open.'

'I know. It's not a perfect arrangement for you. But that's not your fault and it's not mine. It's the fault of small-town society where people have nothing better to do than gossip and lie about each other.'

Anne looked down.

'There's nothing you or I can do to change that. You simply have to try to make the choices that will make you happiest in the circumstances. If you'd feel better back at the Lion d'Or, then I quite understand. Please believe me, I won't be offended. It's your choice.'

'Oh no! I *adore* these rooms. It's the prettiest, most perfect little apartment, I've ever seen. I know I'll be happy here. I just . . . it's silly, but I just wish things were more straightforward sometimes.'

Hartmann's voice rumbled on soothingly. He had a way of making things seem quite clear and reasonable, Anne thought; so much so that he could talk away the most unsettling doubts – talk away, perhaps even the horrors that visited her in the night.

She raised her face to him and he noticed that her eyes were fierce with pleading and determination. 'Monsieur, you must not betray me.'

Hartmann could not know what betrayal she might have suffered before, but he was aware from the hard edge of her voice that she was asking him for something fundamental to her happiness. He also knew, without admitting it to himself, that the more reasonably he put the case for Anne's staying in the rooms he had rented for her, the more he stressed the possible drawbacks, the more he said it was her own free choice, the more likely she was to do what he wanted.

'You can trust me, Anne,' he said. 'I give you my word.'

It was a meaningless promise because it was so vague, but Anne believed in it. Hartmann hardly knew himself what he was saying, apart from assuring Anne that his regard for her was sincere. He looked over to where she stood by the table in the middle of the room, her face half in shadow from the hanging light above. He felt the same onrushing of desire that had made him throw the books towards the rafters of the attic; and mixed with this he felt for the first time a sense of identification with her and with her vulnerability.

Anne at the moment found that her doubts were soothed, as she looked at him sitting at ease in her armchair, in her apartment. With his fastidious gentleness, his niceness of feeling and yet, too, that self-control and confidence in all his dealings – with these qualities she could not be doing wrong, whatever she did. She smiled at him again.

Hartmann stood up, 'I mustn't keep you, now that you've got to get up even earlier in the mornings.'

'It's only ten minutes. You don't have to go.'

'I must. But I'll come and visit you again if you like. One day next week, perhaps.'

'Oh yes, please. I'll make you dinner. I can take an evening off. What would you like?'

'Anything you can do easily. A stew or coq au vin or something like that. I don't mind at all.' He didn't want her to spend too much money.

'Could you come on Sunday?'

'All right. I'll bring some wine, so don't bother about that.'

Once more, Anne smiled at him.

5

IT WAS HIGH summer and the sun shone full on to the small courtyard overlooked by Anne's sitting-room. On her first Sunday morning there she sat in the window-seat barefoot with her arms around her legs, her hands clasped together in front of her, and looked down. There were, as usual, two cats asleep. One, called Zozo by Mlle Calmette, was lying on the half-roof that jutted out over the inner porch by the door to the street. Anne could quite clearly see his grey flanks inflating as he dreamed another impossible dream of his daring. He was a fantasist of a ridiculous nature who, Anne thought, had not been destined for domestic cathood. He would prowl through the patchy grass at the edges of the courtyard in pursuit of a sparrow that was pecking at the gravel, concentrating fiercely on his long, skating steps, seemingly under the impression that the handfuls of intermittent weed gave him the protection of a lush savannah. The bird would always see him coming but continue to peck until it was ready to go. Before Zozo had even reached the stage of preparing himself to spring, the sparrow would be off with a faint, derisive chirp to continue feeding at its leisure elsewhere in the courtyard. After two or three such failed attempts, the cat would leap up on to the high inner wall and patrol the perimeter of the courtyard with a strutting air to recover his dignity. This would last either until he grew tired and curled up to sleep, or until someone came in from the street, when he would hurry round the wall and adopt a waiting position, coiled in as close a resemblance to a spring as he was ever likely to manage. On Anne's first day she had screamed in terror when what felt like a heavy hand, with the fingers slowly spreading, had landed on her shoulder as she walked to her front door. Zozo leaped off and threw himself in her path, lying on his back and waiting for her to stroke him. In this odd dog-like position he demanded the attention of all those who crossed his domain. What strange feline fantasy he was living out as he sailed through the night air to land on her shoulder Anne could never guess, but she had felt guilty at her scream, which must have alarmed the cat, and ever since, like all the other residents, she crossed the courtyard with her eyes turned warily skyward.

Anne turned her gaze back to the sitting-room. What decoration there was had been effected in a style which pleased her, with thick fabrics and solid furniture, the impression homely but not cluttered. It was the first time in her life she had lived alone, and she loved the feeling of pulling the door shut behind her at night and knowing she couldn't be disturbed. She liked the feel of the plain china plates in her hand, of the rough sheets on her face and the alternating wood and rug on her bare feet in the morning; not because there was anything unusual about them, but because they were hers alone.

She pushed back the window and heard the sound of church bells close at hand. She had intended to go that morning, since church was a good place to meet people, and when one was alone one had to risk such irreligious thoughts. Now she couldn't be bothered, but sat gazing out instead on the sun-struck cobbles where the second cat, an awful, brindled creature, was dozing. This cat had no name as far as she knew and was not owned by anyone nearby. Its face was gouged and partly bare from a life of fighting over fishheads, and its mangy fur grew in irregular clumps along its spine. However, it exercised sleeping rights over the courtyard without fear of contradiction, least of all from Zozo who, at the sight of the other, would absent himself on urgent business, hustling off over the rooftops, dislodging stray tiles in his hurry to be elsewhere.

Anne had no work to do that Sunday, and in the evening Hartmann was coming for supper. 'Just something simple' had been his instruction; but she also remembered his mentioning coq au vin, and she wanted to please him. He probably had no idea of the difficulty such a dish caused; it needed long, slow cooking in an oven, and all she had was a single

99

ring of uncontrollable temperature. She had made some soup late the previous night and had bought two kinds of cheese so that, if the chicken went wrong, they would not go hungry.

Meanwhile the day seemed to spread before her like a flat, tree-lined road, winding into sunshine beneath a sky of hammered and immutable blue. She rested her cheek against her knee, gazed down at the sun-filled courtyard and heard the steady clanging of the church bell beyond.

Mme Bouin had not been pleased when Anne told her she would no longer be living at the Lion d'Or.

'I've never heard anything like it in my life,' she had said.

'I suppose it is unusual, isn't it? I just – '

'Unusual! It's unheard of. I don't think Monsieur the Patron is going to like it if his staff are not on hand when they may be needed.'

'But I won't be late for work, I promise. It's only ten minutes' walk.'

'It is the principle, mademoiselle. People will talk. They will want to know where this money comes from. It is not good, not good at all.'

'It was a piece of luck. I've told you.' Anne couldn't bring herself to tell a lie in quite the way Hartmann had suggested. 'A friend has organised it. There was some money in the family. An agreement. They were friends with Mlle Calmette. I can have no money myself by this arrangement, but this plan was worked out so I would get some advantages.'

Mme Bouin looked hard at her before taking up her knitting. Her hands were hidden beneath the desk, so from where Anne stood it seemed as though the metallic clicking was coming from the energetic movement of Mme Bouin's finger joints. 'The Calmette family was never any good anyway,' said the old woman at last. 'The grandmother was in prison, you know.'

'What for?'

'Adultery.'

'But that must have been ages ago! You can't go to prison for something like that nowadays.'

'If you call two generations an age. There's bad blood in the family, the same weakness from one generation to the next. Her sister was the same.'

'What do you mean?'

'She used to work at old M. Hartmann's house. "Secretary", they called it.'

'What are you saying?'

'He was old, but he was a wicked man. An atheist and proud of it, too. Even in his eighties he would have women go out there to clean or do other work for him, but everyone knew what it was for.'

Anne felt herself colouring. 'Perhaps he was lonely.'

'That Calmette woman, the sister. She knew what it was all about. And this isn't going to look good at all, your lodging there, not good at all.'

Anne was perturbed at the news of Hartmann's father. Perhaps it was well known that going to work at the Manor was merely a pretext for something else. Perhaps everyone in Janvilliers was already laughing at her and saying how Hartmann had a way with him, just like his old father. On the other hand, she had decided to trust him; she had to trust someone in her life. And it could be that Mme Bouin herself had tangled with this woman, Mlle Calmette's sister; perhaps when they were younger . . . but no, she found it impossible to imagine Mme Bouin battling for a man's affection. Presumably there must have been a M. Bouin, too. What can *he* have been like? she wondered. She saw him as short and plump with a round bald head, a silver watch-chain and a gruff, aggressive manner which he would have cultivated to keep his wife at bay.

Mme Bouin resumed her more normal manner. 'I shall be speaking to Monsieur the Patron later today and will let you know what he has to say on the matter. Now I'm sure the head waiter has some work for you, mademoiselle.'

'Thank you, madame.'

The same night André Mattlin came into the town bar and ordered a drink. He told Anne of some new plans he had

101

been commissioned to prepare for the Mayor, and watched the pull of her skirt around her hips as she worked.

He lit a cigarette. 'I've got more work than I can handle, that's the problem. When you've had experience of working on major projects in Paris everyone in this tin-pot little place wants to hire you.'

'I don't know why you don't go back to Paris,' said Anne, pouring a glass of beer for another customer.

'Paris is finished. It was fine in the twenties, and till a few years ago perhaps, but not any more. People are scared, there's not enough money, and they're obsessed by the Germans.'

'But aren't we all?'

'I suppose so. I don't suppose there's much we can do about it. If they want to invade us they will. They'll just walk in.'

'They won't *walk* in, surely? We'll fight.'

'No. Never again.' Mattlin swirled his drink around the glass.

'Why did you leave your job in Paris?'

'I've told you.' Mattlin puffed on his cigarette. 'The place was finished. And the company I worked for, they – I – it was ridiculous. I was the only competent young architect there. All the older ones just wanted to build like latter-day Haussmanns, all that monumental stuff, and I was the only one with any idea of the modern movements. So I had to do all the hard work while some of these other time-servers became partners.'

'So you resigned?'

'I – yes.' Mattlin nodded energetically, the curls on his head wobbling slightly as he did so. He had narrow greyish eyes, underscored with a darker grey after too many nights' excess, a long nose which started to hook about an inch before the end, and an upper lip on which the brownness of the pigmentation was blurred into the skin above at certain points, giving rise to doubts about what was lip and what was face and, in the more general sense, what was the difference. His cheeks were slightly concave and, though the chin was firm, there was a suspicion of a second beneath it when

102

he lowered his head, as he often did, to take up a drink or cigarette. Despite these flaws he was a good-looking man, the features somehow fitting together to make a whole that was more impressive than its parts. Perhaps the high bony forehead gave it dignity, or perhaps it was a triumph of proportion over detail, like a building by the despised Haussmann.

'What's this I hear,' he said to Anne, 'about your living in lodgings with that Calmette woman?'

Anne was taken by surprise. 'How did you know?'

Mattlin smiled. 'Everyone knows. And I couldn't tell you where I'd heard it. It's true, isn't it?'

'It's not definite. Monsieur the Patron has got to approve it.'

'Who's paying for these rooms?'

'It's none of your business, monsieur, if you don't mind my saying.'

Mattlin smiled, 'I thought as much.'

Anne blushed, then, feeling ashamed at herself for showing guilt where there was none, blushed even more, so her eyes stung with the burning. 'I don't know what you mean,' she said, fumbling with some glasses below the bar.

'It's nothing to be ashamed of, Anne,' said Mattlin.

'Of *course* it's nothing to be ashamed of,' she said, straightening up and furiously addressing herself to him.

Mattlin smiled. 'Of course.'

Anne took a tray and hurried round the bar to gather any empty glasses she could find. Mattlin watched her as she leaned across the tables. He had no idea who was paying for her rooms and had been surprised when his random shot went home: clearly there was something going on or Anne wouldn't have looked so guilty, but he didn't believe that Hartmann had made her his mistress. Hartmann, to Mattlin's relief, had ceased to be a competitor for the affections of the women they knew, and Mattlin doubted that he would have changed his mind now. If he had, then there were ways of making sure his suit would be unsuccessful. In the meantime it did no harm for Anne to believe that he thought Hartmann was keeping her as a mistress, and it would serve his purposes if confusion on the issue were spread as far as possible.

Anne felt indignant as she loaded her tray, but she knew she lacked even the consolation of having been honest. There was nothing dishonourable in what she was doing, she was sure, yet she was forced to conceal the facts of it with half-lies, and her reputation would suffer in this small town just as much as if the rumours were true.

Before he left, Mattlin made her agree to go out with him the following night. It was the last thing she wanted to do, but she could see that if she refused it would only make him more suspicious.

That had been three days ago and now, as she set about tidying the apartment for Hartmann's visit, Anne had still heard no word from Mme Bouin, so she presumed the Patron had made no objection to her staying there. Or perhaps he had been too busy even to see his manageress.

The butcher who sold her the chicken had also given her an old bacon knuckle, which she had added to the pot, and some beef bones which she had boiled to make stock for the soup. As she went about her rooms, dusting the mantelpiece, straightening the chairs, she had to sniff continuously to make sure the chicken had not boiled over and quenched the flame beneath it, thus leaving the gas to leak freely on to the landing. Usually when she went to check she found that the flame had sunk so low that the liquid in the pot wasn't even gently simmering. The only position in which the gas-ring worked properly was fully open, when it let out a fierce and continuous blast; at lower temperatures it flared and died capriciously, as dictated by the clogged inlets from the pipe to which it was connected.

Anne went to change her clothes. There was not a great selection from which to choose and, after a moment's thought, she chose a wine-coloured dress which was striking but demurely cut. She spent more time going through a box of combs and slides and earrings. In the end, after some minutes in front of the mirror, she was satisfied.

As she changed, Anne reflected that she had spent all the day preparing and waiting. Hartmann, no doubt, had had other things to do. There was his job and those boxes full of papers he had to read for it; there was his wife, and the large house to look after and the workmen to supervise; then there were his friends to see and play tennis and chess with: there was Jean-Philippe, whom she liked best, and his brother Jacques, the jolly one; and the persevering Mattlin; and the other people in Paris to whom he had made vague reference. All day Hartmann would have been occupied with these things while she had had nothing to do but think about him. Since he had last seen her and made the appointment for this evening he had probably not thought about her once, while she, who was so dependent on his bidding, had had to wait and hope that perhaps he might look into the Lion d'Or; that he might send one of his scribbled notes or might request an earlier meeting; might even contact her to confirm that he was coming. Perhaps, she thought, that is why I have reached this pitch of feeling so soon, when I hardly know him, because I have nothing else to think about, no way of my own of influencing events; while he, once he has decided what shall happen next, can merely turn his mind to other things. She felt a rush of resentment as she lifted the lid and peered once more at the now perversely bubbling chicken; but she could think of worse ways of passing a day than in this gentle simmer of anticipation.

Hartmann had in fact divided his day between despatching telegrams to Paris and discussing at some length with Jean-Philippe Gilbert, in whom he had confided, his position with regard to Anne.

Jean-Philippe viewed Hartmann's dilemma with detached amusement. He warned him to be very careful in his visits but couldn't otherwise see why Hartmann was perplexed. 'It's simple,' he said. 'Almost every married man in this town has a mistress. So long as it's kept private, nobody minds. So long as it doesn't cause your standard of living to fall – which distresses the wives – the system works well. Keep up appearances, that's all that matters. To do what you're doing – to worry when you haven't yet done anything wrong – is the worst of both worlds.'

Hartmann laughed. 'I suppose you're right. Here, you must try some of this wine. I don't know what it is, because the labels were all washed off when my father's cellar caved in, but this bottle's very good. Go on, give me your glass.'

'You never used to be like this, you know. You never used to have these scruples.'

'I know. I'm getting older. I thought you stopped changing when you reached a certain age, but you don't. Your good health.' For fear of talking too much about himself, Hartmann made inquiries about Jean-Philippe's life. They forgot the problems of Hartmann's lust and conscience until Jean-Philippe was leaving, when he agreed to tell Christine, if it should be necessary, that Hartmann had spent the evening with him.

At about the time Anne was changing, Hartmann put on an old jacket and went for a walk along the side of the lake and out towards the sea. As he thrust his hands deep into the pockets he felt a crumpled letter and pulled it out. It was the one from Etienne Beauvais, his friend near Bordeaux, inviting him for a weekend. He read again the hearty conclusion: 'Bring yourself a companion. All is discretion here! Do come, Charles; it will be a jolly party and we haven't seen you for a long time.' He looked at the date on top of the letter: it was nearly a month old and he had quite forgotten about it.

An hour later he drove his car at high speed through the pine forest and out into the sandy unwelcoming plain with its small cluster of houses round which children were playing. On the seat next to him was a bottle of the same unidentified wine he and Jean Philippe had been drinking earlier and a bunch of flowers he had gathered on his walk through the woods and stored furtively in the boot before re-entering the house. As he accelerated uphill and back into the pines, he felt the exhilaration of the schoolboy who is breaking bounds. For several moments he enjoyed the feeling along with the rush of air over the windscreen. Then he thought: why should I feel this when I've done nothing wrong? What bounds have I broken? As he slowed the car at the approach to the cross-roads on the edge of town, he felt once more the stirrings of conscience. Then he looked again at his feeling and found in it nothing but pleasure and kindness and an eagerness to please. He swung up into the long boulevard with its stripped trees and powered the car on up to the Place de la Victoire.

Anne's day of waiting ended as she heard at last the ring of the street doorbell and Mlle Calmette wobbling over to open it. Then she heard the old woman's front door close behind her, and there remained only the sound of Hartmann's footsteps crossing the gravel of the courtyard. She felt a pounding in her throat. She heard him on the stairs to her apartment where she knew he would be assailed by the smell of cooking. She stepped out on to the landing, her cheeks a little flushed against the darkness of her hair. She was apologising and welcoming him and her words were falling over each other; she took his proffered hand, the patch of colour in her face not unlike the colour of the slide which held back her hair just above the ear. She noticed that he moved and spoke with slow movements, presumably to calm her.

He opened the wine and poured some for her. She took it and sipped from the glass, looking at him over the rim as though she feared he might vanish if she let her gaze leave him. Hartmann laughed and raised his own glass to her.

'Oh, monsieur, I hope you won't be disappointed in the dinner. It's so difficult with the gas-ring. I'm not complaining, of course, you know, but . . . it doesn't give out a regular heat and it's been very difficult, so I hope you won't be disappointed.'

'Of course not. What are we having?'

'Coq au vin,' said Anne, with a hint of surprise. 'It's what you asked for.'

'Is it? Of course, yes. I'm sorry if it was such a nuisance.

You could have done anything. I don't mind, I just wanted to come and see you were settled all right.'

'You'd forgotten that's what you asked for, hadn't you?'

'I – well, yes. I've no recollection of it at all.'

Anne began to laugh. 'And to think of the trouble I went to.'

Hartmann laughed too. 'I don't even particularly like it, as a matter of fact.'

'Now *really!*'

He gave her the flowers he had gathered in the woods and she went to find a vase for them, glad to have a chance to compose herself a little.

Hartmann meanwhile glanced around the room. On a side-table was a small pile of books and he walked over and picked them up. The first one was a cloth-bound edition of *Essays* by Montaigne. Although old, it had been recently purchased, as the bookseller's pencilled inscription inside the front cover made clear. Recalling their conversation in the attic, Hartmann felt a wave of embarrassment. He put down the books and turned away from the side-table to see Anne coming back into the room with the flowers arranged in a striped blue vase.

Anne had read some of the essays in the book Hartmann said was his favourite but appeared unwilling to discuss them with him. He didn't press her, but deferred to her opinions and tried to guide the conversation into areas where she would feel at ease. Sometimes, he noticed, she would grow quite voluble in her enthusiasm but then would suddenly stop, as though she were afraid of talking too much or too inconsequentially. Then he would begin his slow prompting again, leading her forwards until her self-consciousness was once more overcome by her natural exuberance.

The food at least had turned out as well as could be hoped, and when they had finished the wine Hartmann had brought, Anne went to find the bottle of brandy she had purchased for his previous visit. Hartmann stood with his back to the fireplace and looked around the room which was lit not only by the candles but also by a dangling light above the table that had a white crocheted shade like an old maid's bonnet.

Anne handed him his brandy and stood beside him. She watched as he turned a silver match-box round between the ends of his fingers.

'Talking of friends,' he said, 'I had a letter from a man I used to know in Paris who lives not far from Bordeaux now. He has some sort of farm there, or rather his wife's family does. He's invited me to go for a weekend.'

'How kind. Was he a close friend?'

'Oh yes, quite close. I thought it might be enjoyable to go and see how he's managing. We're in a rather similar situation, really – trying to live in the country after years of the town.'

'And does he like it?'

'I don't know. He's very hospitable and I'm sure he'll make it a good weekend, with shooting and picnics and all sorts of things during the day, and probably music in the evenings. Even dancing perhaps.'

'How lovely.'

Hartmann lit a cigar. He blew the smoke out and said, 'The thing is this: he's asked me to bring someone with me and I don't think Christine would be very interested, so I wondered if you might like to come. Just for a change of air, you understand. No obligations. You could do just as you liked. It might be nice for you to get away from the hotel for a day or two and meet some different people. You'd be entirely . . . independent there, you'd be left alone . . . If the idea appealed . . .'

For the first time since he had known Anne, Hartmann was himself confused, allowing his voice to trail off inconclusively as he was unable to find words delicate enough to express his meaning. Anne, however, was too excited to notice any loss of composure.

'It's very kind of you. I don't know what to say.' In fact she did know what to say, but feared to seem precipitate. 'It would be difficult to take the time off work, and Mme Hartmann . . . are you sure she wouldn't want to come? Or rather if she knew I was going . . .'

'She wouldn't know.'

'No . . . no, I suppose not. But at work, at the hotel, it might be difficult.'

'You've been there long enough. Surely they owe you some holiday by this time? It's the law now, you know. Thanks to M. Blum.'

'I suppose so.' Anne looked down.

'Anne, I don't want to force you. It might be better if you didn't come, if you felt it would compromise you in some way. It was only a thought. I wouldn't want you to do anything unless you felt whole-hearted about it. It would be mad to go there and spend the weekend wondering if what you were doing was the right thing. It should be a time just to relax and forget your worries.' Hartmann appeared to believe sincerely in what he was saying, Anne thought.

In her imagination she saw a country mansion and smart evening parties and herself unsure of the etiquette and being talked about by other women behind her back. But she also saw herself being protected by Hartmann, walking at his side, and borne above all the difficulties of the occasion by his sublime self-confidence. Her decision was immediate, and depended on the simplest of things: it was a chance to be with him.

'I'd love to come. If I can get permission from Mme Bouin.'

Hartmann smiled, and not even Anne at her most timorous could doubt the sincerity of his pleasure.

Not knowing where to look, she picked up the bottle of brandy from the table and poured some more before Hartmann could stop her. He grasped her wrist to prevent her filling his glass with drink he would have, out of politeness, to finish. Anne jumped at the feel of his flesh on hers and he quickly released her lest she should misinterpret what he was doing. The brandy spilled on to the floor and over Hartmann's feet. He laughed as he wiped his shoes with a handkerchief and Anne, seeing he was not annoyed, laughed too.

'I'll come into the Lion d'Or tomorrow evening to find out how you got on.'

'All right. I don't think Mme Bouin is going to be very pleased.'

'Well, don't ask her. Ask the Patron. It's his decision, after all.'

'But I couldn't do that! Mme Bouin says he's terribly busy. And he certainly wouldn't want to be disturbed by a waitress asking about her holiday.'

'Why not? That's his job, running the hotel. And he couldn't be less sympathetic than this Mme Bouin, could he?'

'No, that's true, but even so —'

'Go on, Anne. You're a brave girl. "Robust" – wasn't that the word I used?'

6

THE NEXT DAY she asked Bruno's advice.

'I've never met the old man, as a matter of fact,' he said.

'Never met him? But you've been here for years!'

'I was hired by a man who was the general manager at the time. I was told the Patron was too caught up with his business accounts and other interests to see me. Why should I mind? I have an understanding with the Cow. She lets me take a holiday in August when I can go back to the only part of this country worth living in.'

'That'll be soon, then?'

'Yes. But as for you, young woman, I'm not sure the Cow would be quite so accommodating. Perhaps you'd better go to the very top.'

Anne looked at him uneasily as he slid a pointed knife into the belly of a fish he held from his dangling left arm and spilled its innards onto the table.

'What if I were to ask Pierre?'

'What if you were? He's only the head waiter. He has to take his turn like the rest of us. No,' said Bruno, wiping his hands on his apron, 'I think it's the man at the top for you. Undo another button of your blouse, hitch your skirt up a bit. Perhaps that'll help persuade him.'

'Is he like that?'

'Any man likes to see a bit of young flesh, that's obvious.'

'But I don't even know where he lives.'

'You go along the corridor on the first floor until you come to the mirrored doors. Through there, where it's marked private, is a suite of different rooms. I think his study is facing you at the end, though I've never been there myself.'

That evening Anne arrived fifteen minutes early for work.

She had combed her hair carefully and pinned it neatly back. She wore her newly ironed uniform and working shoes, together with a white apron. She ignored Bruno's advice on her dress. She didn't think a senior businessman would want to be distracted by a coquettish waitress; she didn't think a senior businessman would want to be distracted at all. Apart from the lawyer and magistrate with whom she had had dealings as a child, the Patron, she thought, would be the most important man she had ever met.

After making sure that Mme Bouin was not in her usual lair, she swiftly climbed the main staircase and turned down the long dingy corridor at the top which smelled of something indefinable – old cardboard mixed with cigarettes and dimly remembered plumbing failures. At the end was the door marked *Private*. Anne waited for a moment, feeling the throb of her heart as it rose up from her chest to falter somewhere in her throat. She thought of the huge sums of money the Patron might be negotiating on the telephone with business partners in Paris, in England, or even in America. She thought how much money she herself would give in order not to have to go any further with this venture. Then she thought of Hartmann throwing her luggage on to the rack of the train as they set off for Bordeaux, and she saw her left knuckle rap timidly on the door.

There was no reply. Against all her better judgment, she pushed open the door and was confronted by a dark, book-lined hallway off which several doors opened. She coughed loudly. Nobody came. She called out, 'Excuse me', but there was no sound. Slowly she made her way down to the door at the end. She pressed her ear against it. She thought she could hear a faint shuffling sound. Perhaps the Patron was filing something, or opening a telegram. She closed her eyes and prayed for a moment, then lifted her hand and knocked boldly on the door. There was no response.

She began to panic. She couldn't spend much more time in this private apartment without making her presence known to someone, or people might suspect she was trying to steal something. She would have to go back downstairs and tell

Hartmann later on that she hadn't been able to contact the Patron, so she couldn't come with him to . . .

She found the oval door-knob turning in her hand, as if her fingers had moved of their own volition. In front of her was a large armchair in which a small, bald man was fast asleep, his mouth open, a book abandoned on his lap and a glass of wine on the table beside him. Anne let out a short gasp of surprise and the man opened his eyes.

'I'm terribly sorry, most awfully sorry, I didn't realise . . .'

It was the man who spoke. Anne in her turn was saying words with similar meanings: 'Monsieur, I do beg your pardon, I'm sorry, I did knock but . . .'

For a while they stammered at each other, then both stopped. Then they both began again until the Patron held up his hand and Anne lapsed into silence, caught between fear and an urge to laugh.

He cleared his throat. 'I was doing some accounts and I must for a moment have closed my eyes. Now what can I do for you, young woman?'

Anne looked at the book he had laid down. It appeared to be a detective story.

'My name is Anne. I'm a waitress here.'

The Patron looked at her blankly.

'I arrived about six months ago to take over from Sophie, the girl from Lyon, who had to go back to her parents.'

'Ah yes, yes, of course. I do remember Mme . . . the manageress mentioning something. I suppose you want more money, do you? Well, it's very difficult, you know. There's not a lot of business at the moment. The hard times have come to France rather later than the other countries in the world. If you believe what you read in the papers, that is.' He looked out of the window. 'I don't. Not really. All this political activity. Half the young people are communists one day and in these leagues the next. I don't know what to make of it all.'

'It's not about money, monsieur. It's about a holiday.'

'A holiday? Good heavens, a holiday. Doesn't Mme . . . What *is* her name? You know, the manageress, I always want to call her Briand, she's such a fixer, don't you know. What is it?'

'Mme Bouin?'

'That's it. Mme Bouin, doesn't she make the staff arrangements?'

'I wasn't told about holidays, monsieur. And Mme Bouin wasn't at her desk this evening, so I . . .'

'Oh quite right, quite right. Come and see me, that's it.'

Anne wasn't sure if he was being welcoming or sarcastic. He seemed to be smiling anyway, so she went on, 'I just wanted to take about four days off so I can go and see some friends near Bordeaux.'

'What a good idea. It's a lovely town. I want my son to go to university there, you know, but he's got his heart set on Paris. It makes no difference, anyhow, because by the time he reaches that age he'll have to go straight into the army anyway.'

'May I go, monsieur?'

The Patron rubbed the hairless skin on the top of his head vigorously with a small, square hand. He took a step closer to Anne and looked at her. She could smell a mingled, not unpleasant, odour of garlic and tobacco on his breath. 'Go on holiday? My God, I only wish *I* could!'

'Mme Bouin says you're very busy, monsieur', said Anne, rather regretting the sycophancy of her tone as soon as she had finished the sentence.

'Does she? Does she? What on earth would she know about it? Busy?' The Patron shook his head and walked over to his desk by the window from where he looked down on to the forecourt of his hotel. Some white shirt stuck out beneath his waistcoat and above his trousers, which in turn hung loosely at the back and finished abruptly some two or three inches above his ankles.

'It's not bad countryside round there, you know. Some good shooting. Terrible if you go down into Gascony, though. It's so barren there that even the crows fly upside down to avert their eyes. All this is memory, only memory, of course.' He turned round again to look at her. 'I haven't been out of this town for eighteen years. Do you know why?' He came and stood close to her again. 'Because I'm frightened. What do you think of that?'

'I don't know, monsieur, I – '

'I'm sorry . . . Anne, wasn't it?'

'Yes. Anne.'

'I'm sorry, Anne. This isn't fair to you. You're a young woman who's come to ask me for a holiday. Why should I tell you my problems? I thought you wanted more money, that's what I thought. They pay you all right, do they?'

'But monsieur, surely you . . . surely you authorise the wages and so on?'

'No, I leave all that to Madame Bri- . . . Madame . . . ?'

'Bouin.'

'Bouin. Is it enough?'

'Yes, thank you. It's enough.'

'Do you know what I'm frightened of?'

'No, monsieur.'

'Nor do I. That's the funny thing. It's the trees and the sky and the roads, mainly. It's odd, because I used to love them. The doctor said there was a name for it – agora-something. He says it should get better. But it hasn't yet. Not in eighteen years. It happened at the end of the war. Have you seen the war memorial in the town? Most of my friends are on that slab of stone. We won't do it again, you know. I'll tell you one good reason *why* we won't do it again, too. Because there aren't enough Frenchmen left. The Germans killed too many. If my boy has to go and fight, he won't last long. We can't resist them this time. Dear God, what a mess they've made of it, the politicians, Poincaré, Briand and so on. What did they think would happen to the Boche? Of course they went broke. Of *course* they did!' The Patron turned away in frustration. 'Mind you, do you know who I blame? I blame the Americans. If they hadn't been so greedy we wouldn't have had to squeeze the Germans. They gave the Boche money to pay us, so we could repay the Americans. It was all American money going round and round. So the papers said, anyway.'

Anne watched in silence as the small man walked round his study. He said at last, 'Of course you can go on holiday.

I wish I could come with you. Tell the woman, Bouin, tell her I said you could go. You can come and see me again here, you know. If you want to talk. There's my son, of course, but he's only interested in girls. He hasn't told me so, but I can tell by the look in his eyes. He was a mother's boy, anyhow. He never had much time for me.'

'In two weeks' time, monsieur? I can go in two weekends' time?'

'Yes. You can go in two weekends' time. If it's that important to you.'

Anne wanted to kiss the Patron on the cheek, but restrained herself by thinking that only a few minutes ago she had thought him the most daunting man in the world. He took up a pair of spectacles from the desk and looked at her.

'You can go, young woman, you can go. Enjoy it for me, too. Do one thing in return. When next you pass the memorial in the Place de la Victoire, stop and look at the list of names. Try to imagine that they're not just letters chipped into rock but that each one has a face, a laugh, a look. My life might just as well have ended with them, too. But yours is possible because of them. It won't happen again. You can be sure of that.'

'I'll look, monsieur, I promise.'

Anne left with shining eyes and, quite forgetting herself, went down by the front stairs to start her evening's work. The Patron stared for a few moments through the door she had inadvertently left open and wondered if she had quite grasped his point. Presumably it was for people such as her to have their freedom that so many millions of men had died; there could be no other conceivable reason, he thought.

117

7

CHRISTINE HARTMANN SAID nothing. That, she sometimes thought, would be her epitaph. 'Here lies Christine
Hartmann, who said nothing: 1902–19 . . .' ? 1972, perhaps.
It would be a long time to keep quiet. It might also be unwise,
when there was so much she noticed that could be harmful
if not checked in time.

Sometimes at night she would hear from somewhere in the
depths of the house a sound like a gun-shot. Then the silence
of the night returned, so dense that for a moment she could
hear nothing; until there would come the choking call of a
wild bird that had strayed alone into the small hours of the
morning, and then the low murmur of her husband's breath.

Tensed and flat, she lay waiting, but the sound seldom
came more than once a night. Of course there were other
creaks and groans: the wooden stairs would ease themselves
out against the flanking wall with a mellow timber sigh, or
snap with splintery temper in the contraction of the cold.
There was often a remote, irregular banging from the door
to the scullery in the south tower which the maid, Marie,
after washing the dinner dishes, unfailingly forgot to close
before going to bed. The shutters in the attic could occasionally be heard grating slowly on their thick rusted hinges, and
down the long corridors of the first floor the worn planks
rumbled and squeaked in a capricious but not discomforting
way. At times like these Christine imagined the whole body
of the house and all its contents to be shifting in its sleep,
the immobile outer walls and towers not quite able to hold
in equal stillness all the disparate inner parts. It was hardly
surprising, when one considered the different portions of the
earth and living world that had been plundered to fill the
place: unrelated oxides fused to make glass and flattened into
windows framed by felled and sliced trees; marble quarried

and carved into decorative mantelpieces on which sat lamps compounded of different or unwilling metals; powdery plaster fixed by water in a brittle firmness unnatural to both. It was only to be expected that a little restlessness be shown at night – an aching of elemental parts which stretched to find their former selves. In this way, Christine thought, the house was like a human brain stilled by a temporary sleep which allowed the brash constituents of its personality the indulgence of a brief and limited self-expression, like a dream.

The gun-shot, then, was an intruder. It bore no relation to what the rest of the house was doing. As she went about the rooms in the morning, opening the shutters, Christine wondered what it was. There were no bullet-marks in the window-frames, no signs of violence, though many of the rooms had jagged cracks along the walls, and sometimes in the ceilings. There was a rough grey dust on some of the bedroom floors, she noticed, which didn't look the same as the soft and colourless fluff that gathered along the shelves, most of which, she had somewhere read, was the result of the human skin's frantic self-renewal.

When Christine mentioned the sounds she heard at night to Hartmann, he told her that all old houses made such noises, and when she pointed to half a dozen cracks along the landing and in the bedrooms he said they had always been there and that plaster shrank and had to be repainted. There was time enough, he said, to fix it.

There were other matters more pressing than the odd stray fall of dust, about which Christine also said nothing. She noticed a change in Hartmann's behaviour and in his response to her, but she merely watched and waited. The outward forcefulness of her character was balanced by a sense of delicacy and Catholic shyness which restrained her. In matters of the flesh she felt guilty towards Hartmann and always feared the loss of his attentions. She also thought it tactically best to say nothing. She knew the workings of Hartmann's mind and knew too that, left alone, he was likely to be entangled by his conscience, while if she gave him a chance to talk to her he might sweep her worries aside with his reasonableness.

In particular, she was distressed that he found it necessary to go to Paris for a long weekend to discuss some complicated business matter. Why did he have to make two trips, one now and one at a later, still unspecified date? Why had he not offered to take her with him on either occasion? And why did he seem so elated by the prospect of the trip when only a short while ago he had said he had no desire at all to return to the city?

She had packed his suitcase and he had told her he would be back on Monday night. She stood in the doorway of the house and waved him goodbye. He had said he would drive to the nearest big town to catch a train, since the small branch-line was so unreliable. Christine nodded in silence. She watched as he threw his suitcase in the boot and nosed the old black tourer round the edge of the house and up the bumpy drive through the pine trees.

Hartmann had initially felt some misgivings about telling Christine he was going to Paris, but his guilt didn't last for long. He felt he had already passed a point from which he could not turn back – with the hiring of the rooms, the flowers, the wine, the letter back to Etienne confirming the weekend. The complaints of his conscience were soothed by two reflections as he drove into town under a greying sky: first, the feeling he had for Anne was entirely of a positive and kindly sort; and second, he intended only to give her the opportunity of a break from the drudgery of work.

Anne was waiting for him. It was a short walk from her lodgings near the church, up past the reservoir and out on to the main road. She had gone with her head bowed, nevertheless, and her face concealed by a headscarf. She was worried that she wouldn't have the right clothes for the weekend: her smartest dress looked tawdry when she held it to the light, and perhaps in any case the other women would be wearing long dresses and jewellery. Hartmann had promised her the stay was quite informal, but she was uneasy.

At last she heard the sound of a car slowing down as it crossed the bridge out of town, and of its wheels turning the gravel on the roadside. There was a short blast on the horn and Anne looked round to see Hartmann gesturing from behind the wheel. She grabbed her case and ran over to him.

For some reason it had never occurred to her that they would travel by car. Where she had imagined herself sitting elegantly in the corner of a train compartment she now found the wind rushing back through her carefully brushed hair and lashing it about her face. She watched him as he drove, his face composed and humorous as he told her what he expected to happen at the weekend. Anne found herself almost unable to speak, so great was her excitement. Hartmann seemed not to mind, and, seeing this, she began to laugh at his descriptions of his friend and the sort of house he thought it would be. The tree-lined roads and small towns through which they passed were nothing extraordinary in themselves, but to Anne they seemed lit by an inner radiance, so that even the torpid peasants in the fields and sullen bourgeois in the shops were like figures from a painting or a film.

They stopped briefly for lunch in a café, but Hartmann was concerned that they should not be late. He was also worried about his car, which had never been reliable and which, he said, few garages seemed able to mend.

They drove on through thickening countryside until they reached a small village where Hartmann stopped and consulted his instructions. Five minutes later they pulled up outside a large farmhouse surrounded by stone outbuildings.

'Remember, don't be nervous,' said Hartmann as he took her case from the boot. 'I'll make sure everything goes all right.' He smiled at her. 'And you'd better stop calling me "monsieur".'

Anne nodded mutely and followed him to the front door.

It was opened by a man of about forty with florid cheeks and what seemed to Anne almost comically countrified clothes of wool and leather, with tweed breeches and a yellow waistcoat.

'My dear Charles! How are you?' Etienne Beauvais shook his friend's hand and then embraced him. 'You've arrived at just the right time.'

121

'May I introduce – '

'Of course, of course, you must be Anne. Delighted, my dear. Charles has told me so much about you. Please come in. You're the last here,' he added, leading them over the flagged hall. 'We're all gathered in the morning-room. Now throw your cases down there and Armand will take them to your rooms. Perhaps you'd like a wash, though, after your journey? Mademoiselle?'

'I don't think I – '

'A good idea,' said Hartmann. 'We'll join you in a minute.'

Etienne rang a bell and a small man in an apron arrived to show them upstairs.

'Don't be long now,' said Etienne. 'We're having a terrific time down there and the others are dying to meet you.'

His words had the opposite of their intended effect on Anne, who thought she would like to spend as much time as possible in the seclusion of her room. Armand led the way up the stairs, apparently struggling under the weight of the bags, even though Anne knew for certain that hers wasn't heavy. He paused for breath at the top before theatrically bracing himself for the final haul down the corridor.

'Your room, mademoiselle,' he said, elbowing open a door and putting down her case. 'This way, monsieur.'

Anne's room had low beams, small windows and a large brass bed on which she sat, breathing deeply and trying hard to tell herself not to worry. As far as the other guests and even her host were concerned, it didn't matter: as long as she was polite, then she didn't mind if she made some social error. The difficulty was with Hartmann. She began to unpack, hoping her one good dress would have survived the journey.

There was a knock at the door. 'Come in,' she said uncertainly.

It was Hartmann. 'Don't look so frightened!' He laughed. 'You can leave the unpacking. They'll send a maid to do it later.'

'All right,' said Anne, as if this were the most normal thing to her. 'But don't I have to change my dress for dinner?'

'No. I'm not changing. You saw what Etienne was wearing.'

'Yes,' said Anne, feeling, to her shame, a smile twitch at the corner of her lips.

'Well then! It's not exactly the opera, is it? Comic opera, perhaps . . .'

Anne laughed a little.

'Now listen, Anne.' Hartmann took a step closer. 'You're going to enjoy this. There's nothing that can go wrong. Etienne's a very nice man. I've told him who you are and how I know you. He won't embarrass you, I promise. If the other people are stuffy or difficult, just be polite and smile and give nothing away. You're here because you've been invited and have every right to be here. Is that understood?'

Anne nodded.

'There's nothing to be frightened of. We're here to enjoy it. Now then, have some of this.' He took a hip flask from his pocket and offered it to her.

'What is it?'

'Rum.'

She drank a little and gave it back to him.

'All right?' he said.

'Yes, thank you, monsieur.'

'Not "monsieur".'

'All right.'

'All right, what?'

'All right . . .'

'All right, what?'

'All right, Charles,' she whispered.

No sooner had she stepped inside the morning-room than Anne found her arm taken by Etienne. A drink was placed in her hand and she was seated by a large fireplace and introduced to Etienne's wife, Isabelle, a dark, austere-looking woman whose handshake crunched Anne's fingers, strong as they were from working. Then came Isabelle's brother, Marcel, the man whose ownership of land had brought Etienne down from Paris. He was less countrified in his dress

123

than his brother-in-law and rather more composed, though quite friendly in his greeting. He introduced her to Mireille, a woman whose low-cut black dress revealed metallic rows of jewellery on an unusually bony chest. She offered Anne her hand without smiling, and Anne, who thought she looked like some sort of countess, murmured 'Madame' as she looked towards the floor. She felt the other woman's eyes pass momentarily over her own dress and hair, which she had tied back in the bedroom but which she could already feel beginning to escape, a long strand stroking the nape of her neck when the air from the open window caught it. She felt again the inadequacy of her clothing, but forced herself to raise her eyes. She thought she saw a flicker of amusement in the Countess's face.

Etienne seemed to have accounted for every minute of the forthcoming weekend. Anne noticed that his brother-in-law viewed him with a benign patience as Etienne explained the vagaries of the local climate and how this had affected the production of truffles and the nesting habits of the local game birds. It seemed that there was to be an expedition on the following day in which all twelve of those present would take part. The night would be spent at a place called Merlaut, which obviously had great importance for Etienne. 'It's an enchanted place, my dear Charles,' he said. 'You wait till you see it.'

Although the atmosphere was not as formal as Anne had feared, the party had been carefully chosen, and Isabelle moved assiduously from group to group to make sure all was well. Anne noticed that no one asked about her job or how she knew Hartmann. She presumed that they had all discussed her before she came downstairs, or even earlier. Perhaps that was why they were all having such a 'terrific' time in the morning-room, according to Etienne, when she and Hartmann had arrived: what a scream, the Countess would have said, to think of Charles bringing down his little mistress from the local bistro . . .

She glanced over to where Hartmann stood by the window talking to Etienne's brother-in-law. His head was slightly on one side as he listened to what Marcel was saying, yet his body was relaxed and he had even raised one foot to the wooden window-seat as a man might do in his own house. She looked longingly across at him, seeing in a movement of his hand and rush of laughter the vestigial enthusiasm of his imagined boyhood which had so charmed her by the tennis court. How was it possible, she wondered, to be awed by someone and yet to feel protective towards him too?

Some of the guests were tired from long journeys – one couple had come from Paris – and this increased their sense of relaxation when they saw that Etienne had taken charge and there was nothing more for them to think about. The men drank freely, as if they were anxious to forget where they had come from; and, as they drank, their talk became exuberant and began to include more and more people at a time, until one of them would speak to the entire room.

As they rose to go into dinner, Anne told herself again the words that had been scored into the years of her childhood: be brave, little Anne, be brave . . . Her guardian Louvet's purplish face loomed up in front of her and his philosophical finger wagged: 'Courage is the only weapon, *it is the only thing that counts.*'

At dinner she found herself between the man from Paris and Marcel. They drank different wines with every course, and Etienne loudly encouraged her to drink more freely, himself setting an impressive example. Hartmann and the man from Paris appeared to be teasing Etienne, who was answering back robustly. Anne wasn't sure if they all knew each other already or whether they had simply lighted on a jovial bond that was common to all men. There was talk of Bouvard and Pécuchet who, she knew, were characters in a book. Since she hadn't read it, however, she couldn't see why the application of the names to Etienne was making the men laugh.

After dinner Isabelle said she was fed up with the sound of male voices and invited Anne upstairs where she had something she wanted to show her. Anne obeyed dutifully and the Countess followed them. Although it was a traditional farmhouse, it had been lavishly decorated inside, and Isabelle's bedroom, where she now led them, had beautiful striped drapes and little sofas and chairs of the most delicate and expensive-looking kind. Anne found herself invited to sit at Isabelle's dressing-table. She took a comb from her bag and began to pull it through her hair, even though, as far as she could see from the mirror, it would make very little difference.

'Allow me, my dear,' said the Countess, stepping forward and taking the comb from Anne's hand. 'Such pretty hair,' she said, as she combed it. 'A beautiful colour.'

'Thank you.'

'But why do you tie it back like this? Why don't you use a slide? You must have this one of mine. Here.' She untied Anne's hair then combed it back into position before slipping a thick jewelled comb in one side.

'But won't you want it yourself?' said Anne, who felt uncomfortable at having this stranger organise her appearance for her.

'No, no. Not this evening, my dear. Do have it. It gives you such an air of ... distinction.'

Anne retired, confused, from the dressing-table, and pretended to be looking at the pictures on the wall. Isabelle evidently had nothing in particular to show her; she had just wanted a break from the men.

'This is my son, Gérard,' said Isabelle, taking Anne's arm and showing her a photograph on a chest of drawers.

'How old is he?'

'Nearly fourteen.'

Doing rapid calculations in her head, Anne wondered whether Hartmann and Christine would soon have children.

Through the open door there came the sound of laughter from downstairs.

'They do make themselves laugh, don't they?' smiled Isabelle.

'I wonder who they're pulling to pieces,' said the Countess. 'It sounded smutty to me.'

They returned to the morning-room for coffee. Anne had never seen Hartmann like this before. She could see that he was happy and she found that she had begun to enjoy the evening herself. In any reckless undertaking, such as she considered the whole weekend to be, there was likely to be a mixture of anxiety and adventure. The latter, she decided, seemed to have gained the upper hand.

When one or two of the other couples had decided to go to bed, she went upstairs also. Her bed had been neatly turned back and there was a carafe of water on the table beside it. Her clothes had been put away and her nightdress was folded on the pillow, the recently mended tear above the hem rendered tactfully invisible. She undressed and sank beneath the covers, where she fell asleep at once, on her back, without moving.

In her dream that night she saw a man die. She screamed and ran home, where Hartmann angrily berated her for making such a fuss.

She awoke, still lying on her back, and found herself gasping for breath. There was a small window just near her head, which she pushed open. At once there was the sound of crickets and a torrent of heavy night air, filled with different scents, and cold on her face. In seconds her head was clear, and she rolled on to her side, away from the window, and fell asleep again, her dark hair splayed on the pillow.

Hartmann, whose room was above the kitchen, was disturbed early by the sound of activity. A dog howled; pans were thrown down gleefully on stone flags; cups and saucers were rhythmically beaten together by a skilled cymbalist. His head ached. The dog, or was it Etienne, barked instructions to the staff while overhead he heard the gasping of the water tank as it frantically refilled itself against the depletion caused by rushing taps and cranking cisterns whose every activity was relayed along the rafters by the strained and rattling pipes. How kind of Etienne, he reflected, to have given him this room, between wind and water.

In the middle of the morning they set off for Merlaut. It was not clear to Anne whether this was the name of a house or of a village, but it was a word spoken with great awe by Etienne. Everything at Merlaut would be perfect, unimaginable, beautiful – ah, but they must see for themselves.

Earlier that morning Anne had found that her hands were swollen with small blisters, and that one of her fingers was bleeding where she must have scratched it while asleep. The itching was intolerable, even after she had held her hands under scalding water in the bathroom. She scratched them until they were raw, scraping the palms against the waistband of her skirt.

It had stopped raining, though the air remained damp and cool for all the efforts of a thin sun. Hartmann attempted to let down the hood of the car, but succeeded only in emptying a gathered pool of water on to his trousers. Anne began to laugh. They were in a convoy of cars, set between a shiny Citroën driven by Marcel and an ugly black thing called a Rosengart that carried Armand the butler and two maids. Armand, who had been entrusted with the driving of it, had not mastered the movement of the gear lever, with the result that it emitted an even harsher grinding sound than was standard with the machine.

Merlaut turned out to be a shooting lodge, set in thick woods. It was intended that the party stay the night: four, plus the servants, could sleep in the main lodge, and the remaining eight in out-buildings and cottages on the estate.

The guests separated; some walked over the wooded hills, some went to see where they would be staying and others sat on the balcony outside the lodge, reading or listening to Etienne. Anne walked with Hartmann, who was still suffering from a headache. She teased him a little, the first time she had dared do such a thing, and he seemed not to mind.

'They've been very kind, so far, these people,' she said. 'They're not as frightening as I'd expected.'

'I told you it would be all right. They're not small-town people, you see. Most of them are Parisians who are pretending not to be. Like me. Paris makes you more tolerant, don't you think?'

'I suppose so. There's one woman who gave me a terrible look last night. I'm sure she must be a countess or something. I think she's called Mireille.'

'A countess, yes . . .' Hartmann looked up over the fields in front of them. 'Mireille used to be a singer. She was in the chorus of a cabaret in Paris that was so bad it became something of a cult. It had a snake-charmer who couldn't charm and a muscleman who claimed once to have been in a show with Josephine Baker. Mireille used to appear with several other women wearing feathers down their fronts. One night she had a note backstage from a man wanting to take her to dinner. She refused, being a nice girl, but he persisted. He turned out to be a manufacturer of pneumatic tyres from Clermont Ferrand. He was about sixty, but I suppose he was kind, because she married him. Unfortunately he died soon afterwards.'

Anne was amazed. 'Poor woman.'

'Yes. Though the blow was softened when it transpired that he'd left her several million francs. Now she's married again – that man with the glasses, Pascal.'

'Not a countess, then.'

'No, not a countess.'

There was excitement back at the lodge where the others were taking pre-lunch drinks on the balcony. Even Marcel, the saturnine brother-in-law, was showing signs of animation. The cause of it was a shaggy German shepherd dog called Oscar who had recently arrived with his handler, a short woman in a waterproof coat.

'He came second in the competition this year. Second out of all the dogs in France,' said Marcel.

'Second at what?' said Anne.

'At truffle-hunting, of course. What else? What other reason could there be for us to gather here at the end of a long summer in this remote little spot?'

'And what draws a dog like Oscar to the truffles in the first place?' Hartmann intervened, to deflect attention from Anne.

'Oh, there are many theories, you know. One scientist maintains that with pigs there is something in the truffle that resembles the smell of a male pig. This is why sows are drawn to search for them.'

'Do they do much better than male pigs?'

'No, about the same.'

'So what does this tell us of the love-life of the pig, Marcel?'

'No, no, I am serious,' said Marcel, crossly, as everyone seemed to be laughing. 'And Oscar, he is formidable. When he goes into the field he is like a virtuoso. His body stiffens and tunes to the one pressing thing that animates him ... the little black diamonds. Out of all the dogs in France, he's the second best. And he's only four years old. Next year, he will be the winner. Am I not right, madame?'

'But of course, monsieur,' the dog's handler nodded.

'When can we see the maestro?' said someone.

'Why, this afternoon. After lunch.'

'Lunch,' boomed Etienne. 'A good idea.'

They sat on benches at a long table inside the lodge and an old woman materialised from the scullery with some bread and a tureen of soup. Etienne deferred here to Marcel, who sat at the top of the table. Jugs of wine were passed round and the talk was of the afternoon's expedition. The old woman cleared the plates and brought some salad, and later some slabs of thick greasy terrine. Anne was sitting next to Marcel, who continued to lecture her on the history of the truffle. On her other side was Oscar's handler or, more accurately, Oscar, who rested his furry head on the table between them. When she thought no one was looking Anne slipped him her portion of terrine, which he swallowed at a gulp.

'In 1900 there were four hundred thousand people living in this region. And now?' asked Marcel, since no one else had. 'Less than half that number.'

'Where have they gone?' said Anne dutifully.

'The Germans killed a good number of them. The rest have gone to the cities. Bordeaux, Paris, Clermont. The villages are empty now.'

The old woman brought omelettes with what looked like mushrooms stuck in them. Marcel carved open the dark yellow mass and served his end of the table. Anne had a good appetite but already felt quite full from what she had eaten. She managed to slide part of her portion on to the wooden floor, where the dog pounced on it, before returning his head to the table and gazing fixedly up at her.

'But it's getting harder and harder to find these little beauties,' said Marcel, forking a piece of truffle from his omelette.

Anne, who hadn't realised she had been feeding the dog with anything more than a strange mushroom omelette, was frightened that someone might have seen her throwing this delicacy on the floor. To quell a panicky desire to laugh, she asked Marcel about the training of the dogs.

A dish of boiled chicken was placed on the table and the jugs of wine were refilled.

'When they begin,' said Marcel, 'the trainer will wrap the truffle in meat and bury it. The amount of meat gets less and less until the dog will go for the smell of the truffle alone. Then sometimes they give him a little reward.'

'Have you seen your lodgings for tonight?' Etienne interrupted, turning to Anne. 'You're in what used to be a granary. It's very small, I'm afraid, just a couple of rooms, but it's got a pleasant view. You can't get the car all the way down, I'm afraid. The path's too narrow.'

Anne was by now not sure if the meal was finishing or beginning, and the arrival of plates of carrots, celery and potatoes made the situation no clearer. The old woman went stoically about her work, giving no indication of enjoyment or distaste. The din of laughter grew and Anne found herself caught up in it. Only one thing still worried her: the way Hartmann had behaved towards her in her dream. But she would tax him with it later.

After a green salad came a tray of cheeses which made her think of Bruno and his taste for the goat's cheeses of the Vaucluse; but the dining-room of the Hotel du Lion d'Or had ceased to exist for her. All the world seemed concentrated in this small wooden lodge in the hills, in the mingled sound of speech and laughter. She looked down into her refilled glass of wine and her eyes seemed to penetrate the bright reflecting liquid into the atoms that made it.

Before the coffee the old woman had one more surprise: an enormous open flan with a yellowish egg filling. For this she brought fresh plates, and Isabelle would take no denials from the guests as she sliced it into equal pieces. Oscar was once more Anne's private beneficiary.

After lunch they set off to see the dog perform. Hartmann

walked with Etienne, who was sweating as the sun bore down on them. He glanced back towards the three women.

'My God, Charles, you've done all right there,' he said.

'All right?'

'Don't be coy, you old badger. How's it going?'

'To tell you the truth, Etienne, it's not going at all.'

'Too young, eh? Too religious? You'll soon talk her out of that.'

'I'm a married man now.'

'Don't talk nonsense. What did you bring her down here for? I tell you, if you don't want to sleep in the granary tonight there's others who'd like to use it.'

'It's difficult, Etienne. I can't explain.'

'Listen, Charles. For well over five years I saw you capering about in Paris. I *know* you. Now either you've lost your touch or the girl's stringing you along in the hope of bigger presents than you've so far given her. You *have* given her presents, haven't you?'

'In a manner of speaking, I – '

'Well, there you are. Girls with her looks can extract a good price.'

'She's not like that. She's very innocent.'

'She *looks* innocent, I admit, but you know what women are like.'

'Do I?'

'Stop pulling my leg, Charles. Are you in love with her or something?'

'I don't think so, no. I don't know her well enough to be.'

'Well, if it's not that, what is it? You do want her, I take it.'

'Yes, you could say that.' Hartmann laughed. 'Listen, Etienne, I want that girl more than anything I've ever wanted in my life.'

'So what on earth is stopping you?'

'I don't *know!*'

They tramped up the hill towards a coppice of oaks, where the search for truffles was due to take place.

'I suppose,' said Hartmann, offering his handkerchief to

Etienne so he could wipe his brow, 'I suppose it's some sort of instinct. A certain kind of delicacy.'

'Scruples?'

'Something like that.'

'Well, I can imagine that to you, Hartmann, such feelings must seem extraordinary.'

'Thank you.'

Etienne gave him back the handkerchief. 'Perhaps you're growing up at last,' he puffed as they reached the top of the hill.

'Is this where we see the champion dog at work?'

'Yes. Just over there. Where the earth is scorched. That's how you can tell that there are truffles. It's an interaction between the oak and the soil.'

'You and Marcel should write a book about all this.'

'Be quiet, Hartmann. How could I expect a city dweller like you to understand the beauties of our country life?'

The dog-handler arrived with Oscar and a smaller, grey-muzzled bitch she said was his mother. While the guests stood round in a clearing she handed the lead of the second dog to Etienne and herself took charge of Oscar. She gave a continuous series of calls to encourage him in his search and told Etienne what to do with the mother. Oscar rambled over the dry ground, sniffing here and there, before sitting down and turning to look at his handler with a long accusing stare. The mother, who was called Gyp, had a faster working style, keeping her muzzle well down among the twigs and scorched earth and suddenly digging fiercely with her front legs. Etienne pulled up what looked like a clump of earth, about the size of a conker, and displayed it in triumph to his guests, who nodded and murmured appreciatively. Gyp pulled him back to work with a tug on the lead, and was soon scrabbling at the surface of the earth again with her paws. 'What a beauty,' said Etienne, as he again held up the result.

'You look at Oscar now,' said Marcel. 'He takes his time, it's true, but when he gets the scent there's no holding him.'

Anne looked at Oscar, and he looked back at her. His handler made some more encouraging noises and pulled him over to a different tree, against which he lifted his leg.

'In this competition they buried six truffles deep in the ground in an area of twenty-five metres,' said Marcel, 'and Oscar, he got all but one of them in record time.'

As Oscar sniffed around the bottom of the dampened tree his mother unearthed another truffle and Etienne gave charge of her to one of his guests. The dog seemed barely to notice the change of handler but continued on her workmanlike course.

'I don't know about you, but I find myself slightly disappointed in Oscar's performance,' said Hartmann to Anne, while Marcel continued his eulogy of the dog. 'I wonder if perhaps he may have over-indulged at lunch time.'

'Oh, I expect he's just getting warmed up,' said Anne. 'It was a big lunch, wasn't it?'

'I wonder,' said Hartmann, 'whether Oscar should have sampled *all* the courses.'

'All the courses?' said Anne. 'I only saw her feed him some chicken.'

'And the terrine, and the omelette and the – '

'Oh my God,' said Anne, 'did you see? Did everyone else?'

'I don't think so.'

Despite Marcel's increasingly irritated urging, Oscar had moved from a sitting to a lying position and closed both eyes. He was only roused from his torpor by the arrival of an old man with a pig. The memory of his lunch seemed to leave him, and the sight of the pig fired his limbs with all the animation Marcel had predicted in his truffle-hunting. He had to be restrained by two men as he leapt and snarled at the fat pink intruder.

'The pig and the dog,' said Marcel, who had a developed sense of the obvious, 'together they make a bad household.'

The box was finally filled with the labours of the greymuzzled bitch, and whatever could be rescued from the jaws of the pig.

'Branches too heavy, not enough light and air for the truffle,' muttered Marcel, 'and that wretched pig. Dying out, the pig, you know. Once everyone's got cars you won't see them used any more. Too nasty to transport.'

*

After the truffle hunt they went off to their separate resting places. Hartmann drove down a narrow track that forked away from the road behind the lodge. The car juddered as its axles took the strain of the uneven ground. Finally the road petered out into a glade of pine-shaded grass and they stopped beneath a tree. In front of them was a path through the woods that dropped steeply out of sight. Hartmann took the suitcases and walked ahead as Anne looked round about her, up through the overhanging branches. Although such dense countryside was quite familiar to her from her childhood, she looked at it in wonder. Hartmann, who must have been more at home in the long carved boulevards and tangled sidestreets of Paris, remarked only that it would have been difficult getting carts full of grain up and down such a steep and narrow path: perhaps that was why they had turned the building into sleeping quarters. The path at last issued into a flagged yard on to which backed a small stone granary.

The inside was simple. The original floor ran throughout the building, though it had mats on it in the sitting-room, which had had a fireplace installed, and in the bedroom from which double doors opened out on to a recently and roughly built terrace. This gave a view down over a patch of grass to a fence with an apple tree, and thence into a valley that stretched as far as the eye could see. They could look down its whole length, seeing both flanks steeply converge in their hectic fertility, with bushes and trees tumbling and milling together into the valley floor. They stood for a moment, straining their eyes to find where it finished, but could see no end to the varying shades of green that ran on and on in their prodigal growth.

Hartmann made a bed for himself on the sofa in the main room, despite Anne's protestations that she should sleep there, then went to investigate what was held in the small storeroom that acted also as a kitchen. Armand had done what was strictly necessary to prepare the place, but not much more. There were lamps and candles under the table and a crate of wine. Hartmann left the granary and went back up the hill to the car. There was something in it with which he intended to surprise Anne later.

Anne unpacked her clothes and washed in the tub in the corner of the bedroom. She looked over to where the evening sun was coming in through the open doors, flashing rectangles over the floor and up to the edge of the wooden bedstead, and she felt her final misgivings leave her under the pressure of an intense and rising delight.

Hartmann secreted his package beneath the sofa and went to wash and change while Anne unwrapped the parcels of food that Armand had left. She had chosen to wear not her smartest dress, because it didn't seem appropriate, but a skirt she liked that was dark and tight around the hips, yet of a cool material, with a pale top. To this she added her favourite red earrings. Hartmann came in to join her in the musty storeroom and started as she turned to greet him, caught unawares by her radiance.

They took two chairs on to the terrace and watched the sun begin to sink at the end of the valley. There was not a house or a human or an animal in sight.

'No birds,' said Hartmann, pouring some wine. 'I suppose they've shot them all.'

Anne smiled and said nothing, looking down into the valley ahead.

'I wonder what's happening at the Lion d'Or,' he said.

'I wonder too. But I don't care.'

'I expect Mattlin's just looked in for his evening drink. He'll be asking where you've got to.'

'Do you like Mattlin?' said Anne.

'Yes, up to a point. Why?'

'He's not very nice about you. The things he said, when he asked me to go with him for a drink one evening. And other things I've heard him tell M. Roussel in the bar.'

'What things?'

'I don't think I should repeat them. I'm sure they're not true.'

'Go on. I'd like to hear.'

'He said you used to walk round to his apartment in Paris to use his telephone because you were too mean to use your own.'

'I never went to Mattlin's apartment, let alone used his telephone. I don't even know what street it was in!'

'But I thought you were his best friend.'

'Hardly. I knew him, but I seldom saw him.'

'But don't you mind if someone says all these things about you?'

'Yes, of course I mind. I was outraged when I first found that Mattlin was making up stories about me, but there's nothing I can do to stop him. Whenever you tax him with it he just denies it. I think he tells lies about other people too.'

'And is it true that he arranged for you to act in this big case – something to do with marsh reclamation?'

'Of *course* it's not true. How could it be? Mattlin doesn't know anybody involved, and even if he did he'd be in no position to influence the choice of lawyers.'

Anne drank some more wine. She was relieved to hear what Hartmann said, though she didn't understand his attitude. In his place she would have punched Mattlin on the nose.

'Why do you think he does it?' she said.

'I don't know. I used to think it might be jealousy, but I can't believe that any more. He has as much money as I do, he has as good a life – better, he would say. His career is just as good as mine. I think that some people are just liars. They do it for no reason.'

'Perhaps it makes him feel more important.'

'Perhaps.'

'It doesn't matter,' said Anne. Nothing mattered to her, except that she should be exactly where she was. To make her peace of mind yet more complete, she nerved herself to put a question she had meant to ask for some time. 'When I was in Isabelle's bedroom she showed me a photograph of her son. It made me wonder if you and your wife had . . . had ever thought about . . .'

'About children?' Hartmann turned to look at her. 'It's impossible. Christine was pregnant, but she miscarried. Now she can't have children.'

That Christine had been pregnant before they married, and that her pregnancy had been the main cause of his proposal, he thought it better not to say.

Anne said, 'I'm sorry, I didn't know.'

'That's all right. It's quite a normal question. You weren't to know the answer would be . . . sad.'

Neither of them spoke for a time. Anne was thinking how strange their marriage must be, with both of them knowing that there could be no children. Hartmann, who had long been resigned to the idea, felt no embarrassment at Anne's question and knew he could trust her to tell no one else. His peace of mind was troubled only by her physical proximity. The silence deepened, and he began to feel in it an uneasy power, like the force that had made him stride away from her when they stood side by side in the attic at the Manor. Anne thought the quietness was like a stream that washed away the barriers between them. But the density of it gradually lessened; Hartmann poured some more wine, and caught her eye. She smiled back at him, then lowered her eyes.

'I suppose we'd better go and have dinner,' she said.

He nodded and went to light the lamps in the main room. He fiddled with matches and wicks until the lamps flared into life and lit up the rough walls. Anne apologised for the dinner, even as she brought it through. There were smoked sausages, heated in stock, and potatoes with mayonnaise. She had found some red beans already cooked, and had made a salad. There were some gherkins and mustard on a shelf, and Armand had provided a loaf of rough bread large enough to last a week. Hartmann opened another bottle of wine and they began to eat.

'It was very good,' said Hartmann when they had finished. 'I think it was the best dinner I've ever had.'

She laughed.

He said, 'I've got a present for you, Anne.'

Already taut with delight, Anne thought she might snap. He pulled out a heavy package from under the sofa and gestured to her to open it. She pulled away the paper to discover a gramophone, not unlike the one she had had to sell before she left Paris.

She couldn't find any words, and, seeing this, Hartmann spoke for her. 'I bought some records. I don't know if they're what you like. I asked the woman in the shop for dance music and she gave me half a dozen.'

He handed her the parcel and watched the emotions passing over her face. Still she couldn't speak, and Hartmann found himself moved by her response. He had intended the present merely as a light-hearted gesture, or so he told himself.

'I'll take the plates into the kitchen while you look at the records,' he said. In the connecting darkness between the rooms, he caught his foot and almost dropped what he was carrying. He heard Anne's laughter.

By the time he returned she had composed herself again.

'Can we dance?' she said.

'Now?'

'Why not?'

'What, in here?'

'No, no, out on the terrace.'

'But it's dark and I can't dance.'

'Come on.'

Anne took a lamp and hung it from a hook on the back wall of the granary. Then she carried out the gramophone and wound it up. As she looked down into the darkness of the valley she saw two moths blunder into the lamp. She remembered her hands, and wondered what Hartmann would say if he noticed their rawness. But it was too late: she had already put on the first record.

'Won't we disturb people?' said Hartmann, from the threshold of the bedroom.

'Come on, you know there's no one near. And it's not very loud anyway.'

'But I can't da – '

She took his hand, and pulled him on to the terrace. They danced to *I Was Only Fooling When I Said I Didn't Care*, *It's Spring-time When You Smile*, and *My Only, My Angel*. Hartmann was as good as his word: he stumbled over the rough paving of the terrace, but Anne seemed always to keep out of harm's way and to guide him onwards. She played the records again and again until Hartmann begged to be released. At last she agreed, and they carried the gramophone, the lamp and the records back through to the main room.

Hartmann poured himself some more wine and stood with his back to the fireplace. The sleeves of his thinly striped shirt were rolled up; he pulled at his tie to loosen it and ran his hand back through his hair. His face had its usual gravity, given by the weight of the head and the dark evenness of the features, offset by a liveliness in his eyes that always had at their centre a point of light, however deep they seemed sunk. It expanded when, as now, he smiled.

It was cool in the room and Anne took her shawl from the back of a chair. She said, 'I haven't said "thank you" for the present yet. It's wonderful.'

'I hoped you'd like it.'

'Last night, you know, last night I had this terrible dream. And it was all your fault.'

'My fault?'

'Yes, you were horrible in it.'

'What did I do?'

'You shouted at me.'

Hartmann laughed. 'I'm sorry. I can't think what came over me.'

'It wasn't funny at the time.'

Hartmann looked at her curiously.

'But it doesn't matter,' she said.

'No. I don't think so. What matters is whether you've enjoyed yourself.'

'Enjoyed myself? Oh.' She seemed to lose her breath. 'It's been the happiest day of my life.'

Again he found himself caught off balance by the intensity of her response. She took a step towards him. It was dark in the room; the one lamp shone on the floor between them. She moved into the light so she was only a pace away from him.

'I love you.'

'I know,' he said, 'I know.' He gathered her in his arms, so that her face was pressed against his chest, where her tears wetted his shirt front. He stroked her hair and felt the outline of her skull beneath it. He thought of the coils of her brain

140

beneath his hand, teeming and looping; he wondered what was thought and what was feeling, what was soul and what was cell – and all the other imponderable things to which he would never find an answer. She clung to him with all her force as if she might draw from him something of himself, some essence which she could keep and take away with her. He could feel her breasts against him and the beating of her heart, and knew he must disentangle himself from her touch before it was too late. He pushed her away, trusting himself only to keep one hand on her shoulder.

With the other he lifted up her face. Over the bridge of her nose and the top of her cheekbones were a dozen freckles, which seemed to him to have the colour and density of those in an opening lily.

Seeing them, he lost control at last. He meant only to kiss away the wetness on her cheeks but the surge of desire was so strong he felt himself beginning to tear at her clothes. He seized the corner of the pale top she had chosen with such care and pulled it from her shoulders.

She murmured, half in remonstration, half in pleasure as she stroked his hair. 'I love you,' she said again, as if the words would dignify the clumsy actions of his hands.

Hartmann felt the material of some softer undergarment rip beneath his fingers and saw her breasts, patterned with freckles like those on her nose, fall forward, and he lowered his head to them. He felt his hair combed up between her caressing fingers. He sensed in her touch a certain passivity, almost a remoteness, which he welcomed because it foretold submission.

He guided her backwards to the sofa against the wall, his lips not leaving hers. He tried to protect her from his weight as he moved on top. His hands ran up her legs, pushing the tight black skirt upwards, and his eyes, through a panic of urgency, saw her thighs and the dark, stretched fabric at the top of her stocking and the white inner thigh above, before his fingers met softer, fine material. He wrenched his arms free from his shirt and could hear the collar tear away from its stud. He pushed and lifted at the frustrating tangle of her clothes until he saw a soft column of fine hair, like a puff of

141

smoke or a feather, and when he touched her there, she gasped.

'The light, the light, please turn out . . .'

He felt a moment of desperation as if what he most wanted might be denied him at the last instant and then, after a brief resistance, there was a relief, a sensation of having come home, somewhere from which he should never have been away. Her fingers were harsh on his back where the shirt had torn sideways, and as his chest bore down on her he inhaled the hot blast of his own breath as his face and tongue moved over her upper body. He was aware of the muscles convulsing in his back and the effort that dampened the tips of his hair against his neck. Very quickly he squeezed her with all the strength of his embrace and gasped in her ear as his body arched and emptied itself in her.

Later in the night he made love to her more calmly, taking slow pleasure in her submitted privacy, feeling the softness of her skin and inhaling the smell of her hair and her neck. Enough light came through the window for him to see the distant pleasure in her eyes.

When he heard her deeply asleep, Hartmann slipped away from the bed, pulled on his clothes, and went outside, down to the apple tree. He sat there, sated, guilty and amazed, until the grudging dawn made each different green of the valley distinct. Then he returned to the terrace and looked through at Anne's motionless form beneath the blanket. He moved quietly in beside her and felt her arm sleepily reach out to him.

The next thing of which he was aware was the sound of Armand clearing his throat theatrically in the storeroom. He had brought some fresh milk and was moving about the room with noisy tact. Hartmann pulled on his dressing-gown and went to say good morning. Armand told him he was required to be up at the lodge by ten o'clock when the shooting party would leave. He showed Hartmann how to make coffee in the antiquated copper pot and went wheezing back up through the woods. Anne emerged from the bedroom in a long white dressing-gown. Her face was pale from sleep; it contrasted with the darkness of her eyes and of the hair that fell on to the just-visible whiteness of her shoulders. Hartmann put the bread and some jam on the table and poured out the coffee. Anne lowered her eyes, took a large cup and drank in silence. She seemed taken by a heavy stillness, a quality emphasised by her pallor and her soundless movements. Hartmann had feared she would be embarrassed, but she seemed, on the contrary, relieved; she acted as though a burden had been taken from her. He was impressed by her calm and was himself infected by it. He watched her intently, and when she rose to go back to the bedroom his eyes followed her to the door.

When Hartmann went to join the men to go shooting, Anne decided to go for a walk on her own. He looked at her for a moment, to see if she was hiding some emotion, but could see none and so went up the hill to the car.

Anne walked through an adjoining field and discovered a path that seemed to loop round through some distant woods. By now the sun had risen sufficiently high to take the chill off the morning and to shine through the tangle of branches above her as she walked. From time to time the path came out into a clearing, and once she came upon a small cottage with geese enclosed in a wire pen. A little further on she sat for a while on a bank and surveyed the sinking fields below. The countryside was similar to that in which she had spent her childhood, until it had been interrupted. She thought back to the house she had lived in and to her parents; to her own self-absorbed innocence. Would Hartmann understand if she told him what had happened? Or would he react like the people in the local town when they discovered? Did she dare to gamble his love on his reaction?

She walked on through the morning and heard a rare outburst of birdsong from the trees: not everything, then, had been shot. Be brave, Anne, she heard Louvet drunkenly saying to her; courage is the only thing that counts. If she did not tell Hartmann, then he would not truly know her and could not therefore come to love her as she loved him. But then again, it seemed mad to risk losing such feeling as he might have for her merely for some perverse idea of honesty.

Anne could hear the distant sound of a gun being fired as the heat of the sun began to grow. It was a day in which everything around her seemed to be in harmony; it was impossible to imagine that the hedgerows and the fields and the woods and streams and isolated cottages were in any other than their appointed place. Only she, a human, with her illusion of free will, couldn't find her true position in it all.

If only the consequences of a deed ended with the grief it caused, she thought, then one could bear up until it passed. But there are some actions which dislocate the arranged order so badly that their effects are never finished, but go on and on through the years, breaking out from the lives they originally affected and contaminating all who come in touch with them. Evil, she thought; perhaps that is what evil does.

By midday, however, when she reached the lodge, her spirits had lifted; and by the time she had gone with one of the maids to the spot where the others were converging for lunch they were buoyant. The men returned from shooting in their shirt sleeves, carrying their broken-barrelled shotguns and discussing the morning's bag – not a large one, it seemed, since only Marcel was a practised shot. Some of the guests would be returning to dinner at the farm, but those with further to go, like Hartmann and Anne, would leave that afternoon. This did not spoil lunch for Anne, since she viewed the journey back with Hartmann as something to be enjoyed even more than the picnic in the sun. She looked at him as he lay on a rug, partly shaded beneath a tree, talking to Isabelle. One or two strands of hair on the back of his neck were damp with sweat, and she could see a slight patterning of it on the back of his shirt.

They returned in Hartmann's car to the granary to pack their bags. Anne looked around her and tried to score into her memory as many details of the place as she could. The worn little rug, the bed, the roughly constructed terrace, the apple tree at the foot of the garden – all now seemed fixed in her mind with immutable precision; but she knew how details could gradually be lost from such pictures until even the outlines became faint.

The convoy of cars rumbled down from Merlaut and out on to the road. Back at the farm there were farewells to be said and Anne was made to promise that she would return. Isabelle shook hands, and Anne thanked her for what she said was the best weekend imaginable, wishing there was a way of indicating that for once there was sincerity in the polite phrases which were all she could muster. Hartmann managed to disentangle himself from the other guests, and at last they were on their way, the car creeping over the stony drive until they met the road.

They talked about the weekend and what they had thought about the other guests.

'I don't think I'm made for life in the country,' said Hartmann. 'My shooting was terrible, and these comfortable shoes – they're agonising. I'd rather wear the ones I wore in Paris.'

After they had been driving for about two hours the wheels abruptly stopped turning. The engine made a loud clanking sound and there came a smell of burning metal. Hartmann steered the car to the edge of the road and stopped.

'What's the matter?'

'I haven't the faintest idea. We'll have to find a garage.'

'But we're miles from anywhere.' Anne failed to sound disappointed.

'Yes, I was aware of that, Anne. Why are you laughing?'

'I wasn't.'

'It looked like it to me. Look, there you go.'

'Well, so are you.'

'No, I'm not. We might be here for days.'

Three hours later they had arranged with a local farmer to have the car towed to a garage. The proprietor said it was a difficult job and it wouldn't be ready until eleven o'clock the following day. With some difficulty they persuaded him to drive them to the nearest town, an isolated place with a solitary hotel.

The manager was able to offer them a room, the last for fifty kilometres or more, he assured them.

'Aren't you expected back at work tomorrow?' said Hartmann. 'We could get a taxi and try to get you back by train.'

'No, I've got the week off. The Patron said I could have a whole week.'

'All right,' Hartmann told the hotelier. 'I'll have to telephone Christine,' he said to Anne. And tell her I'm still in Paris, he thought to himself.

Anne had now become almost hysterical with pleasure at the thought of the hours stolen back from nowhere. She began to giggle as she helped Hartmann with the luggage.

'Will you be wanting dinner, monsieur?' said the hotelier.

'Yes, please. And my cousin would like to take a bath.'

'Your cousin, monsieur?'

'Yes, the young lady I'm with.'

'Oh, I see, monsieur. Your cousin. Well, I'll show you where it is.' He scratched vigorously at his moustache as he preceded Hartmann up the squeaking staircase.

It was nearly eight o'clock, and Hartmann went for a stroll while Anne was changing. Over dinner he told her more about his past life. He chose his words with care, so that he should give an honest account of what it had been like. He never seemed satisfied until he had selected the correct combination of words, and would sometimes go back and verbally cross out what he had said before, until he was sure he had conveyed exactly what he meant. Then he looked satisfied, as if he expected that Anne would herself now register the experience precisely as he himself had done. As he spoke she watched and reflected how much his trust in her was growing, and how kind his face looked when animated. She was surprised by how little her declaration of love for him the night before, and what had followed, seemed to embarrass her, and she was encouraged by the way it seemed to have made no difference to the way he acted towards her.

After dinner he ordered brandy and they sat in the walled garden at the back of the hotel where it was still warm. No one else was in the garden, though they could hear the sound of voices from the restaurant. As their own conversation began again, Anne felt she would inevitably tell him what she had dreaded. Probably there were still good reasons not to do so, but she had always trusted more to instinct than to reason. Neither the time nor the place was perfect, but nor would they ever be. Then, once she had decided and could sense the anticipation in her stomach, the conversation would not come round to a point from which she felt she could properly begin. Hartmann's delicacy was such that he avoided areas where, for once, she wished he would intrude.

It took her in the end some abrupt changes of course.

'My life in Paris seems to have been very different from yours,' she said. 'I think I missed the glamorous times of the twenties.'

'I'm not sure they were as glamorous as people always tell you. I remember collapsing governments and fear about the franc as much as nightclubs and artists' exhibitions.'

'We lived too far from the centre of Paris to know about all the attractions and the nightlife. Though we used to read about it in the newspapers of course.'

Hartmann nodded.

'I lived with M. Louvet, my father,' said Anne.

'I've heard you mention him.' He smiled. 'It's very formal of you to refer to him in that way, your own father.'

'He isn't my father.' Anne leaned forward slightly in her chair. 'My father's dead. He was killed in the war.'

'I'm sorry. So many men . . .'

'It wasn't like that. He killed a man. And then he was shot for it.'

Anne's voice had a cold quality, as if she were reciting words already written. Hartmann watched to see if she would go on. She clenched her hands a few times in her lap.

'I may as well tell you.'

Hartmann said nothing but watched her face, which was impassive as she stretched her mind back into her childhood. She had been born, she told him, in the Cantal district at the southern tip of the Massif Central, in a house buried so deep in the countryside that no one would have known of its existence unless directed to it.

147

'My father was a shopkeeper. In the years before the war, when there were plenty of people to work the land, he became a sort of wholesaler as well. He used to arrange transport for all the local cheeses, and other produce too. It went to Aurillac and Clermont, then on to Paris. My first memory of him is when he came back on leave from the war. He had been fighting on the Marne and had done well. He had a citation for bravery. He used to play with me in the fields and tell me stories – you know, all the things a father does. It was terrible when he went back. I was far too young to know what it was all about, just that it was something awful he was going back to.

'I used to sleep in bed with my mother at night and we would say our prayers together. She wanted to have brothers and sisters for me, but she said we would have to wait until after the war. She told me we were sure to win soon and then it would all be over.

'My father used to write to us quite often and we were thrilled by his letters. So many people in the village had had bad news already. There was a woman called Mme Hubert, a widow, who had lost both her sons in the first year. My mother said I must be nice to her, but I hated her. I don't know why. She became a "godmother" to two young soldiers – you know how women used to adopt young men like that. She was always writing to them and then telling us how brave they were.

'Then my father was wounded and he came back on leave. He was at home for three or four months. I think it must have been in 1916. As he got better he would tell me stories again, but never about the war – just fairy tales and funny stories. My mother was very happy to have him home and she hoped his wound would take a long time to get better. He took me all around the fields and hills where we lived. I was only a tiny girl and I couldn't walk far, so he carried me on his back. He said I would easily fit into his knapsack and if I was lucky he'd drop me inside and take me back to war with him.

'Mme Hubert, she said if he was fit enough to play with me he should be fighting. She said both her soldiers, her

148

godsons, had been wounded but hadn't left the front. I think she was jealous of my mother because my father was still alive and she had lost everyone. Anyway, he went to the military doctor at Clermont and they said he was fit to go back. His regiment was at Verdun.

'We didn't know much about it. He never talked about the fighting to us, or certainly not to me. I think he just wanted to talk about the things any father would, not about war and death. In the village, people had heard of Verdun and they said it was a glorious fight.

'My father kept on writing. He didn't say much about what he was doing. He just talked about my mother and me. He said he was the luckiest man at Verdun, with his two pretty girls to come home to . . . There were three friends, him and Uncle Bernard, who came from our village, and another man whose name I can't remember. This other man was killed and my father was very sad about that. I think they'd kept each other going, the three of them, since the beginning. Also he said he couldn't sleep for the noise. At one time he said they hadn't slept for twelve days. Mostly he just talked about what he wanted to do when the war was over, and of the fun we'd have together. He worried about our safety. He'd brought in his old shotgun from the barn and showed my mother how to use it in case we ever had intruders. In fact it was a very peaceful place, but it was funny that he was worried about us when you think what he was doing.

'He was at Verdun until the end. He said most of the army had been there at one time or another. When he came home again on leave – it was in winter, I think it was January – he had changed. He still looked handsome, with his big moustache and his brown eyes, but something had happened to him. I used to hear him talking in his sleep. But that wasn't it. It was as if some light had gone out in him. When he looked at me his eyes were blank. Even as a small child I could see this. He still took me on his knee and he still carried me over the fields. Once he took me on his back all morning and we sat by a stream and he took out some bread and cheese and we ate it by the water. Then he squeezed me and he said, "I love you so much I can't bear it," and then he cried.

'That night he told my mother and me a little bit about the war. We had a small black dog, it was something my parents had been given by a local farmer when they married. My father said it was just like the black spaniel that belonged to the commanding officer in one of the famous forts at Verdun – I can't remember what it was called. They held out there for days. So my father said we were to be very proud of the dog. He wasn't really a spaniel, he was a farm dog, but we didn't mind. We pretended to give him the Légion d'Honneur, and my father laughed then, for the first time really since he'd been back.

'My mother by this time was working in a factory. She still believed we'd win the war and my father would come back safely. I think there was this feeling then in our village. Everyone thought it was a matter of honour. But I could see her look at him in the evenings, when he was sitting by the fire, and even I could see how worried she was. Perhaps other people could sense a change in him. I remember Mme Hubert saying to my mother that she hoped he wasn't going to be a waverer. She said "her" boys would carry on whatever the cost. "Whatever it costs, Madame, whatever it costs," she was always saying.

'The last night before my father went back he gave me a bracelet he had made from part of a shell. He had done a lot of carving on bits of metal and he had made a ring for my mother. He hugged us both in the kitchen and called us his two little girls. He told us to look after one another. My mother held on to him and cried, so he couldn't pull himself away. I watched him at last walking up the road. He didn't turn round or wave, he just walked away.

'The weather went very, very cold. Do you remember? We had a letter from my father saying there was a new man in charge of the army and they were hoping for a quick victory. And then we heard nothing. All through the spring it went quiet. The papers said our army had been defeated some-where. Still we heard nothing from my father. My mother said we were certain to hear if something was wrong. Eventually there was a letter from Uncle Bernard saying my father had been wounded in April and couldn't write, but that he was fine and sent his love.

'We never heard again. All through that year and the next the only word we got was from Uncle Bernard who never referred to him by name, but just said something about the other fellow, you know the one I mean, he's doing all right too. My mother said it was something to do with censors. But she was worried out of her mind. If he was so badly hurt, why didn't he come home?

'By now I was just about old enough to go for walks by myself, and I went over the fields to the places I had been with him and I prayed to God he would be all right. I used to play a game of pretending I was in his knapsack and then I'd jump out and surprise him and Uncle Bernard. I was quite happy in a way. I was convinced he'd be all right because he seemed so powerful to me. I couldn't imagine him letting anything go wrong. I knew men did die in this war, but at that age I'd no idea what it was like and I was sure he wouldn't let it happen to him.

'My mother, though – she was worn down by worry. Mme Hubert had lost one of her "godsons" and now she wanted to know where my father was. She was always sniffing around our house, and although my mother told her everything was fine I think she could see from my mother's face that something was wrong.

'When the war ended we had a letter from Uncle Bernard saying my father had been affected by shell-shock and had gone off to live with a cousin in Switzerland until he was better. My mother convinced herself this was true. My father loved the mountains and it was obvious on his last leave that he had been affected by something. I was just heartbroken that he wouldn't come back to us. Uncle Bernard was living in Paris now, and my father had asked him to keep in touch with us.

'But another year passed, and then they put up the war memorial in the village and they put my father's name on it. The local people believed he was dead, even though they had

had no official word of it. In my heart I never believed it. I was sure he was alive. I was sure he wouldn't betray us.

'One night when I was asleep upstairs there was a knock on the door. It was Uncle Bernard who had come all the way from Paris. We went and sat by the fire and he told us what had happened. He said my father had asked him never to tell us the truth, but to make up a story of how he had died in battle. Uncle Bernard said he couldn't bring himself to tell us this, so he had invented the story about Switzerland. Uncle Bernard said he loved us and didn't want to tell us anything that would upset us, but now he had to because there was going to be something in the papers.

'After my father had left us that very cold winter they had to prepare for a big attack. But the men were exhausted, they couldn't take any more. When the attack began they walked straight into the German guns. The Germans were just waiting for them. After Verdun, after all they had been through, some of the men thought they were being asked to do something impossible.

'Uncle Bernard didn't tell us everything that night, but he sent a letter to my mother in which he described exactly what happened. They were attacking somewhere called the Chemin des Dames. There was a restlessness among the men. One of the young officers had gone mad and my father and Uncle Bernard had pulled him out of a shell-hole where he had been screaming. Now the men wanted rest, but they couldn't have it. They were being sent over the top straight into the guns. Uncle Bernard said if it had been at the start of the war it might have been all right, but after Verdun it was different. They were kept at the front two weeks longer than the officers promised. Finally they were sent back down the line. Sometimes they would go to quite nice billets in a town, a little way from the fighting, but this time they were in some place underground.

'Here, behind the lines, they were allowed to sleep a little and mend their clothes. Perhaps my father did some more carving. Then after only two or three days this officer, a man who came from an important family near where we lived, came to tell them to go back up the line. The regiment that was supposed to go had mutinied and wouldn't take its place. The men hated this officer and they refused to go. There was no plan, no plot. They just refused point blank, all of them. My father pleaded with the officer. He said the men needed a few days of quiet to get their strength back. He said they weren't cowards, but they had been through more than any man should have to do. He said they were prepared to defend but they refused to attack. This is what was happening everywhere. They weren't cowards but they had had enough.

'The officer was furious. He said he would make them all into water-carriers so they would get killed crawling around the trenches. The other men were urging my father on. There was a terrific argument and the officer took out his pistol. He said if the men didn't pack their bags and start to move straight away, he would shoot them. My father said, "Go on, shoot me." They stood face to face and the officer put his revolver in my father's ear and told the men he would shoot if they didn't pack up their kit. By this time some of the men were crying.

'My father shouted at them not to move. Then he and the officer stood toe to toe shouting at each other. A sergeant came in and said he had carried out his orders and that the young officer my father and Uncle Bernard had pulled out of the shell-hole was to be tried for abandoning his position. Then there was a terrible screaming between my father and the officer, with the sergeant trying to intervene. My father tore the revolver out of the officer's hand. Uncle Bernard said the noise of the commotion was so great that for the first time in a year you couldn't hear the guns. All the men were shouting and stamping and my father put the revolver to the officer's head and he shot him.

'There was a long silence. Eventually the men began cheering and they wanted to congratulate my father, but he pushed them away and went to give himself up. A few days later, in the middle of the night, Uncle Bernard and the others were woken by a senior officer and told to fall in. Then they were marched at gun-point for half an hour till they came to a small copse. Uncle Bernard said he had a terrible feeling what was going to happen. A man with a blindfold was brought

153

through the wood by a sergeant and told to stand against a tree. They knew it was my father. Uncle Bernard and his friends were told that if they didn't shoot straight they would be shot themselves. The commanding officer gave the order and they all fired. They didn't have a choice. They killed him.'

At this point Anne leaned forward in her chair and held her head in her hands. Hartmann reached out to touch her, but she pushed him away, smiling a little, determined to finish the story. Uncle Bernard told her that the extent of the mutinies had been kept very quiet so that morale would not be affected. Then after the war the newspapers had had a story about two young officers who had been shot without trial for cowardice at Verdun. It seemed that in fact they had acted sensibly and there was a public outcry.

'According to Uncle Bernard the army had been looking for a way to get over that embarrassment for some time and the story of my father was a good way to do it. What he had done was not mutiny but murder, and the man he killed was apparently an inspired soldier, so he had damaged the national cause. This was the story the newspapers would tell, anyway. Uncle Bernard had come to warn us. He told us it might be better if we left the district.

'My mother was too shocked to do anything. I just cried because he was dead. I felt no shame. That night I slept in my mother's bed. She lay there trembling. She didn't cry at all.

'Uncle Bernard stayed with us for a bit while the story appeared in the papers. It was terrible. Even some of the big papers, the national ones, they printed some of the story because they said the crime was bad and the man he shot would have been a great officer. Also he came from a rich family. In our village and round about the papers had nothing else in them, it seemed. There were pictures of him, and the stories were full of lies. When we went out people would shout at us and throw stones. Mme Hubert was the worst. She met my mother in the shop and said, "I always knew he was a coward, but I never knew he was a murderer too." And still the papers were full of stories. I don't know where they found all the things they printed, but none of them were true. I just had to try to remember the father I'd known.

'It was worse for my mother. You know the custom in some places of sending letters, anonymous letters. She was getting lots of these. Once she took me to one side, and even though I was small I could understand her. She said: "Your father was a good man. You must remember him as he was, remember the truth, and never, ever, believe the things other people will tell you. There are some things in life which are too great for someone to endure."

'I remembered those words. The next week a stonemason came and chipped my father's name off the memorial to the dead in the village square. I watched my mother's face. I will never forget it. When we got home people had put things – horrible things – through the door.

'There were one or two people in the village who were nice to us. One man had been in the same place and he said he didn't blame my father for what he'd done. He said the full story of the mutinies wasn't half known yet. But most people took their lead from the papers, and Mme Hubert kept up her campaign against us.

'Still my mother refused to leave. She said that would be giving in. Anyway, she didn't want to leave the house she'd lived in with my father. But the letters didn't stop. The trouble was, it was more than mutiny, it was murder. This was what people said, and I could see as the weeks went on that my mother was looking ill. She wouldn't eat, and I could hear her crying at night.

'One day she came back from work and she found that the little black dog, the one we had given the Légion d'Honneur to, was dead. A man from the farm said it must have eaten poison and my mother said she thought she knew who'd done it. I think this one small thing must have been too much for her. The next day, when I came back from school, I found a policeman at the door of the house. He took me to one side and told me that my mother had been found in a barn. She had taken my father's shotgun and killed herself. I ran into the field behind the house and

155

screamed. And then I ran and ran. I didn't want to go home. I didn't want to see anyone again, ever. I wanted to die.'

Anne's account became disjointed for a time. No one had wanted the responsibility of looking after her. Her mother's sister had taken a strong line against Anne's father, and Uncle Bernard proved untraceable. A local lawyer, who wound up the family affairs, discovered that Anne's father had left quite a reasonable sum from his business and it was agreed that they should advertise for a guardian for the girl. After a while a certain M. Louvet applied and removed Anne to his house in Clermont Ferrand. She was sent to the local school, where she took Louvet's name to hide from the shame the papers had brought on her family. What she felt on that first day at school, even she could no longer remember.

'But what happened to this M. Louvet?' said Hartmann.

'I don't know.'

'But didn't he help you? Wasn't he your saviour?'

'Oh yes, he was very kind for a time. But we moved from Clermont to another town nearby and the people started whispering. It was hateful, I can't describe it. I . . . I won't talk about this part.'

Anne looked down to where her hands were tightly clenched in her lap. She swallowed and smiled thinly.

'When I was twelve the money ran out and I had to leave school anyway. We moved to another town where I was sent out to work, but the same thing happened. People began to talk, and the following year we decided to move to Paris. Louvet said we could lose ourselves there. We lived in an awful place near the meatyards in Vaugirard, then we moved to the other side of the city, to Saint Denis. Louvet was supposed to be a businessman, but he never seemed to have any work. I went to find jobs as a waitress, but it was disheartening because Louvet seemed to give up hope. His wife had left him years before and he was still disturbed by that. Although he was kind to me he used up all the money that my father had left and when I was sixteen I think he hoped I'd be like a wife to him – look after him as he got older.

'But I didn't want to stay in our little apartment. I wanted to be in the countryside again, where I'd come from. Paris was a terrible place to be. My wages actually grew less, not more. Do you remember the riots, a couple of years ago, when they tried to storm the Chamber? Louvet took part in them. He'd joined some league – one of these things you were talking about – something he said would make France great again. He got shot at and trampled in the Tuileries gardens. I think he was drunk. He came back with his hand bleeding. It wasn't very serious, and I put a dressing on it and he went to bed. That night he had a fever and he raved in his sleep. It was awful, the things he said. About me . . . He said he wanted . . . you know. And then he disappeared. I don't know where he went, though he sent me a letter a week later saying he was emigrating. The letter came from Lyon. I've never heard from him again. I think perhaps he went to America. He sometimes talked about it.

'Although I wasn't sure I liked him very much, I missed him in a way. I was alone, then, in this place. I thought I had to do something for myself. Delphine, one of the girls I worked with, said there was a spare room where she lived. It was in a house near the railway leading from the Gare Montparnasse, but it was a nice room and I didn't mind the noise. That's when I got my gramophone, on my birthday. Delphine loved music too and we used to have dancing parties there. It was all right for a time, but I wanted to be out of Paris. I was desperate to see fields and open air. One day when I was walking past the station I picked up a newspaper on a bench. It was a country paper that someone coming into Montparnasse had left behind. I saw the small advertisement for the Hotel du Lion d'Or. I had nothing to lose by answering it. I had learned to write quite well before I left school. Perhaps that helped. Or perhaps it was the fact that I was prepared to accept low wages – anything to be out of Paris. Anyway, I packed my case and left.'

Hartmann looked at the wall of the small garden in silence and then back to Anne. Between the freckles there were small dry marks where the three or four tears, which were all she had allowed herself, had run. Her eyes were deep and shining in the darkness, alive with hope as she turned to him.

'Monsieur?'

'What?'

It was the Patron. 'Monsieur, do you mind? It's nearly two o'clock and we must have some sleep, my wife and I.'

'Yes, of course. We hadn't realised it was so late.'

Anne stood up, smiling towards Hartmann. She gathered herself quickly, picking up her handbag and her shawl from where they had lain on the chair beside her. There was something of a willed resolve in the brisk normality of her actions after the emotion of the experiences she had recounted; but there was also a new and unforced lightness about her, as though relief and growing hope had quickened the movements of her body.

Hartmann rose more slowly from his chair, looking down for a moment at the table where he pressed his hand flat. He stood aside to let Anne go into the hotel before him, moving his arm with gentle courtesy. When he looked into her face she saw that his eyes were filled with compassion.

Anne put her hand gently on his arm as she passed. As they climbed the stairs they heard the Patron lock the door behind them.

PART THREE

I

HARTMANN WAS SUMMONED to Paris by a former army friend and business associate called Antoine Lallement who worked for the government. He needed informal legal advice on a matter of some delicacy concerning a government minister. Hartmann would normally have been intrigued by such an offer, but on the train he found his thoughts elsewhere.

The story of Anne's life had tapped a weakness in him he hadn't known existed. For some days he was persistently troubled by the thought of the small girl running into the field behind her house. He thought of the moment at which she screamed and of what hopelessness that sound must have signalled. When he imagined the policeman giving her the news he thought of the incongruity of the lumpish official in his uniform and the minute, uncomprehending girl. The man had brought a simple message: her world, her life as she had known it, was finished. Then Hartmann put himself in her place and tried to imagine what his reaction as a small child might have been. He found it impossible.

At the start of 1917 it had been easy enough for him to make an under-age entry into a demoralized army. In the ensuing eighteen months he had seen men die in their hundreds, some of them known to him, some in terrible pain and some obliterated by shells so that no part of them remained except some ragged piece of flesh in a tree. Although he had felt briefly shocked Hartmann, like the other soldiers he knew, required only a day or two away from the front to find the wash of normality restore him. He had felt fear for himself and sorrow for the men who died, but it had not gone deep; some instinct, of self-protection perhaps, had shut out any excess of feeling.

Anne's story troubled him in a low, destabilising way. The unfairness of the persecution by the villagers outraged his sense of justice. What further courage had her parents needed that neither had been able to find? Yet Anne herself, starting from nothing, had contrived it. With none of the basis of family love he took for granted, she had confronted this evil and created a life for herself. From a brief remembered experience of normality she had fashioned a convincing and proper identity.

Hartmann put these thoughts aside and tried to concentrate on work. As he watched the countryside slipping past the window of the train he wondered what business of Antoine's could be so urgent and so confidential that he couldn't give even the merest hint of it by telephone. Antoine was someone who enjoyed the exercise of power and discretion, as Hartmann had discovered when they first met in the army; but he was also a trusting and expansive man who wouldn't have taken pleasure merely in trying to tantalise an old friend.

Hartman took up a book, but after reading a few pages he put it aside. His thoughts kept returning to Anne. He couldn't understand what resilience and courage lay inside her. For the first time since it had ended he was forced to think about the war, an episode of such surreal horror that most people could only face it by ignoring it. Yet here, in Anne's life, was the clear domestic connection with the bizarre nightmare of the trenches. Some parts of her story had seemed a little vague, but Hartmann recognised the events to which she referred. His first job as a junior officer, fresh from hasty training, had been to tell the weary veterans of Verdun that one more push under the dashing General Nivelle would bring them victory. He was roundly disbelieved. There were things, as Anne's mother had remarked, which are too much for human beings to endure. When the men came down the line after their spell at the front many of them refused to go up again. They had reached a limit beyond which no amount of urging from a fresh-faced officer would propel them. They would defend, but they would no longer attack.

Antoine Lallement, a respected and senior officer, had taken the view that the men could be pushed no further, but that some sort of formal obedience to orders was necessary

162

until the doomed attempt on the cruelly named Chemin des Dames was abandoned.

In the first week of June there had been near-panic at the scale of the mutinies in the regiments around Soissons. There were rumours that exemplary measures had been taken. An entire unit was said to have been rounded up and machine-gunned by its comrades. Hartmann was sceptical of the stories. By this time many junior officers had come up from the ranks and identified too closely with their men to have allowed such things. Nevertheless, as officer in charge of communications with the press, Hartmann was shown an order from the Ministry of War instructing that no news of executions be released without the ministry's approval, for fear that the Germans or, just as bad, the British, should learn the extent to which morale was beginning to break down.

He had put such events from his mind, thinking only that in the end more lives would be saved if the army stood firm. He wondered now what men like Anne's father must have felt. He had never heard of murder behind the lines before. It was not exactly surprising but it argued extreme provocation. Yet in the world of continuous noise and death which men had been able to describe only with words like 'hell' or 'inferno' normal morality was already violated. No one felt inclined to pass judgement on the private actions of others, even on murder. And yet – and here was the pity beyond his imagination – such single actions were connected; they were not entirely random or alone.

He remembered well the public outcry Anne had talked about which followed the newspaper stories that came out after the war concerning two young ensigns, Herduin and Millaud, who had been shot without trial for cowardice at Verdun. It seemed that both men had in fact been exceptionally brave and that their platoons, who had been forced to carry out the executions, did so with tears in their eyes.

He also had a vague recollection of the case of Anne's father. There had been some uncomfortable stories about the true extent of the 1917 mutinies, and the army, or some of its senior officers, had been anxious to put themselves in a better light, particularly after the bad publicity of the Herduin-Millaud case. The story of how a private soldier had murdered his commanding officer must have seemed a good way to redress the balance and show that severe discipline had been necessary. Many of the newspapers, owned or run by members of the small élite that wielded more power than the ever-changing governments, were only too happy to print stories about the heroism of the murdered officer. Among the people Hartmann knew in Paris it was dismissed as a small attempt at propaganda and quickly forgotten. He had not paused to think how such an event might affect the lives of those intimately concerned.

He was moved also by the picture Anne had given of her parents. He thought of the small girl on her father's shoulders and wondered what this poor man had been like, with his big moustache and tired eyes and his beloved little daughter. Anne, he thought, could only have been a child of great gentleness, big-eyed, excitable and trusting. And her mother: she sounded a simple woman, dependent on others and presumably beautiful if it was from her that Anne had inherited the light femininity of her bearing. In the brief and mundane connections between the three of them that Anne had sketched he saw a life of tenderness that was enviable. He wondered at how quickly Anne had absorbed its elements to be able to make such a person of herself.

In the past Hartmann had felt sympathy for friends who were distressed, even the odd rush of unexplained compassion, like the one he had felt for Roussel when they surveyed the house together; but what he felt for Anne was something more unsettling, a feeling which was complicated by his continuing desire for her, which one night at Merlaut had not dispelled.

As well as this aimless pity he felt awe at her composure. Her life began to look like a rebuke of his own – or so he thought – with its privilege and hedonism. It appeared to him that through no fault of his own he was now faced with the responsibility for her happiness; that by playing with her feelings he had invited her to place her trust in him, and now it was his duty to redeem the horror of her childhood.

2

HARTMANN'S CAR HAD finally been mended, and the journey back to Janvilliers had been quickly accomplished – too quickly for Anne, who found that in addition to her usual tasks at the hotel there were a number of extra jobs she was expected to perform as an unofficial penance for having been away. It became difficult to keep alive in her head the bedroom, the terrace, the apple tree and the other details of Merlaut that she had tried to imprint on her memory. She didn't mind too much, however, since something more important had been salvaged in the understanding Hartmann had shown her. The risk she had taken seemed to have been worthwhile, and the love she had felt for him was now justified and fulfilled.

While his train sped towards Paris, she went about her work in the kitchen. There came a sound of coughing from upstairs. There was always someone coughing in the Hotel du Lion d'Or. Sometimes it was a bullet-headed Marseillais who stayed once a week in the course of his work, which entailed travelling up and down the coast. Sometimes the sound was of gentility at war with a thin painful choking and came from the dark recess beneath the stairs. Often it was the rich chest-clearing roar of Bruno, preparing himself for a morning's work in the kitchen; at other times the coughing was spectral and thin and seemed to echo down the corridor upstairs, past all the bedrooms, coming from no one knew where.

It was occasionally reassuring for Anne, when she stood in a deserted dining-room, to know that there were other people alive in the building. At times it seemed so lonely, leaning against the sideboard, swinging her foot backwards and forwards, waiting for a customer, that any noise was welcome. But then, when people came, the sense of isolation didn't necessarily diminish. So much of what she did and said was repetition. There were always salt cellars to be filled, and bottles of oil and vinegar to be replenished from the slippery containers in the kitchen. There were always the same questions to ask: Have you decided yet? What wine would you like? What would you like for dessert? Worse than the repetition were the long spells of idleness, with only the thoughts in her mind to keep her company. While she stood by the sideboard, describing circles with her foot in the dusty parquet, her head was full of sound, and in her imagination she was dancing. When the visitors addressed her it was not necessarily to make contact with her, but merely to obtain information or give orders through a series of set phrases, so that her actual personality had not been engaged at all.

When company did arrive it was frequently in the almost indiscernible form of the head waiter Pierre, whose soundless step carried him unheralded through the hotel. He had learned to give a little warning cough when he entered a room, having often startled people who were unaware of his presence if he began speaking at once. When he organised the plates and glasses on the sideboard or in the bar, his movements always seemed to leave a thin layer of air between his hands and the objects he was touching, so that they appeared to have changed position spontaneously. Anne liked this delicacy in him, and she liked him also because he asked after her and she sensed he was no happier in this hotel than she was. Beneath the softness of his manner there was a toughness she admired, even if it showed itself only in the end as resignation. Sometimes on an afternoon off he took her to the cinema. It was always packed with people and they often had to queue, but both were entranced by what they saw.

Anne also made friends with a girl called Mathilde, a great-niece of Mlle Calmette, with whom she went for walks in the public gardens when they could not afford the pictures. Both were devoted to Jean Gabin, and Mathilde had a yearning for Maurice Chevalier. Anne told Mathilde certain things about her life. Her childhood she glossed over, as she had done with everyone she had ever met, except Hartmann; but she told her something of her present situation, without revealing names. Mathilde, who had a young man to whom she was engaged, listened patiently, and they exchanged their views of men.

When work was finished, she would go back to the rooms that Hartmann had rented for her and play with Zozo the cat, if he was anywhere to be found, listen to her new gramophone, or read one of the books she had been lent by Mathilde. She was usually tired after a day beginning at six, especially if she had been on duty in the bar, which sometimes didn't close till one. The compensation for working so late was that she had the chance to talk to people there, and after the initial order of the drink most of them treated her like an ordinary person.

She passed her day, when she examined it honestly, in the hope of a communication from Hartmann. She resented the way her life was so dependent on the whim of another person, but not so bitterly that she was unaware of what she had to do, which was merely to wait and to be patient, and not so bitterly, either, that it changed her affection for him. As far as the strange terms of their relationship permitted, he was punctilious. He showed consideration for her position and he did his best to see her when he could, but the unforgivable thing was that he was not hers, and he was not there when she wanted him to be. She wondered if he had any idea at all of the eagerness with which she waited once he had made an assignation to see her; of the obliterating importance of these meetings in her day. In her more doubtful moments, she was sure he had not, and that there was only a painful and rather ridiculous inequality of feeling between them. Then, when she was on the point of despair, she received a telegram from Paris: 'Delayed here. Returning Friday. Meet Saturday evening?'

She placed it on the table in her sitting-room next to the small vase of flowers and felt that the waiting had been worthwhile.

*

At the same time that Anne was reading his telegram, Hartmann sat down in Antoine's office overlooking the Seine in the Quai Voltaire.

'Have you seen the latest *Gringoire?*' said Antoine.

'Certainly not,' said Hartmann. 'I'm surprised they let *you* read such dangerous nonsense.'

'You should look at this.' Antoine threw a copy of the paper across the room. 'They're going to nail Salengro by whatever means they can. They want blood, and the sort of blood they'd like best is the blood of a leftist minister. That would be the first step to bringing down Blum's government.'

'But nobody believes this story about Salengro having deserted in the war. Who'd believe the word of these fascists against that of a minister?'

'*Gringoire* says they've got fourteen witnesses to his desertion. Blum's going to announce an inquiry.'

'But why? He can't believe in stuff like this.'

'Of course he doesn't, but he can't afford to have a government in which one of his major ministers is suspected of having deserted under enemy fire – not when everyone is in a state of hysteria about the Germans invading again. So he'll have to clear his name.'

'I don't think Blum should give people like this the respectability of a reply,' said Hartmann, waving the paper in the air.

'Have you ever met Salengro?'

'No. What difference does it make?'

'None at all. You're right, in any case. He's charming – perhaps too sensitive to be a politician – but utterly honest, and patriotic.'

Antoine rose from his desk and looked over the river. He was an imposing, grey-haired man who liked to present his worldliness as cynicism. He was ashamed of enjoying his work so much, so pretended he was only a minor functionary in a system no longer under control.

'Our problem, Charles, is worse than that of *Gringoire* and Roger Salengro. I haven't asked you here for your advice about a small right-wing periodical. The newspaper I am concerned about is a serious national daily. The story they

168

have is no more scandalous and no less, but if they print it they will be believed, because unlike *Gringoire* they are widely circulated and respected.'

'I know. Though in their way no less venal.'

Antoine looked quizzical.

'Be sensible, Antoine. You're as aware as I am how much the papers are in the pocket of the bankers and the politicians – those of the right colour. Even the sainted Poincaré used to bribe them, as well you know.'

'Poincaré was a fine man.'

'Perhaps. All I said was that he bribed the press. Once he'd retired to Lorraine people forgot that in their rush to beatify him as the saviour of the franc.'

'Be that as it may, we are dealing with a proper daily newspaper with a huge circulation and, in the peasant's eyes, the authority of an oracle. The minister in question is the head of my department.'

Antoine named a man who was one of the youngest in the Cabinet, and who was said, even by opponents, to be one of the ablest. The man's detractors had been unable to find examples of poor judgement in his career and so tended to say he was too ambitious, or too clever for his own good.

'And what has he done, or not done?' said Hartmann.

'It's a question of sex,' said Antoine, sitting down again, and settling his glasses on his nose.

'A woman? What's the problem? Good heavens, look at Reynaud and that monstrous mistress of his.'

'Not exactly women. Girls. Young girls.'

'How young?'

'Too young for the press to find tolerable, when it's thirsty for blood. Too young for the government to be able to withstand.'

'Are you sure?'

'I think so, Charles. I fear so. Even if they don't fall on this one it will destabilise them further.'

'How far has the paper got with the story?'

'They say they've got all they need to run it, but I'm not sure.'

'And is it true?'

'You're going to have a chance to find out. We're meeting him this afternoon and he can tell us all about it.'

Hartmann lowered his head. 'My God,' he said. 'Can you imagine how hard that man's worked to get where he is? How he must have fought, what dedication . . . And he's an outsider, too, isn't he? To break into that coalition of old pals, to realise an ambition he must have been consumed by all his life . . . And then to risk it all – for this?'

Antoine nodded. 'Exactly.'

Christine was sitting in the morning-room with her embroidery. From somewhere underground she could hear the intermittent thump of a workman's pick-axe; through the window she could see where a thin wind was agitating the trees on the other side of the lake. It was two months since Hartmann had last made love to her. She remembered the occasion because it was in itself unusual, having followed an earlier gap of five weeks. When, so many months ago now, she had become pregnant she had feared that Hartmann's reaction would be hostile and that he would abandon her; but Hartmann, whom she had loved but not trusted, had shown his worth by accepting fully the responsibility of his actions, and for the brief period of their engagement and subsequent marriage all had seemed well. Even the difficulty of the miscarriage had been overcome with equanimity, and the later discovery that she would never again conceive had seemed if anything to bind them more firmly together. Although she had misgivings about making love with no possibility of procreation, she took his continued desire as proof of his true feeling towards her.

Now that it seemed to have waned she found all her old fears returning. She knew she was not beautiful, and she knew that, whatever Hartmann might have said to the contrary, he was disappointed that she was now sterile. She felt guilty towards him for this failure, but had hoped that she alone would be enough to satisfy and keep him; and so, since their marriage two years previously, it had seemed she was.

Christine stood up and walked over to the window. She

gazed across the water, thinking of the trial that lay ahead of her and hoping she would have the strength for it. She had no idea whether Hartmann had lost interest in her because he was making love to other women, because he no longer loved her, or whether all men went through periods of uninterest. Her instinct suggested that other changes were taking place simultaneously in her husband which might in some way be connected, though at the exact nature of those changes she could only guess.

She walked across the black and white marble hall and up the broad stairs, feeling the risen banister against her palm. A handle turned loosely in her fingers and she peered into the gloomy corridor ahead. In one of the bedrooms she paused and looked around her at the hectic confusion that spilled from the cupboards.

Above the mantelpiece she saw a long jagged crack in the plaster that ran up to the picture rail and reappeared above it in splintery tracks that crawled up through the cornice and out on to the ceiling above. She put her finger over the crack above the mantelpiece and ran it downwards, watching the thick grey dust tumble out.

'Bring me some rum in a glass of warm milk, will you?' said Antoine to the waiter.

'Still the same problem?' said Hartmann.

'I've seen every liver specialist in Paris and I don't think they have the slightest idea what to do. They wanted me to go to some awful spa and take the waters. My God!'

'You drank too much when you were young, Antoine.'

'Of course I did. So did you, Charles, and you seem to be all right.'

'I wasn't in the army long enough to learn the bad habits you had.'

'What was it, six months?'

'Two years. You know very well. And I tried to join up before, as you also know, but I was only – '

'All right, all right. You'll be showing me your medals in a minute. What are you going to eat?'

They had taken a taxi to a restaurant in the rue du Faubourg St Honoré. Every sound seemed to be muffled by the thickness of the velvet drapes and the plush upholstery of the chairs and benches. The talk around them was in murmurs, and the loudest noise was that of corks being slid from wine bottles by the assiduous waiters. Hartmann turned the conversation to the minister he was due to meet.

'Have any other newspapers got this story?' he said.

'No, and you can be sure they won't be getting it if your friend the editor has his way. Only he and the reporter know about it.'

'And the minister.'

'Yes.' Antoine sipped the milky liquid in his glass.

'And does he seriously expect that I can dissuade the editor on the grounds that I've worked for the paper in the past?' said Hartmann. 'Does he think I can stop them printing something which is not only a good scandal in itself but which would also serve their political ends?'

'But the editor *is* a friend of yours, isn't he?'

'Not a close friend. And this is like giving a dog a juicy bone then saying, "Please don't eat it".'

'Or a man with a young girl,' said Antoine, 'and saying, "Please don't touch her".'

Hartmann looked up from his fish and saw Antoine gazing at him in the half-mocking, half-bullying way that had frightened him when he had first encountered him as a senior officer. What did Antoine know? Was the reference to him, or to the minister?

'Exactly,' he said.

'In that case, Charles, if your personal magnetism is not enough, you'll have to find some very good legal reasons.'

Hartmann went over the possibilities in his mind. 'That may not be easy.'

'But that's what you're paid for. I've told the minister you're the foremost expert in Paris on newspaper law.'

'Thank you,' said Hartmann unenthusiastically.

'And naturally you want the Popular Front government to continue in power?'

'I do or I don't – what does it matter? I take the brief to

172

do the job as best I can, that's all.' Hartmann paused. 'And because it was you who asked me.'

Antoine inclined his head in acknowledgement. He went on, 'But you do want Blum's government to continue, don't you?'

'I think Blum is an honest man, I've said that, and I think France needs someone who can hold it together against the Fascists in Germany and those within who want to destroy the country – the people who tried to bring the Republic to its knees a stone's throw from where we're sitting just two years ago.'

'The riots, yes indeed the riots . . . But what a ragbag of a government, don't you think? And a pact with the Communists?'

'If the support of the Communist party is the price you have to pay to keep the Republic intact, then we have to pay it. Though I think they'll stab Blum in the back whenever it suits them.'

Antoine ordered some more rum in milk. 'Did you vote for them?' he said.

Hartmann smiled. 'I wouldn't tell you, Antoine. I think the only imperative in voting today is to vote for any government that does not contain Pierre Laval.'

'Pétain says Laval is the man of the future.'

'What the hell does Pétain know?'

The waiters plied them with further food and drink. Hartmann was surprised by the way Antoine seemed to accept what appeared to him to be a political disintegration, but supposed that when one's masters had changed as often as Antoine's had in the last ten years one became resigned to turbulence.

'I take it,' he said, 'you don't like Blum's government.'

'I'm a public servant. It's not for me to have opinions. Just like you, Charles, I accept my brief and – '

'Come on, don't be pompous.'

Antoine laughed. 'Well, do you honestly think from what you know of me that I would like a government led by a socialist and supported by Communists? A government whose accession to power brought the largest strikes this country has ever seen? And which threatens the possessions and livelihood of the fat bourgeois like me?'

Hartmann smiled. 'You're not a fat bourgeois, Antoine. A trifle corpulent, some might say, perhaps, but – '

'I know what you think of me, Charles.'

'Do you? Do you really?'

'A time-serving middle-aged bourgeois with a house in the country, who – '

'You can go on as long as you like, but you won't dissuade me from my good opinion.'

'Fine words from a lawyer. To tell the truth, I don't think it makes much difference. If Blum doesn't fall this time, there'll be others.' Antoine wiped his mouth on a huge linen napkin. 'I'd give M. Blum one year at the outside.'

'And then?'

'Daladier, I should think.'

'Daladier! Good God, not him again. Not even he can be thick-skinned enough to come back after that humiliation. Riots and deaths and – '

'You don't believe all that Daladier the Killer nonsense, do you?'

'Of course not. It wasn't his fault, but the fact remains that he was in charge when the mobs ran riot and he lost his nerve. A show of force the following day was all that was needed.'

'He was an infantryman. He was appalled at the sight of blood on the streets of Paris.'

'We were all infantrymen, Antoine, and none of us liked seeing blood.'

'But he's durable, Daladier. Don't underestimate him.'

'There have been worse,' Hartmann acknowledged. 'I think he's honest, all right, but hardly the man for the hour. You might as well say we'll have the ludicrous Chautemps back next year.'

Antoine called for the bill. 'I wouldn't put that beyond the bounds of possibility, either. Come on, Charles, try to look a bit more cheerful. We're going to try to save a minister. The least we can do is cheer him up.'

*

Anne was helping to clean the town bar after lunch when Mattlin came in. He gave her a half-smile, revealing a broken or possibly twisted canine on the left side of his mouth. Anne could never be sure if he was pleased to see her or not. He came in often enough, yet seemed irritated at having been distracted from more important matters. He always made Anne feel apologetic, even before she had said anything.

'How did you enjoy your weekend away?' he said, the half-smile stretching out a little further.

'Very much, thank you.'

'And how were your friends down there?'

'Very well, thank you, monsieur. What would you like to drink?' Had she imagined the sarcasm in the word 'friends'?

Mattlin had some coffee. He watched Anne move about the bar and briefly wondered what she would look like with no clothes on. The doctor's widow on the boulevard had told him she no longer wished to see him, since she had had an offer of marriage from a respectable businessman in le Mans. Mattlin had been forced to recall Jacqueline, the postman's daughter, and seduce her afresh. She had initially been proud and unwilling after the abrupt way Mattlin had earlier dismissed her, but she was quickly flattered into submission. Still, it could only be a temporary arrangement.

'Would you like to come out to the pictures with me one evening?' he said.

'Thank you, monsieur. It's very difficult for me to get the time off in the evening.'

'Or on your afternoon off, then? Surely the old boy lets you have one afternoon from time to time?'

'Yes, but I have to go to work sometimes. And the next free evening I have I'm going with Mathilde, a friend I've met.'

'Working, eh? Is that for Hartmann, down at his house?'

'Yes, monsieur. It's kind of him to let me work there. But I work hard.'

'I'm sure you do, Anne. He was away about a month ago too. I wanted to organise some tennis, but Jean-Philippe told me he'd gone to Paris. A strange time to work, at the week-end, don't you think?'

'I don't know. He hasn't discussed his business affairs with me.'

Anne, who had been evading questions all her life, did not find Mattlin's prying difficult to handle. All that worried her was that he would tell stories to other people.

'I'm surprised Christine lets him go away to Paris on his own like that,' said Mattlin. 'I'm sure he's still got a lot of old friends there, if you know what I mean.'

'Not really, monsieur.'

'I'd have thought Hartmann would have preferred a week-end in the country.'

As Anne disappeared into the kitchen with a tray full of dirty ashtrays and glasses, Mattlin was struck by an idea.

Christine's name reminded him that she had a cousin, Marie-Thérèse, who lived not far away. He had met her once at the Hartmanns' for dinner, and, although she was snobbish and rather silly, she had a bright look in her eye, a pert manner and a large, dull husband. She was a woman whose nerve-endings seemed close to the surface. The patina of respectability, though hard, was probably very thin. The prospect excited him.

A few moments later, the door from the street opened and Roussel came in, looking distracted.

'Ah, the very man I want to see,' said Mattlin, moving over from the bar to shake his hand.

Roussel, who was unused to such greetings from his social superiors, looked nonplussed.

'The work you're doing on the Hartmanns' house, you remember – '

'Oh God, don't mention that, M. Mattlin. It's turned out badly. I can't complain. It was all my fault, I priced it badly and I – '

'Never mind about that. Do you remember the lady who recommended you?'

'What? No, no . . . I just didn't know it was going to cost so much. And the boy's been ill again, coughing, and soon there'll be a penalty clause for running late, even though M. Hartmann says he won't enforce it – '

'Just try and remember where she lived, the lady who recommended you. Mme Hartmann's cousin.'

Roussel looked blank. He said, 'I don't know what I'm going to do.'

'Her first name was Marie-Thérèse. I don't remember the second. She lived near here.'

Roussel looked at him. 'You mean Mme Collinet? Roof work, I think it was. Renewing fillets and flashings. Some painting and – '

'Thank you,' said Mattlin, shaking Roussel's hand again. 'Collinet. That should be enough.'

Anne came back into the bar as Mattlin left, to find Roussel staring anxiously into space.

A young man showed Hartmann and Antoine into the minister's office. It was a wood-panelled room with glass-fronted bookcases and a large polished desk with a small library lamp that threw a yellow circle of light on to the leatherbound blotter and some single sheets of paper. The dim afternoon was visible through the window behind his head. Beyond the wind-whipped slick of river they could see across to the obelisk in the Place de la Concorde. After shaking hands, he gestured to them to sit down on a small sofa.

Antoine was firm. He was some years older than the minister and seemed to take a more detached, political view of their visit than did the minister himself who, though dignified, was agitated.

'Hartmann is going to find out how far advanced they are with this story,' Antoine said. 'He will then try to see what legal expedients we can draw on to forestall publication. And, failing that, what personal pressure can be applied.'

The minister nodded. As he did so, the stiff white collar of his shirt dug into the folds of his neck. He had the pallid complexion of a man who has spent too much of his life indoors. Although he was not yet forty, his flesh seemed to have died on him. His eyes looked tired from too much reading, and although he could, had he lived differently, have

177

been a handsome man, his untended body seemed to hang on him like a rebuke.

Hartmann was uncomfortable. He felt corseted in his formal clothes, and he was sitting rather too close to Antoine on the small sofa. He watched the lowered eyes of the minister as he prepared to explain himself.

'It's probably not worth worrying about,' the minister began. 'Probably just a lot of inventions which you can put a stop to with no difficulty.'

'I think not, minister,' said Antoine. 'We've had a report on the information they have. I sent you a private memo, which I think you have.'

'Ah yes.' The minister fumbled through some papers on his desk. 'This thing.'

'Yes. The documentation seems quite conclusive.'

'But so it does with Salengro. Can they prove it? That's the point.'

'With respect, minister, that is *not* the point.'

'I know Salengro well and the only court martial he had was for refusing to work for the Germans when they captured him.'

'The point is not whether they are right or wrong in your case, minister. The point is, will they print it?'

The minister said nothing. He turned his chair and looked out of the window. Antoine persisted. 'I'm sure you're aware that your party has few friends in the press and – '

'Yes, I am aware of that.'

'Perhaps M. Hartmann had better see the memo and then you can tell him what the position is.'

The minister walked round the desk and handed Hartmann a piece of paper without looking at him. Hartmann read the memo, which was written in bland, legal terms and looked up.

'Well?' said the minister.

'How much of this is true?'

The minister shrugged – a huge movement that seemed to ripple down his whole body. 'I will tell you. I will satisfy your legal curiosity, monsieur, and you can give advice from

178

the safety of your respectable position.' He walked over to the window again and looked out on to the river.

Hartmann felt uneasy at the minister's attitude and was about to speak when he felt Antoine's restraining hand on his arm.

'I was in Corsica last summer,' said the minister, 'as the memo correctly states. I was on holiday, which it does not state. It was the first holiday I had had for seven years. I had rented a house near a beach where I intended to read and to prepare for what I thought would be our inevitable victory at the polls the following year. I was alone. One morning I had gone to swim. I don't sleep well, and I had been up since six, reading. On my way back I heard the sound of voices. I don't know why, but I retreated behind a tree. I saw three girls run through the wood at the edge of the beach and out on to the jetty. They stood there laughing, and then they jumped in and swam. They were all naked. I don't know what age they were, so don't ask me. They were physically on the border of development, half-grown. Is this salacious enough?' The minister sat down at his desk, so that his face was hidden by the lamp.

'I followed them, and discovered they came from a little summer school on the island – I don't know what its function was. In town that day I saw a dozen of them out for a walk with their schoolmistress. Later I fell into conversation with her in a café. She was a very upright woman and was impressed that I had known people like Poincaré and Briand. She asked me to dinner at their school, which was a broken-down building not far away, at the north of the island, hidden by trees. We were waited on by the girls at dinner. They caught my eye. One thing the papers will never tell, one thing you cannot explain, is how these girls are not innocent. They have power. One of the girls who waited on me – a girl with long fair hair – was one of those I had seen that morning. I knew what her body looked like beneath the little dress. It was almost like a woman's body – almost. She knew it and I knew it, but the schoolmistress thought she was a child, and when she served at table she looked like it. All that night I lay awake thinking of it.'

The minister looked up, and his face, which seemed to have grown paler than before, became visible from behind the lamp. 'They were there again the next morning, and I watched them. Afterwards, when they lay down to dry in the sun, you could see that some innocence was missing from their movements. I walked on to the beach and they screamed and ran away, but one of them, the same fair-haired girl from the previous evening, stood for a moment and stared at me.

'The next day they came to my house after their swim and I gave them tea and lemonade. They were dressed, of course, but not properly. One of them sat on the rocking chair on the wooden balcony and she wore nothing under her little skirt. She rocked backwards and forwards, backwards and forwards . . . They did it on purpose. Day after day they came to see me. Just for half an hour, and then they would say they had to go back for fear of being found out. There were three of them. The girl in the rocking chair, the blonde one who had stood and stared at me, and a taller one who looked half gipsy, with Moorish blood perhaps. They knew I was alone. It was obvious. But they also sensed something else. They seemed to sense I was . . . unfulfilled. They knew more than their teacher. She was impressed because I came from Paris and because I knew famous men. She thought that must be all a human being needed. She had heard my name and thought I had a reputation, which I suppose I did. But the girls were unimpressed. They never said it, but they knew.

'All my life I've been dedicated to politics and to improving our poor country and trying to keep the peace. The papers say I'm ambitious, and I suppose it's true. But I'm ambitious for France as well as for myself. I'd never been able to get on with women. I've never had time, and I've never taken the trouble to find out the best ways of getting on with them – like noticing what clothes they wear. Even these little girls could sense there was this gap in me.

'Day after day they tormented me. One day they wanted to explore the house. In an upstairs room they found a trunk full of old clothes and they wanted to try them on. They called me in to see what they looked like. The gipsy girl was dressed up, but the girl from the rocking chair was naked. Soon they were all changing, and sometimes they had clothes on and sometimes they didn't. They made me join in. They were all laughing and it seemed quite innocent in its way. So I deluded myself. They ran around upstairs, in and out of all the empty bedrooms, shouting and laughing. The girl from the rocking chair took my arm and led me to a box-room. Then she took my hand, and placed it beneath her skirt. I made love to her. It was over quickly. I can't tell you what it was like. What does it matter? They came back again the next day, and she must have told her friends, because they all wanted me to do the same thing – though I didn't. But I let them do things to me, and each time I felt my life and all my work slipping away. With each weakness I undid everything I'd laboured for, but the pleasure was so intense that it hardly seemed to matter. To them, it meant nothing at all. For the one I made love to it was not even the first time. When they left, they were laughing.'

The minister stood up. 'There, gentlemen, you have it all. Disgusting, depraved. I'm sorry if I've made your stomachs turn. There are many more details I could give you – extenuating circumstances, provocation, but I don't think they're relevant.'

There was a silence in the room. Then Hartmann said, 'How did the story get out?'

'I don't know. One of the girls did tell her mother but they were both given money by an intermediary. They were perfectly happy with it. Certainly neither of them had any idea who I was. The mother, who was illiterate and doesn't know the law, just thought the girl had been rather clever.'

'And how did the reporter find out?'

'I don't know. But he's got no proof. I'm sure of that.'

'How can you be sure?'

'The girls didn't know who I am. They were never introduced. I told them I was a writer and they believed me. It accounted for all the books and papers I had. I said I was writing a history of the island. They called me "the Professor".'

Hartmann shook his head. 'It doesn't look very good to me, I'm afraid.'

'What are you going to do?' said the minister.

'Speak to the editor. Find out exactly what they know, and see what pressure I can bring to bear. I suppose.'

'You don't seem very certain.'

'I'm not. I'll speak to Antoine, and he'll let you know.'

'There's nothing else you need to know?'

'Not at the moment. Well, one thing. Not a legal point, just a matter of curiosity.' He paused. 'Wasn't there a moment when you could have stopped it happening?'

'I don't think I knew it *was* happening until it was already too late,' said the minister. 'There was no moment of decision, just a series of lost opportunities, moments when I could have resisted. I didn't see it as a deed, an action, until it was too late.'

It had grown dark by the time Hartmann and Antoine parted on the Quai Voltaire.

'You look upset, Charles. It wasn't an edifying story, was it?'

'It's not that, Antoine. It wasn't pretty, but worse things have happened. I know what he means about those young girls, too. They're not so innocent, and sometimes they don't feel things at that age. Their emotions are not engaged, and so in a way it matters less.'

'I wouldn't mind betting that my minister has suffered a good deal more anguish than the girls.'

'Probably,' said Hartmann. 'But there are things that people do as thoughtlessly as that which matter terribly, where the feeling goes on and on.'

'Like what?' said Antoine.

'I don't want to keep you in the cold.'

'It's all right. I've nothing left to do today.'

'Walk along with me. I'll buy you a grog or some coffee.' He took his friend's arm and steered him into the rue du Bac.

182

'Do you remember once you took me to a concert? Beethoven, it was.'

'I was always taking you to Beethoven.'

'Yes, this was a particular one, though. It was a quartet, though I don't remember what it was called, or what number it was.'

They went into a café and Hartmann ordered drinks. 'When I heard it with you that night I was so moved by it I cried.'

'Had that never happened to you before with music?'

'Of course. You know I'm not an expert like you, but I've been moved by it. Only this was different. There was a feeling in the music greater than any emotion I had ever experienced, or even imagined. It was frightening. It wasn't the sadness or the triumph of a symphony, or the exhilaration of something classical, it was colder and far greater.'

Antoine stirred his grog. 'I'm glad I educated you just a little in all your years here.'

'But you didn't. That's the point. I went back four times to hear that piece of music. And I couldn't bear it. I listened to it again and again, because I was trying to get on top of it, to comprehend it, but I couldn't. The power of the feeling in it was too great.'

'You sound surprised.'

'I *was* surprised. Until that time I'd thought that every feeling could be taken on and understood. I thought it was all a challenge – that any emotion could be assimilated if you tried hard enough. This was the first time I realised my mind was just not large enough to comprehend properly what some other people have felt.'

'What has this to do with our minister?'

'Not a great deal, I suppose,' said Hartmann, looking out through the steamed windows of the café. 'I think the connection is this – that I understand his temptation. When he said it seemed innocent when the girls were running around upstairs, I could feel your scepticism. But in a way he may have been right. There is a contradiction. How can such a powerful impulse, such a propulsion as he felt to perform a natural act, how can it be thought of as anything but innocent? When I was younger I would have been quite sure that there exists a ground of argument somewhere on which one can explain such things, and I would have been quite sure that I would eventually find it and so explain them to myself. Now when I think of the sublime but frightening feeling of that piece of music and what you might call the base but equally frightening feeling of the temptation your minister underwent, I can see no way in which to explain them. I can see no way in which they can be brought within my experience and reason, and I have to admit this. And so, instead of taking on every challenge and finding a way to assimilate it, you have to shy away, and say, "This is too disturbing. This is dangerous".'

'Or: "I desist", like Montaigne.'

'Yes. I thought it was a coward's response, but now I can see that it's the only reasonable way to react – to admit that your life will be, in some senses, incomplete.'

Antoine beckoned to the waiter for more drinks. 'And what will you do about the minister?'

'What I said. I can certainly delay the story with various legal tactics, but if they've really got the facts it'll only be a matter of time.'

'And so goodbye to another government.'

Hartmann nodded. 'What is the matter with this country? Why can't we produce a single man to run efficiently what should be one of the most civilised nations in the world?'

'Because we're only drawing on half the proper capacity,' said Antoine. 'The men who should be leading this country are dead and buried on the battlefields of the Western Front.'

'So ensuring that history will briefly repeat itself.'

Antoine lifted his glass and looked at Hartmann over the steaming brim. 'A truce for twenty years, that's what Foch called it.'

Hartmann said goodbye to Antoine and walked down the boulevard Raspail to the Sèvres-Babylone intersection, near where his apartment had been. Resisting a temptation to call in and see who lived there now, he pressed on through the early evening down to the junction with the rue de Rennes, at the end of which was the Gare Montparnasse. He thought of Anne picking up a newspaper left by a traveller just arrived from a distant and no doubt attractive-sounding part of the country. Anything must have seemed preferable to the life she had lived till then, he thought, as he found himself walking on towards the station. It was the wrong way for his hotel, but he was in no hurry to return.

It was a cold, autumn evening with a thin drizzle beginning again as he plunged into the small streets behind the station, wondering which one she might have lived in with her friend, Delphine. He tried to picture them dancing to her gramophone in the evening. He tried to imagine the resilience of her spirit that had made her dance, but he could not.

He continued walking towards Vaugirard, where she had first gone to live with Louvet. The rain was dripping from the brim of his hat, and such people as were on the street ran between the doorways. He walked down the rue de Dantzig where pavilions purchased after the Paris Exposition had been reassembled on the waste land to make studios. They had been ruined during the war by refugees who had broken the windows to make outlets for stoves on which they'd burned wood from the surrounding trees. Now the wind droned through the shattered glass and echoed in the thin fabric of the temporary buildings.

He cut across the rue des Morillons and looked around him where the rain was dropping from the eaves of the slaughter-houses. Was this where Anne had lived? In this house, here, with the broken shutters dangling from their hinges? Or in that apartment, above a boarded-up shop? Was this where her friendless life of sheer determination had brought her? Had her life really been shaped by a single act in which a man, pushed by circumstance beyond what he could suffer, had killed another? Or was the key moment her mother's loss of courage? Was there a single instant at which a greater effort could have stopped the chain of events; a second at which some restraint, some passionate reserve of will, could have been called on? His pity ran far more for Anne, who had survived, than for either of her parents. He could see how they had been victims of circumstances they could not control; yet when he tried to think clearly of the act of murder he didn't see it as part of an inevitable sequence of events. He saw the big soldier's hand close on the service revolver in the half-light, could feel the weight of the gun and ribbed texture of the handle in the soft palm, heard the explosion in the confined space of the dug-out behind the lines. He could only see the act then as existing on its own – a single, self-willed deed without reference to anything else.

Hartmann could feel himself sweating beneath his coat in the rain. He thought of Anne's mother and her poor hands holding the cumbersome shot-gun. Was anyone of sufficient moral stature to call her action selfish? He thought of the minister and of what could be seen as his failure of will but which seemed in some ways to Hartmann more like an assertion of belief.

What is happening to me? he thought, as his mind swung suddenly back, for no reason he could see, to the conversation he had had with Antoine in the café about the piece of music that awakened feelings it was dangerous even to try to comprehend, because they aroused too much longing.

Then, like a series of extinct lights which are linked and illuminated by an electric current, the disjointed thoughts seemed suddenly to be connected by a terrible sadness which made him lean against the wall of the street and hold his face in his hands.

3

ANNE, LIKE MOST people, cared little about politics. She was aware that the Germans were once more a threat, but had read in the newspaper that they would find it impossible to breach the line of fortifications erected by M. Maginot. She was grateful that the new government had introduced the idea of paid holidays, but otherwise could see little to distinguish it from the other governments which had succeeded one another with such bewildering rapidity throughout her life. What did it matter who was in power when the same people seemed to be in each government anyway? She had a certain admiration for Marshal Pétain, the hero of Verdun, because he had been so warmly spoken of when she was a child, but had now done her best to forget about this since Hartmann had spoken so dismissively of him.

There were other, far more important things to be considered. The first of these was the visit Hartmann had proposed by telegram for that evening. As she swept the corridor between the kitchen and the back stairs of the hotel she wondered what he would have planned. She would not be free to go till ten o'clock, at which time Pierre had said that he would either shut the bar or take over the service himself. She had arranged to meet Hartmann in the rue des Ecoles at ten-fifteen rather than walk all the way back to her rooms. She wondered if she would have time to change before meeting him. He had once expressed a liking for her waitress's skirt, but she couldn't be sure if he was sincere or merely being polite.

Since she had told him the story of her childhood Anne had felt an increasing sense of relief. She had, at first, been frightened that he wouldn't want to know her any more; but as every day passed and he showed none of the cruelty or revulsion she had found in others, her trust in him grew.

To the people who had written anonymous letters to her mother and thrown stones at her, she had seemed tarnished; but his attitude seemed unchanged, except for the increase in concern he showed when he reassured her of his feelings.

As her trust in him grew firmer, the frustration of being separated from him became correspondingly more acute. She wanted him to hold her and put his arms around her in a way that would take the world away from her, and would deliver her into his orbit of strength and security where the loneliness and pain and deceit which had made up so much of her life could no longer touch her. In the meantime she could only wait.

Hartmann was glad to be back at the Manor after what he had heard and felt in Paris. After greeting Christine, he went for a walk by the lake, breathing in the salty air that blew from the headland. It was Saturday afternoon, and the pleasure of being home again was increased by the prospect of seeing Anne in the evening. He thought of her slight figure with its hint of undisclosed fullness, the light-filled eyes and gentle girlish trust. This picture alone was not enough to obliterate the memory of the anxious forebodings he had felt in Paris, though it seemed, temporarily at least, to soothe them.

On his return to the house he went to find Christine and discovered her in the morning-room, looking over some household accounts.

'How's the building going?' he asked.

'Going? I'd say it's gone. The man Roussel hasn't been here for three days, and you know how much the others do.'

'It looks as though we made a bad choice. Still, it hasn't been too expensive. And they've done most of it now.'

'Most of it!' Christine stood up and two specks of colour came into her cheeks. 'They've done about half the work and you've paid them the entire amount of money. It's no wonder that stupid little man hasn't been back.'

'I haven't paid all of it, my dear. There's still the completion payment to be made.'

'Yes, but you've paid them for all four stages of the work and they've only completed two!' Christine was angrier than Hartmann had expected. He couldn't see that it mattered so much if he had been hasty with the schedule of payments to the builder; the amount of money involved, if not negligible, was not large. He didn't see that Christine had other reasons for her anger.

'I'm sorry, my love. But these things are always happening. Roussel isn't a rich man. He has no capital, he was desperate for work, he – '

'He's an employer, he's a businessman. He should know better.'

'No, he isn't. He's a workman. These days it makes no difference if you have two other workmen with you on a day rate.'

'Then we shouldn't have employed him.'

'Obviously. But you said Marie-Thérèse recommended him and – '

'That reminds me,' said Christine, who knew when an argument was slipping away from her, 'Marie-Thérèse tells me your friend Mattlin has invited her and Albert to dinner. Rather strange, don't you think?'

'Why?'

'Does he give a great deal of dinner parties, your bachelor friend?'

'I haven't a clue. But why shouldn't he?'

'I just think it's odd, that's all,' said Christine.

'Perhaps,' said Hartmann. He was still too taken aback by the heat of Christine's response to the trifling matter of Roussel's payments to be bothered by speculation into Mattlin's continuous plotting.

'I'm sorry,' gasped Anne, as she opened the door of Hartmann's car, 'I couldn't get away. Mme Bouin insisted I polish all the tables in the dining-room before I left. And then I had to sweep the floor.'

'It doesn't matter.' Hartmann put the engine into gear and moved off up the rue des Ecoles.

'Where are we going?'

Hartmann knew of a café which stayed open late where they wouldn't be seen. Anne chattered on in her excitement, and it was not until they were nearly there that she realised she hadn't stopped talking since getting into the car.

She fell silent abruptly, ashamed of her girlishness. She said, 'I missed you.'

'I missed you too,' said Hartmann. 'But you wouldn't have liked it in Paris. It looked awful. Grey and dismal.'

'Even the Seine?'

'Especially the Seine.' He was thinking of Vaugirard.

The café had high-sided wooden stalls, so the people in each table were invisible to the others. A wireless was playing at the bar.

A waitress brought a candle and some drinks. They raised their glasses. Hartmann couldn't remember when Anne had looked as beautiful as this before, her eyes shining with excitement in the half-lit darkness.

'You're so pretty,' he said almost in disbelief.

Anne laughed. 'And what did you do? Did you see old friends? I wish I could have come.'

'I saw Antoine, who was the same as ever, acting the cynic but thoroughly enjoying the exercise of power. And I saw the editor of the newspaper I used to advise.'

'Was that fun?'

'It was difficult. I was trying to stop him from printing something, but I didn't know how much he knew. I had to find out without giving away how much we in our turn knew.'

'And did you succeed?'

'For the time being.'

'So you'll be all right? They won't print the story?'

'We *may* be all right. It's better than I thought in that respect. But then again they may find the people involved or they may simply invent them. They may even bribe people to testify. That's what *Gringoire* is doing with the Salengro case. Claiming to have witnesses to something that never happened.'

'How awful! And will this editor do that?'

Hartmann stroked his chin as he weighed the possibility. Anne glanced at his hands. 'On balance, I think perhaps not. But I wouldn't bet a sou on it.'

'And then did you go out with your friend in the evening?'

'No. Antoine had to go to a dinner at the Treasury. I went for a long walk and ended up going to the pictures.'

'What did you see?'

'It was called *La Belle Equipe*. About some people who win a lottery and – '

'I know. Mathilde and I have seen that.'

'Did you like it?'

'I didn't like it at the end. I didn't see why it had to be so sad.'

'But there were lovely things in it, weren't there?'

'Oh yes.' Anne paused for a moment. 'And then what did you do?'

'I went back to the hotel and went to bed. I was tired.'

Anne wanted to find out if he had seen another woman but didn't dare ask him directly. She looked down at the table.

'And what have you been doing?' he asked.

'Oh, the usual things. I went to the pictures one evening with Mathilde. I've listened to my gramophone. I've read some more books.'

Hartmann liked listening to Anne talk, and kept asking her questions just for the pleasure of hearing her voice, indignant or excited, as she told him about her day.

Eventually he called for the bill and drove her back to her rooms. He didn't try to pretend that he should not come in with her. Once in her sitting-room, neither of them could finish the unwanted coffee Anne felt she should offer for decency's sake. They put down the cups and fell on each other, she moaning endearments to him which saved her from the embarrassment of her physical passion.

Afterwards Hartmann looked down at Anne, who lay with her head on his chest. He hated it now when he had to leave her; he hated it in fact even if Anne left the room for some reason, feeling agitated until her return. Yet he was not satisfied with what he felt. When he stroked her hair he tried once more to force his imagination to help his failed understanding of her life. Because the effort always came to nothing, it left him with a sense of anguish that had no proper outlet. It blended with the tenderness he felt for her, but it was not the same feeling.

Anne turned her head so that she was looking up at him.

'Don't frown so much,' she said, running her forefinger down the furrowed skin between his eyes.

When Hartmann left her rooms that night Anne discovered the cat sitting in the courtyard. After she had heard the street door close, she took the animal upstairs in her arms and lay down on the bed. 'What am I going to do, Zozo?' she said. 'What am I going to do?'

4

THE ONSET OF autumn brought even fewer visitors than usual to the Lion d'Or. Mme Bouin marched along the corridors with her bunch of keys to check that the bolsters were neatly in place on the beds, that the old linen sheets were clean and newly starched, and that the shutters were properly secured against the westerly winds that rattled them. Thus the rooms hibernated in a state of unused readiness through the winter months, while draughts began to sigh in the passageways.

Anne was briefly entrusted with Mme Bouin's key and despatched to the linen store to fetch further blankets for the half dozen rooms that were being used. There was a pungent smell of mice and mothballs in the warm wooden darkness of the cupboard. She pulled out a handful of bed-covers and found that the slats on which they rested were loose; two or three of them fell to the ground. One of them, she noticed as she put it back, was cracked. She held up the blankets in the light of the corridor to see which were the most suitable for use. Most were threadbare and dull, but still usable. One, however, bore the imprint of what appeared to be a large boot. Anne replaced it in the linen store, wondering what visitor had been standing on his bed in his shoes. She went to the bathroom next door to wash off some of the old dust and dirt that had stuck to her as she groped in the darkness of the cupboard. She hadn't used the bath with its brown encrusted stain for months now, she thought, as she remembered her first night in the hotel when she had risked Mme Bouin's anger by doing so.

She carried the blankets back along the corridor, humming a tune to herself. She left them at the top of the stairs and went down to return the key to Mme Bouin.

The old woman looked up from the ledger in which she

was writing and took the key. 'How is Mlle Calmette?' she said.

'Very well, thank you, madame. I don't see her very often, but sometimes I go and have a cup of chocolate with her.'

'And do you like your lodgings?'

'Yes, thank you, madame.'

'Better than your room here, I dare say.'

'I liked my room here, too, madame. It was cosy, being up there on my own. I know most people would have had to share.'

Mme Bouin set down her steel-nibbed pen on the glass rest. 'I'm not sure you'd be quite so pleased with yourself if you knew what people were saying about you.'

Anne felt herself blushing. 'What? What things?'

Behind the thick lenses of the spectacles the old woman's eyes came as close as Anne had ever seen to smiling. 'I'm sure you don't need to have it spelled out.'

'But madame, I don't know what you mean. I've done nothing wrong.'

'I warned you when you took the rooms in the first place, didn't I? I told you it wouldn't look good. Now naturally I did everything I could to keep the good name of the hotel. But people will talk.'

'But what do they *say*?'

'Please don't be pert with me, mademoiselle.'

Anne had learned that there was little to be gained from arguing with Mme Bouin. In any case she had no wish to hear her fears confirmed. She looked down at her feet.

'Is there anything else, madame?'

'Not at the moment.'

Anne went to the kitchen and found Roland sitting at the table reading a magazine and running a finger over the pocked and greasy skin of his forehead.

'What are you reading?' she said.

'The Young Patriots' magazine.'

'Aren't they the people who support the Germans?'

'Don't be stupid. They just think we shouldn't fight them. They've got the right ideas. Better than this bunch of Communists we've got in power.'

194

'But they tried to overthrow the Republic, these people of yours. Those riots in Paris . . . I was there.'

'Good thing, too. The Republic's done nothing for people like me. Now it's a Jew as Prime Minister.'

'Why shouldn't we have a Jew?'

Roland laughed. 'Everyone knows about the Jews. They're not reliable. It's just money with them.'

'Get your nose out of that and do some work!' shouted Bruno, coming in from the back yard. 'Come on, you pus-ridden little wretch. What are you reading? Smut, I expect. That's all you think about isn't it?' He caught Roland a glancing blow on the head with the flat of his hand.

'No, it isn't, it's – '

'Go and unload the van. Now. And you, girl, go and help him. We've got a special menu tonight. A gastronomic menu.'

'Oh God,' said Roland.

'Quick!' Anne laughed, and grabbed his arm to pull him out of the way of Bruno's swinging boot as together they ran into the back yard.

She had grown to like Roland, for all his surly manner. He made her laugh when he imitated Bruno behind his back, and he was truly unafraid of Mme Bouin. He had fixed the seat on his bicycle for Anne to ride and had lent it to her several times. There were other little grudging acts of kindness he had performed, and once a small bunch of flowers had arrived for her unaccountably in the kitchen. Roland's snort of disdain when it was suggested he might know where they came from was not wholly convincing.

Roland for his part felt excluded from what mattered to him most. He feared that accidents of birth and nature meant that he would never make love to a girl as pretty as Anne and he felt constantly resentful of those whom pure luck, untouched by merit, had singled out to have such pleasures. He looked at the awful old women in Janvilliers and supposed that one day he would be married to a hag like that. Someone must have married them, he thought; someone must at one point have said yes even to the old crows in widow's black. He had an awful feeling that the someone had been an older version of himself. Perhaps the passage of time would take away the physical pain of frustrated lust that moved like a slow mist through his waking hours.

He looked at some of the men who brought attractive wives to the hotel and wondered what it must be like to have an object of such desire at your disposal. When the men went home they could sate themselves each night. What was more, their indulgence of their longing was sanctioned by society, which called their wives 'Madame', and even by the Church!

When Roland read accounts of young men gathering in small provincial towns and running riot in the name of patriotism and the old France he didn't feel that something sacred, the Republic, was under threat. He thought it sounded a better way of spending the evening than cleaning boots at the Hotel du Lion d'Or. Protecting some ideal was the privilege of those who profited from it, he thought, but for people like him whose wages had been reduced by previous governments, there was nothing to lose in responding to the rallying call of old soldiers and young men with whom he felt a vital sympathy.

He felt no fear when people talked of another war against the Germans because he felt no part of what his country had become. Until such a day, he watched Anne closely, dredging the depths of his memory to recall what he had seen on those precious evenings looking through the bathroom wall. He also spent time practising his imitation of Bruno, because he saw she liked it.

The next day Roussel made his first appearance at the Manor for a fortnight. Hartmann walked out to meet him in the driveway.

'Have you been ill?' Hartmann asked, as Roussel leant his bicycle against the side of the house.

'No, M. Hartmann. In the best of health, thank you,' said Roussel unconvincingly. 'My little girl, she's been bad, mind you. We've taken her to see the doctor.'

'Ah yes, the doctor. Everyone goes to see the doctor nowadays, don't they? And was he any help?'

'He's given her some medicine. She seems a little better.'

'Good. Now what about this work? I've been down into the cellar today, and it seems to me you're still a long way from being finished.'

'Oh no, not that far.'

Hartmann looked carefully at Roussel. He might have called the doctor for his daughter, but clearly it was he who needed help. He looked pale and vacant, yet also curiously relieved, as if he had taken some decision which was going to free him from responsibility.

Roussel began to wander over towards the lake, as if he were in a daze. He stopped and looked out across it, then put his hand on top of his head where the hair had thinned out.

'Oh yes, M. Hartmann.' He spoke more quietly than usual. 'We'll be finished one day.'

'But you know I've paid you all the money, don't you?'

'Oh yes. Oh yes. I know that.'

Roussel's face, which was expressionless at first, broke into a thin smile as he felt Hartmann's eyes on him.

'It seems to me you're never going to finish,' said Hartmann.

'It's all right, we'll finish.'

'Are you really sure? Don't just say that to please me.'

'We'll stay.' Roussel's voice was now almost a whisper.

'Did you have to move any beams or joists down there?'

'We just put some supports in where there was a load-bearing wall. It should make it stronger. There's not much left to do now. Just the floor and the wine racks.'

Roussel began to walk along towards the woods. 'It's a nice house, isn't it?' he said.

'Yes, I suppose it is,' said Hartmann walking beside him.

Roussel held out his hand. 'I think I'll go now, monsieur.'

Hartmann felt the passive hand in his and Roussel smiled at him. 'Thank you,' he said. 'I just wanted to say that. Thank you.'

Hartmann watched curiously as Roussel climbed on to his bicycle and pedalled with difficulty up the potholed drive. From the top of the drive, where it met the road, he heard the thin ringing of a bell.

*

197

The following Wednesday afternoon Anne was working in the kitchen. Christine was sitting next door in her small morning-room, embroidering with snappish movements of her fingers. She had said nothing to her husband, though she found the strain of silence increasing. The rasp of the broom from next door played on her nerves. She thought of the girl's hands that held it, and how they must have run through her husband's hair; how her fingers would have run down his back. Christine couldn't imagine how the woman had the cheek to come to the Manor and wash and scrub as if nothing had happened. It seemed an impertinence of a grotesque order. Hartmann, she noted, had gone off for the day to see a client; presumably he no longer had any need of their stolen moments together in his study or wherever it had been – not now they were lovers.

The rough-bristled broom rasped again over the stone-flagged kitchen.

Christine didn't know how to approach the servant girl without losing her own dignity. She vigorously disapproved of the new licence granted to workers by the Government, and hated the thought of meeting such people from the big towns on their holidays, but her own family was not of such grandeur that she was able to show to servants that sense of natural contempt and casual sympathy which she had noted in some of the aristocratic people she had met.

When Anne passed the door on her way to scrub the hall floor, Christine called out to her.

'Yes, madame?' said Anne, stopping in the doorway.

'Come in here a moment, would you? Put those things down outside.'

Anne left the pail of water and brushes by the door and wiped her hands on her apron before trying to tidy her hair and push back the long strands that had escaped from their combs on either side. She walked a little way into the room.

Christine had no idea what she was going to say. 'It's getting cold, isn't it?' she began, looking out of the window, where the sky was already colourless.

'Yes, madame.'

'I think it's going to be a hard winter. It gets very cold here, you know.'

'Yes, madame, I arrived here in February. I remember it was cold then.'

'Is it cold in the hotel? In your room?'

'I – no, it wasn't too bad. They'd left a lot of blankets on the bed.'

'So you'll be all right, now that the winter's coming on?'

'I think so.'

Christine admired the way the girl had moved away from her question without actually lying, merely by transposing it to the past. She seemed practised at evasion.

She put it to her more directly. 'Do you still have the same room as when you arrived?'

Anne felt a slow blush rising in her neck. Her heart began to judder and pound at the entrance to her throat. Christine saw her discomfort and noted without pleasure that even this seemed to make her prettier, more vital and more varied in her looks than she herself could ever be.

'No madame. I've moved. I have a room near the station.'

'*Do* you now?' said Christine. The plummeting sense of disappointment as the rumour proved to be true gave her the calmness she needed to appear detached. 'That's an unusual arrangement, isn't it? To have the staff not living on the premises?'

'Monsieur the Patron is very . . . understanding.'

'And how do you afford it? Surely my husband can't be paying you so much for what you do that you can afford to rent accommodation?'

Anne couldn't believe what she was hearing. From an afternoon of casual loneliness she had been thrown into something worse than she could have imagined. 'Your husband, madame?' she managed to say.

'Yes.'

'For what I do?'

'We're not in the habit of hiring servants and not paying them.'

'I see, I see, of course.' Anne fought to recover from her misunderstanding. 'But surely, madame, it is you who authorises the payments to the servants? And you must know that – '

'Yes, yes, of course,' said Christine, feeling the advantage slip away from her. 'But my husband is so ludicrous in the way he gives money to servants. Take that idiotic builder man, for instance.'

'Oh yes,' said Anne. 'I like M. Roussel.'

'We don't want to talk about *him*.'

'No, madame.'

There was a pause, and Anne shifted back a couple of steps towards the door. Christine looked up and caught her eye. She stayed quite still as she spoke. 'So how do you pay for these rooms in town?'

'I was left some money by . . .' Anne couldn't remember if it was supposed to be an aunt or a cousin ' . . . someone in my family. Not very much, but the income is just enough.'

Christine noticed that Anne had not resisted the change from 'room' to 'rooms' and felt a tug of despair as Marie-Thérèse's story seemed to be confirmed still further.

'And do you like it here in our town?'

'Yes, thank you, madame.'

'Have you found it easy to make friends?'

'I have one or two. Pierre, the head waiter at the hotel. And a girl called Mathilde. It isn't easy because I spend so much time working.'

'And you must have admirers? A pretty girl like you.' Christine found the words easier to say than she had expected.

'No, I . . . Not really, madame.' Anne looked at the floor.

Christine stood up and walked over to a table on which was a pile of books. She picked up an old photograph album that lay on top and walked over to a small sofa. She had had no plan of how she would proceed, but she felt that the album could be put to some use.

'Come and sit here, next to me,' she said, arranging herself among the cushions.

Anne looked down at her dress, which was dirty from the work she had done, and at her apron, which was splashed.

'I – '

200

'Come on. It doesn't matter if your dress is a bit dirty.'

Reluctantly Anne walked over and sat down where Christine indicated.

'What do you want, madame? I have so much work left to do before I go.'

'I won't keep you long. I just wanted to have a little chat.'

Christine opened the photograph album and placed it on the sofa between them.

'This book belonged to my husband's father,' she said. 'He was a very distinguished man. He was quite an influence on my husband, as you can imagine.'

Anne said nothing, but looked at the brown pictures in the book as Christine turned the pages. 'This is the Manor when his parents first moved in. You can see what a state it was in. But they soon restored it. Mind you, those were the days when servants and workmen knew their job.'

The pictures gave a history of the house from the time Hartmann's father had first bought it. Family, friends and visiting relations were shown in front of it. Anne hated looking at the photographs in this way. She would have liked to have them explained to her by Hartmann, not shown by Christine who overlaid them with a glaze of bitterness. There was a page or two which seemed to have intruded from an earlier time.

'This is Vienna . . . and this, I think, must be Rome.'

Anne looked away from the photographs, but Christine moved closer to her and opened the book wider, so that one half of it rested on Anne's thigh where she was obliged to steady it with her hand. Free for once of the irritating eczema, the skin was soft and clear. She could smell Christine's scent when her arm moved to turn the pages.

'And here is my husband. This must be just before he left to join the army. Look at it. Doesn't he look fine in his uniform? Go on, look at it.'

'Yes, madame.' Anne's voice was barely audible.

There were more pictures of him, and one of a party outside the house with long tables laid on the terrace and beneath the trees. It looked like a marriage or a first communion. Anne felt her body tighten from the longing she had to be free of the room.

'Ah, now look at these.' This time there seemed to be a genuine note of enthusiasm in Christine's voice. 'The Arctic swans.'

Anne looked down at a blurred picture of two large birds in flight and a clearer one of them standing by some water's edge.

'They're very rare, these birds,' said Christine. 'They come all the way from the Arctic during the winter to find somewhere warmer. These pictures were taken just here. Do you recognise the lake and the woods behind?'

'No.'

'Look carefully. There, you can just see the edge of the dyke. Look, there.' Christine's short finger with its brightly varnished nail pointed at the old photograph.

'Yes, I see.'

'Do you know how far it is from the Arctic to this lake here?'

'No, madame.'

'Nor do I. Not exactly. But it's a terrible journey. It takes them weeks, and many of them die on the way. They came here for three or four years, and then they stopped coming. They haven't been for ten years now. So my husband says.'

Anne tried to move away, but felt Christine's hand take her wrist.

'Do you know why they do it, these birds?'

Anne shook her head without speaking. She felt the older woman's grip tighten on her wrist.

'Because they have no choice. That's why.'

'Please let me go, madame, I – '

'Look at me!'

Anne raised her eyes to Christine's. 'Can you imagine what courage it must take?' she said.

'No. No, I can't.' Anne at last managed to wrench her arm from Christine's grip and ran from the room.

That night the wind began to blow from the Atlantic. Anne

heard a scratching at her window and found the cat, Zozo, trembling outside. She took him in, pretending that she was doing him a favour, but in fact glad of his company.

Hartmann had called in at the Lion d'Or on his way home and he and Anne had spoken in the guarded way they had now adopted in the vicinity of others. He left at ten o'clock and arrived back at the Manor to find Christine bolting the shutters in the lower rooms.

After greeting him she said, 'Neither of the workmen came today. I think Roussel must have stopped paying them.'

'I'm afraid so,' said Hartmann, sitting down and stretching out his legs against the fender in the sitting-room. He expected her to berate him further for placing too much trust in Roussel and had decided not to respond to her criticisms.

Christine prepared herself a tisane, and Hartmann drank some brandy.

She said, 'I had an interesting conversation with whatshername, the servant girl, today.'

'Anne. Did you?'

Hartmann's voice registered only faint interest.

'Yes, we talked about this and that. She seems a bright girl, really.'

'Yes, I think so.'

Hartmann found the deadpan response he had prepared for dealing with Christine's expected nagging about Roussel was useful too for this more delicate subject.

Christine placed her cup carefully on its saucer and folded her hands in her lap.

'Sometimes you wonder what girls like that expect from their lives, don't you?' she said.

'Do you?'

'I mean all she must want to do is find a nice husband, don't you think?'

'I imagine so, yes. She has no money – as far as I know. So she must want to settle down with someone who'll support her. And then she'll want children.'

'That's right. Children. Lots of children.' Christine paused. 'That class of person – sometimes I think they have too many, don't you?'

Hartmann shrugged, 'Oh, I don't know. We need the labour now, apart from anything else.'

He picked up a magazine from the table and thumbed through it as he sipped from his brandy glass.

Christine pursed her lips. 'The girl – Anne – she's good company for me, I think. It gets quite lonely out here sometimes.'

Hartmann laughed. 'Really, Christine. After all you've been saying about the peasantry and the lower classes and their idleness and their breeding habits . . .'

'But they're not all like that, Charles. I'm not a snob, you know.'

'No.'

'All I was saying is that sometimes it's nice for me to talk to someone during the day. It's all right for you with your work, but this house can be quite bleak.'

'I thought you liked it.'

'Oh, don't worry, I like it. I know how much it means to you and of course I can see that it's very nice here with the lake and everything . . .' She tailed off, allowing another pause to develop.

'Anyway,' she said, picking up her sewing, 'we had a nice little talk today. I showed her some photographs from your father's album.'

'What?'

'I showed her some photographs from your father's album.'

Hartmann put down the magazine. 'What on earth for?'

'Oh, I don't know, we were just having a chat about this and that. Then I came across the album and thought she might like to see what the house looked like in the old days.'

'But why?'

'You're not angry are you?'

'No, I just want to know why,' said Hartmann, taking his feet off the fender and swinging round to face her. 'Why did you show Anne those photographs?'

'I told you. We were just having a chat,' said Christine, toying with Hartmann's attention now that she had finally secured it.

He picked up his glass, trying to appear calm. It was difficult. 'Mme Monnier and Marie – you don't show them the photograph album, do you? You don't spend the afternoon going through your jewellery with Marie and asking Mme Monnier to come and have a look round the cellar with you.'

'Of course not, Charles. Poor old Mme Monnier! I don't think she could even manage the stairs, let alone – '

'You know what I mean.'

'Not really. Are you angry with me, Charles? Just for showing your father's pictures to a servant girl?'

Hartmann, who was trembling with an anger he couldn't explain, said, 'Yes, I am. You had no right to.'

'But she enjoyed it. You're the one who's always saying I'm too dismissive of the servants and I think you're right. She understood exactly what they were about.'

'But of course.'

'There was one of you in uniform, about to go off and fight.'

'You showed her that?' Hartmann stood up and walked to the window, still clutching the glass.

'Yes, and there was one of those swans from the Arctic. And lots of your parents.'

'Why do you have to be so cruel?' said Hartmann.

'Cruel?'

'Yes. You were taunting her, weren't you? Because she's what you so subtly call a "servant girl". You wanted to show her the things she couldn't have.'

'You mean the house?'

'Yes, the house. And the money and the parties. And the family and – God, if you ever thought what lives some people might have lived.'

He could hear himself becoming incoherent, and so tailed off. There was something in the way Christine had said 'your father's pictures' that implied an inadequacy in him. It had touched him on an area of weakness he hadn't known existed but which she, in some strange way, had guessed at. He felt guilty towards Christine as much as towards Anne, though for reasons which barely seemed his fault.

Christine's eyes were sparkling as if the sight of Hartmann's anger thrilled her.

'I've never seen you like this before. But really there was nothing wrong. It's the way we're supposed to be now. All equal, isn't that it?'

'You taunted her, Christine, you know it. You didn't show her those photographs because you wanted a companion.'

He had begun to shout and when Christine saw his hand tighten on the glass as if to crush it in his fist, she lost her nerve. Unable to confront him with his infidelity, she finished peevishly, 'What does it matter? She's just a waitress. She's strong and young enough to get over it.'

Hartmann banged the glass down on a table and left the room, slamming the door behind him. Christine leaned forward where she sat and held her face in her hands. She started to sob, thinking of the girl's pretty eyes and of her own dry womb.

That night they lay on opposite sides of the bed, separated by a vast expanse of linen and blankets. Christine had gone up early, her head aching with tears, and had curled herself into a small knot of self-pity. Hartmann had walked along by the lake for an hour or so, trying to calm himself. He was glad he had left the room when he did, before he had said anything he might have regretted.

He lay on his back, staring upwards into the darkness. He felt guilty towards Christine and for his part in her unhappiness. The reasons for it were clear enough, however, and it was a feeling which would pass. With Anne it was different. He felt it was the first time he had seriously confronted the nature of his own past life, let alone that of another person. He thought once more of the small girl running into the field, and his heart ached for her. His inability to comprehend fully either the emotion itself or what implications Anne's life might have for his understanding of greater patterns and meanings in the world made him clench the bedclothes in his fists as he screwed his eyes shut, trying to see backwards into darkness.

206

He knew Anne was robust – how else would she have survived? He knew she didn't view her own life in a sentimental or obsessive way. But a sense of his own weakness, buried for so long by the layers of acquired experience and sophistication, had been tapped at a low level by Anne's story, and now her pain ran through him as if it were his own.

5

IN THE MIDDLE of the night Hartmann was awoken by what sounded like a pistol shot. He sat up in bed.

'Did you hear that?' said Christine, taking his arm.

They listened for a few moments, but could hear only the wind coming in from the sea. Then there came a louder sound, more like a snapping oak tree than a pistol. Hartmann felt Christine's fingers tighten on his arm.

He craned his head forward. Both sounds seemed to have come from within the house, from the direction of the north tower.

'I'd better go and see,' he said.

As he leaned forward to lever himself out of bed he felt Christine's hand grip him again suddenly as a loud series of shots began to ring out, an odd staccato with no set pattern but with growing volume and spite.

'Charles, I'm frightened. What is it?'

Hartmann looked out of the window where the wind had blown back the shutter. The night clouds were charging over the woods beyond the lake. It was a typical gusty night on the headland. Then, slowly, the pattern of gun-shot sounds changed and became a single, continuous noise – a martyred groaning, as if the whole house were shifting and stirring, desperate to free itself from the elements that made it.

Christine began to cry. 'My God, Charles, what's happening?'

Hartmann sat where he was, fixed by fear and by a strange sense of guilt. The noise began to grow louder: he could feel the house begin to pulse and teem as if the earth were quaking beneath it.

Then the rumbling stopped and the natural quiet of the night began to re-emerge, until the wind was audible again outside the window. It resumed its low howl, interrupted only by a sporadic groan, as if in afterthought, from the tower.

Hartmann flung on his dressing-gown and went along the corridor in the direction of the noise. He looked in the bedrooms, turning on one light after another, illuminating the dusty jumble of possessions. There seemed to be nothing wrong. He retraced his steps and went on to the main landing in the middle of the house. Everything was in order as he descended the stairs. It was not until he was almost in the kitchen that he became aware of a smell that was both damp and powdery.

The room itself was wrecked. Part of the floor had fallen into the cellar below, leaving a gently smoking hole. The range, a vast antique system of ovens and boilers, had been torn away from the wall and half of it now lay in the cellar too. There had been a fall of plaster from the ceiling and this clouded the darkness that the electric light, another casualty of the event, could not illuminate.

Hartmann went outside. By the indifferent light of the moon he could see that it was only plaster which had been shaken from the ceiling of the kitchen; although the fall was heavy, the structure above looked unimpaired. The noise made by the range as it fell had made him fear that half the Manor had collapsed, but from outside, the building still looked massive and untroubled.

He went inside and telephoned Mattlin.

'It's a terrible imposition at this time of night, but it's possible that another part of the house could collapse and there's something we could do to stop it.'

He gave Christine a tisane and assured her there was nothing to worry about. There was some structural damage, he said, but nothing serious. He told the weeping maid, Marie, the same thing.

It was starting to grow light by the time Mattlin arrived, his eyes narrow and ringed with grey. He inspected the damage in silence, focussing a powerful torch on to the kitchen ceiling. Hartmann watched him swiftly weighing up the possibilities.

'Didn't you have any warning?' he said.

'Not really. Christine mentioned that she'd heard some strange noises and there were a few small cracks in the walls upstairs, but nothing more than you get in any old house. I suppose I should have paid more attention to what she said.'

Mattlin poked around amongst the rubble on the kitchen floor. He laughed. 'It must have made a hell of a noise!'

'I thought the whole place was falling down.'

'I'm just going to have a look at the back,' said Mattlin, disappearing with his torch.

Hartmann felt slightly irritated by Mattlin's attitude but also relieved. Not even Mattlin would be laughing at this hour if there were something seriously wrong.

'There's the root of the problem, of course,' said Mattlin when he reappeared, pointing at two supports which stuck up from the cellar. 'Your builder has put those in to strengthen the cellar but he's succeeded only in putting pressure on the rest of the structure.'

'So what's going to happen?'

'Nothing.'

'But if there's pressure on the whole house – '

'It can take it. That's why it was just the floor that fell in. These outer walls are very strong. They deflected the upward pressure. And that's why part of the ceiling collapsed.'

'And nothing else is going to happen?'

'I shouldn't think so. I'll get a structural engineer to come and have a look later today. But I shouldn't worry if I were you. It's just going to be a messy job to clear up. If you'd had an architect to supervise the builder it would never have happened in the first place.'

'I'd no idea he'd done anything so drastic. He said there was nothing structural to do and that he would just put in a couple of supports to give extra stability to the roof of the cellar.'

'Yes, but there are ways and ways of doing these things. For a start they need to go in straight, not at any old angle like these.' Mattlin smiled. 'But don't worry. Nothing else is going to happen. It's just a mess, that's all.'

Christine appeared in the doorway of the kitchen in her

nightdress and Hartmann noticed Mattlin's eyes instinctively run up and down her distraught figure.

'Nothing to worry about, Christine,' said Mattlin. 'Messy and noisy, but nothing serious.'

Hartmann wondered if there had been a woman in Mattlin's bed when he had telephoned. He certainly seemed anxious to be off.

'I'll get this man Conturier to come and have a look later,' he said as he moved towards his car.

Hartmann shook hands and watched him disappear. Christine returned to bed, her brief bout of tears having given way to what Hartmann viewed as a more healthy response of vigorous criticism of the standards of the average labourer.

Before going up to join her, he looked once more at the rubble in the kitchen and into the gaping cellar below.

At lunch-time the next day Christine received a telephone call from Marie-Thérèse who was in the state of nervous excitement which meant she had bad news to tell. It concerned Roussel, the builder. Little Jacqueline, the postman's daughter, had gone round that morning to deliver a parcel and discovered his house locked up. There was a note on the door addressed to the local doctor, to whom Roussel owed money. It appeared he had absconded, taking his wife and children with him, and leaving no indication of where he had gone. He had left in the middle of the night and no one had heard a sound. Marie-Thérèse said this showed he must have been planning it for weeks.

'What time did he leave?' said Christine.

'I don't know exactly, but in the middle of the night.'

'So he couldn't have heard about our house then?'

'What about it, dear?'

It was a good morning for Marie-Thérèse.

There was no shortage of conversation that night in the bar of the Lion d'Or, though there was a considerable lack of information. It was first understood that the whole of Hartmann's house had collapsed and that there were at least three dead. A man whose sister knew the maid was able to assure them that there had been no fatalities. It was, however, not unnaturally assumed that Roussel had absconded because of what had happened at the Manor.

Anne, who was behind the bar, listened as various opinions were put forward.

One theory was that Roussel had disappeared to escape the shame of having syphilis. 'It's everywhere, you know,' said the fisherman who introduced the idea. 'The country's riddled with it.'

At about ten o'clock Mattlin's curly head appeared round the door, and he joined the noisy discussion.

'It's really quite simple,' he said. 'The answer is money.'

'Money?'

'When the police look through his books they'll see that Roussel had gone broke. It's impossible for people like him to make a living these days – especially with this Government in power.'

'How do you know this about Roussel?' asked the fisherman, disappointed to hear his own theory supplanted by a more mundane explanation.

'I'm an architect. I deal with builders and surveyors. We know each other's business – informally, of course. If I'm to recommend a builder for a job I have to know what sort of shape he's in. We all know about each other.'

'And Roussel, he was in a mess, was he? I always thought he seemed a smart one, with his business cards and whatnot.'

'It doesn't matter how smart you are if you don't get paid,' said Mattlin. 'And if you've got a sick child, like Roussel had, as well as all those other hungry mouths – well, you can imagine.'

There was more muttering and shaking of heads around the bar as people tried to resurrect their own more lurid theories for Roussel's disappearance. But Mattlin was persuasive. 'Take the job he was working on at the end, at the Hartmanns' house.'

'The place that's fallen down?'

'That's right,' said Mattlin. 'There he was, working for

212

months with a complicated schedule of payments, forced to buy all the materials in advance. And Hartmann never paid him for them.'

'What, even when they were going into his house?'

'That's right. And he'd only paid him for a quarter of the work though Roussel had almost finished.'

'It's a bad business.'

'How do you know about all this?' said the fisherman.

'I've been called in as a consultant.'

'That's a bad thing, if it's true, M. Mattlin. A man should pay what he owes. Especially a well-off man like M. Hartmann.'

'He's always been like that,' said Mattlin, ordering another drink. 'It's the Jewish blood, you know.'

Anne passed him a glass and took the coin he proffered.

'I didn't know he was one of them,' said Collin, the local butcher. 'Old Mme Hartmann, we used to deliver to her for twenty years or more and I never knew.'

'It's on the other side,' said Mattlin. 'The father's.'

'Well,' said Collin, 'I remember she used to order up all sorts of pork and that for him, and I thought these Jews didn't eat pig.'

'Just because he didn't practise doesn't mean it wasn't in the blood,' said Mattlin.

'Jew or no Jew,' said the fisherman, 'it's a bad show when a man doesn't pay his debts. And now look what's happened.'

Mattlin lit a cigarette and pulled a loose shred of tobacco from his lower lip. 'You mustn't blame Hartmann alone,' he said. 'Roussel's business was in trouble before he started the work at the Manor.'

Anne had not seen Hartmann for five days, and the sound of his name brought him closer in her mind. She was sure he was unhappy. Whatever the truth about the damage to the Manor, she knew how much he loved the house and how upset he would be. She sensed a further sadness and struggle in him, something greater and more abstract than his worry about the building. When she pictured him now she saw him

213

in the guise of a boy, as in the photograph of him about to go to war, with the protective layers of manhood stripped away. Since she had first seen him at the tennis court she had imagined his boyhood and sometimes sensed its influence in his adult actions, but she had been too awed by him and too frightened of saying the wrong thing to let this more vulnerable side of him figure much in her picture. Since she had come to know him better, however, and since she had also seen photographs of his youth, the earlier period of his life seemed more real to her. Her love for him held some degree of understanding in addition to dependence.

Her shift behind the bar finished at eleven o'clock, and she prepared to walk back to her rooms in the rain. She recognised as she walked up the rue des Ecoles that her sense of Hartmann's needing her was in part a projection of her own wish to be with him. She battled with the feeling almost as far as the church, then could bear it no longer. She ran back down the glistening streets to the hotel and down the narrow alley at the side to the courtyard behind the kitchen. She let herself in and went to the small room off the scullery where she discovered Roland playing cards with a friend.

'Roland, I must borrow your bicycle,' she panted. 'Please. It's terribly important.'

'At this time of night? In this weather? You must be barmy.' Roland turned back to his cards.

'Please, Roland. It's desperately important. I'll do anything in return.'

'Anything?' Roland looked up, a slow smile spreading across his face.

'Anything.'

'What about doing all these boots for the morning, then?' he said, pointing to a pile in the corner.

'All right,' said Anne.

Roland seemed taken aback. 'And I'll want a kiss.'

'All right.'

He grabbed her round the waist and pressed his face against hers. She let him kiss her hard on the lips then pushed him away. He wiped his mouth.

'Where is it?' she said.

214

'Round the back. Against the wall in the corner.'

'Thank you. I'll do the boots when I get back.'

Roland smirked and took up his cards again while Anne ran out into the night.

There were no lights on the bicycle and once she was out of town it was hard to see where she was going, as the rain drove into her face. She knew that what she was doing was foolish, but she barely noticed the juddering of the seat or the rain seeping in through her clothes. By pedalling hard, she was just able to control her fear. She began to breathe heavily as she rode faster and faster along by the pine trees whose long dripping branches stretched downward over the road in damp theatrical despair.

At last she found herself at the end of the drive and swung the bicycle down it. Only then did she pause to think that Hartmann might have gone to bed, or that he might be with Christine. She muttered hasty prayers that he should be alone as she flung the bicycle into the bushes by the side of the drive and went cautiously forward on foot.

There was a narrow moon over the woods on the other side of the lake, and by its light she could see the clouds spitting and surging round it. She crept up to the corner of the south tower, her hand flat against the stone wall, then looked round to the front of the house where she could just make out the lamp swinging by the glass-panelled door. She trembled and took a step or two backwards. It was impossible, ridiculous, she told herself. But her nerve was strong, and she inched forward again round the corner of the house.

Through the shutters of the study on the ground floor she could see a light. She raised her hand and knocked gently. There was no sound from within and the light was not shadowed or changed as it would have been had someone moved in front of it. She knocked again, a little more loudly. This time she saw the light darken for a moment, and she knew that someone inside the room had moved. She knocked again. She heard a hand on the bar of the shutters and she pulled away ready to run if it should be Christine. She heard his voice. She whispered back.

'Go round to the scullery door.' He sounded shocked.

He let her in, and she flung herself against him, holding on to him, sobbing and laughing in relief.

'You're soaked,' he said. 'What on earth are you doing?'

'I — I,' she gasped, but he put his finger over her lips, saying, 'Ssh, we mustn't wake Christine. Let me get you a towel.'

'No!' She grabbed his arm as he moved away. 'Please, don't go.'

She looked up at him, holding his arm. 'I was in the bar tonight and they were all talking about Roussel.'

Hartmann nodded.

Anne said, 'And then they talked about what had happened here. I felt . . . I don't know.'

'Felt what?'

'I felt . . . I felt you needed me.'

'My dear girl.' He smiled and held her to him.

He made her some coffee and they sat on the bench in the corner of the scullery. At first she was worried about the damage to the house, but when Hartmann had reassured her that it was no more than a nuisance, she seemed satisfied. She thought so little of Mattlin that she didn't think it worth telling Hartmann what he had been saying in the bar. Hartmann talked to her, but Anne said nothing as she sipped from her cup, resting her body against him. She seemed to withdraw into a contented calm, and slowly a thin, remote smile spread across her face, as if she were transported. Gradually he spoke less and less. He assured her he was all right, and that she had no need to worry on his account. He told her he didn't mind her having come to the house, even though it had been an appalling risk. Then gradually he too fell silent.

'It was lucky I decided to do some work,' he said at last. 'Normally I would have gone to bed by this time.'

She nodded. He lifted a damp strand of hair from her forehead and kissed the skin where it had lain. She wrapped her arm across his chest, feeling the dry warmth of his shirt beneath her hand. She allowed her eyes to wander slowly round the room, dwelling on the arrangements that had been made to press the scullery into service in place of the kitchen.

For some minutes she imagined what she would have done with this room and the whole house if she had been mistress of it. She seemed disinclined to talk at all and when she had been there for half an hour or so Hartmann told her she must leave.

'I'd like you to stay,' he said. 'But you understand.'

'Yes,' she said. 'I don't mind now. Not now I've seen you and know you're all right. You did need me, didn't you?'

He looked at her big eyes fixed on him. 'Yes,' he said, 'yes, I think I did.'

Anne looked through the window where the rain still fell, and pouted in distaste. Hartmann laughed and went to find her something to keep out the wet.

When he had said goodbye, she retrieved Roland's bicycle from the bushes, and, with an old waterproof of Christine's on her shoulders and with the imprint of Hartmann's lips still on her own, set off for the town.

The rain had eased a little, and she rode more slowly on the way back. She deposited the bicycle in the back yard and prepared to fulfil her side of the bargain by polishing all the boots. It would take her an hour or more, but she felt it had been worth it.

It was past midnight, and there was only one light on in the hotel, on the second floor at the back, above the servants' quarters. Just as Anne was about to let herself in by the side entrance she saw a woman with long hair sitting down beneath the light, framed by the window. She was wearing a white, frilled night-gown, and began to brush the waist-length hair with long, even strokes. She was obviously looking into a mirror that wasn't visible from where Anne stood. The woman kept up the brushing for some time before carefully massaging her face with cream. Her fingers moved deftly down and outwards from beneath her eyes in a motion of pampering gentleness. Suddenly Anne saw something familiar in the colour of the long hair released from the prison of its bun, and she recognised with a pang that the woman was Mme Bouin.

*

217

With the shutters closed to the rainy night, Mme Bouin prepared for bed. She arranged her hair over her shoulders, the way she had done every night since, at the age of fourteen, she had first been considered old enough to grow it, and then made sure her door was locked. She folded back the bedclothes in a careful V-shape and placed the striped bolster in the cupboard. Then she knelt down to say her prayers, the knotting of her finger joints exaggerated by the intertwining of her hands.

Her prayers were mostly incantations, well-known phrases repeated for their solemnity and the sense of continuation they gave her. She believed in everything she said – the ever-present nature of sin, the need for vigilance, the death of Christ which had made redemption possible for all sinners, even for herself.

She liked to pray for not less than fifteen minutes, but as she grew older she permitted herself to steal occasional glances at the small clock which was positioned on her bedside table where she could see it by opening her stronger eye for just a moment. She remembered all those who had died and all the saints they had been named after; she prayed to the Virgin Mary and then allowed some of the staff of the hotel into her thoughts. She didn't consider them individually worth praying for, but she asked for a blessing on the place and on its work. Secretly she worried about the boy, Roland, and the girl, Anne. She thought they were too interested in the cinema which had recently opened, to say nothing of the other rumours that had reached her. She worried for the head waiter Pierre also, thinking that at his age he should be married. The Patron was an absolute authority to her who did not need either her prayers or her solicitude. She had been shocked when she heard Bruno laughing about him once, saying he was a coward.

When the hands of the clock signalled her release, Mme Bouin stood up and fetched her book from the dressing-table. It was a novel that one of the guests had left behind, and although she had opened it with trepidation she now found herself enjoying it. It was a frivolous story, but so far she had found no real harm in it.

After one chapter she laid it aside to prepare for sleep. She checked that her clothes were ready for the morning and that the alarm was set, then she went to the dressing-table and picked up a picture frame which held a photograph of her son. He had a long thin face and a somewhat vacant expression. He looked to be no more than fourteen or fifteen, but had in fact been eighteen when despatched to the front. She had had only one letter from him, posted from Verdun. Some months later she had received official notice of his death, but not until the end of the war did she learn how he had died, when the mother of another soldier wrote to her. The two boys had been friends and were found together in a wall of French dead where they had lain for twelve days before the bodies could be moved. He was, she learned, one of almost a million men who died in a mere ten-month siege, and she was only one more mother to be informed.

She lifted the photograph, touched the glass once with her hand, then turned off the light and climbed back into bed.

6

TWO NIGHTS LATER Hartmann went to visit Anne in her rooms. He parked his car near the station and set off on the short walk to the rue des Acacias. At the end of the street he saw a faintly familiar figure buying a newspaper. He was a short man in a thick coat and a black hat; his trousers finished two or three inches above his ankles. He was standing on the pavement, apparently unsure what to do next.

Hartmann went up to him. 'Monsieur?'

The other man looked at him. There was no recognition in his eyes.

'You don't remember me, do you, monsieur?'

The older man took off his hat and rubbed his bald head vigorously. 'I can't say I do.'

Hartmann said, 'The Lion d'Or, yes?'

'Yes, I know it.'

'But you're the Patron, are you not, monsieur?'

'Yes indeed. Yes, I am.'

Hartmann introduced himself.

'Good God, I do remember now. I remember your father. He used to come to the hotel. That was years ago. Before the war, I think.'

Hartmann smiled. 'You remember him?'

'Oh yes. Quite well.' The Patron frowned a little. 'Quite well.' He seemed less certain this time.

'I used to come in myself when I was young. Sometimes I had to run errands or pick things up from someone there. It was a good meeting point for us, you see – half way towards where we lived.'

'Absolutely. It's still a good meeting place for people.'

'That's how I recognised you,' said Hartmann. 'I remembered your face from when I was a boy.'

The Patron looked increasingly confused.

220

'But I never see you in the hotel now,' said Hartmann.

'Good God, no. That woman, she runs the place. I have my other – other interests.'

'Of course.'

Hartmann wasn't sure if he was embarrassing the Patron; perhaps he too was on his way to some illicit rendezvous. He tried once more to see if he remembered anything about Hartmann's father, but the old man looked perplexed and began clenching his newspaper.

'Here,' he said, thrusting it towards Hartmann. 'Did you see this?'

The headline read: SALENGRO CLEARED. The Chamber had debated the result of General Gamelin's court of honour inquiry and had cleared the minister of any suspicion of desertion by the margin of 427 votes to 103.

'That's excellent news,' said Hartmann.

'I suppose so. I don't follow half of what's happening, though. I don't know whose side I'm supposed to be on.'

'I know. It's confusing. Would you like to come and have a glass of beer with me? There's a café just nearby.'

'No. I mean, thank you, but I must get back. I don't go out much, you see. I just thought I'd try a little walk today, but I want to go back now.'

'Of course. One thing, monsieur. There's a waitress on your staff. She's called Anne. You let her go away for a few days. She was very pleased by it and I know she wanted to thank you.'

'Anne?'

'Yes, she hasn't been there long. She took over from a girl called Sophie.'

'I remember. She came and saw me in my study. I thought she wanted more money. That's what it's usually all about.'

'It was very kind of you to let her go.'

'I thought I had to! I thought it was the law nowadays.'

'But even so.'

'Hmm.' The Patron began to fiddle with his newspaper again. 'Probably get pregnant before the year's out. They usually do. Bring them in from the little villages, teach them to speak so they can be understood – not all that dialect –

221

and by the time they're able to do the job some local boy's seduced them.'

'Well. Let's hope for the best.'

'Absolutely. Now then . . .' He seemed to be searching for a name. 'Hartmann,' he said firmly. 'I must be off.'

'Of course, monsieur. Goodbye.'

They shook hands and the Patron shuffled off down the boulevard. Hartmann bought a paper, stuffed it in his pocket, and hurried on.

It had grown cold, and Zozo the cat no longer prowled the perimeter wall but lay curled beneath the gas-ring in the recess of the stairs. Hartmann's breath left cumbersome trails on the frosty air as he crossed the courtyard. He knew as if by telepathy exactly the effect that the sound of his footsteps was producing in the waiting girl.

While Anne went next door to return some sewing things she had borrowed from Mlle Calmette, he glanced around the little sitting-room which was full of objects whose provenance Anne had at one time or another explained to him. On the mantelpiece was a china figure that Louvet had given her for her sixteenth birthday. On a low shelf by the fireside was a pallid doll which was all that remained of her rustic childhood. He had seen in her bedroom the photograph of her mother. The view of Parisian roofs, painted in a shaky watercolour, had been bought, she had told him, from savings she had made from working at her first job in Paris when she and Louvet lived in Vaugirard. On her dressing-table was a china box that had belonged to her mother, in which Anne kept pins and slides. She made coffee in an enamel pot given to her by Delphine, her fellow-waitress at Montparnasse, when she left Paris. On a table by itself, proudly displayed, was the gramophone, with half a dozen heavy black records in brown paper sleeves beside it.

Each object was charged with meaning; their combined significance made up her life. He thought of the profusion of his unknown possessions in the Manor: their number and anonymity gave him refuge, but these few things, each with its treasured reference, laid Anne naked.

She returned, flushed and smiling. Hartmann took a half

222

bottle of brandy from his coat pocket and poured two glasses. There was a silent tension between them, as if each expected the other to move first.

She gazed at him, looking into the eyes beneath their black brows, focussing on the narrow gleam of light that shone there. He looked back at her, seeing her own eyes glowing against the pale white of her skin, the handful of freckles visible beneath them.

After a moment Anne went to her bedroom and took a small box from the top drawer of the dressing-table.

'Charles,' she said, returning to the sitting-room, 'I've got a present for you.'

'For me? Why?'

'It's just something I saw,' she lied. 'Something I thought you'd like.'

'You're wicked, Anne. You shouldn't be buying me presents. I'm not at all pleased.'

She laughed; he showed no sign of displeasure.

Carefully he opened the box. Inside was a pair of oval gold cuff-links joined with narrow chains.

'But Anne . . . this is ridiculous. These are beautiful. You .can't – you shouldn't . . .' She laughed again. 'How on earth did you manage it?'

'Never mind about that. Do you like them?'

'Of course I do. They're the nicest pair I've ever had, but I just hate to think how – '

'Please don't worry about that. Put them on if you want. I wasn't sure what shape you liked,' she added, which was untrue, since she had taken careful note of all the cuff-links he had worn over the past month.

Hartmann fitted them to his sleeves as Anne watched excitedly. She had saved the money she had made working at the Hartmanns' and had also borrowed some from Pierre. She had done some sewing for Mlle Calmette, who took in a small amount of work to augment her income, and although it had meant sitting up late into the night it all seemed worth it now as she saw Hartmann pull back his jacket sleeve and insert the links with his long, articulated fingers, twisting his wrists so the flat palm of his hand became visible as he fitted them into place.

Anne couldn't quite understand his response. He seemed pleased, as she had hoped, but also troubled. She had told him not to worry about the expense, yet, unusually for him, he looked embarrassed. There must be some other reason, though she couldn't think what it might be. When he took her in his arms he squeezed her so tightly it felt as if he were struggling with some feeling in himself and were using the physical exertion to control it. Then she felt his hand lift up her chin, and when he looked into her face his body relaxed. He smiled and kissed her gently.

Four days after the visit of the surveyor, Hartmann rose early to read some papers. He asked Marie to make some tea and take it up to Christine in bed. It was seven o'clock and barely light outside, with a sleety drizzle coming in off the lake. As he looked through the glass panels of the front door a boy on a bicycle appeared and shoved a newspaper through the letter-box. Hartmann picked it up, tucked it under his arm and made off through the dining-room towards his study. As he did so, his eye was caught by three letters: SAL. He stopped and opened the newspaper to find the headline: 'Salengro Found Dead.'

The opening paragraphs were written, or rewritten, in the style favoured by editors seeking to impart a sense of urgency.

> Roger Salengro, Minister of the Interior, was found dead in his apartment in Lille yesterday. Police were called to the house after neighbours reported a smell of gas. M. Salengro was found in the kitchen.
>
> The apartment, in which M. Salengro lived alone since the death of his wife last year, was unheated. A cold supper left by his maid the night before had not been touched.
>
> Four days ago M. Salengro was given an overwhelming vote of confidence in the Chamber after allegations in certain parts of the press that he had deserted during the war.
>
> Jean Zay, a cabinet colleague, commented last night: 'He was a sweet, timid and extremely sensitive man.'

He is said to have been depressed by the death of his wife and upset by allegations made against him in the press. Police do not suspect foul play.

Since their argument over whether Christine should have shown the photographs to Anne, relations between Hartmann and Christine had been tense, but Christine felt that her long period of waiting was nearly over. It had taken courage to control her natural urge to confront Hartmann with his infidelity, but she was glad that she had managed it, because she sensed that the struggle in him was reaching a climax. It was beginning to turn out just as she hoped: Hartmann was growing entangled in the coils of his own conscience, without any prompting from her.

Just before lunch Antoine telephoned from Paris to say that Salengro's death was being hailed by the right-wing press in Paris as a confession of guilt. They had kept a flame of hatred burning for Salengro since he had signed the government decree outlawing the fascist leagues in June, and now they felt they had their revenge.

When Hartmann told Christine of his conversation with Antoine, she said, 'You mustn't take it so personally, Charles. These things happen.'

'Apparently.'

Marie brought in some artichokes and a vinaigrette. Christine began to talk about Roussel and how badly he had let them down. While she spoke, she watched Hartmann closely. In all the time she had known him she had never seen him so listless. She kept up her chatter, but all the time with one eye on him. She waited till Marie had brought in the main course before she moved into the vacuum left by Hartmann's lack of spirit.

'Why were you so angry with me the other day, Charles, when I told you I'd shown those photographs to the girl — to Anne? Perhaps it was a little indiscreet, but I wouldn't have thought it mattered that much.'

'No. Perhaps it doesn't. I felt you'd taken advantage of her position to taunt her, but maybe I'm wrong.'

There was silence except for the sound of their cutlery on

the china and the remote ticking of the grandfather clock in the hall.

Christine braced herself. 'Charles, there isn't anything going on between you and that girl, is there?'

Hartmann stopped with a glass of wine half way to his lips, his eyes suddenly alive again. 'Going on?'

'Yes, it's just that . . .' To her mortification and surprise Christine found herself blushing. 'I heard rumours . . . I don't know how to say it . . .'

'Well, don't say it,' said Hartmann. 'Don't even allow yourself to think it.'

He looked down at the table and tore off a piece of bread, not noticing for a moment that Christine had begun to cry, the tears running over her round cheeks. Then he stood up and walked round the table to where she sat. He put an arm around her shoulders.

'I'm sorry,' he said. 'I haven't been myself lately. So much has been happening . . . so much strain. And I haven't been kind to you, Christine, I know that, and I'm ashamed.'

Christine took the hand that rested on her shoulder and stroked the long fingers.

'I have no excuses,' he said. 'I've neglected you and you've been very patient. Just give me a little more time. Just a week or two – '

'Two weeks?'

'All right, a week. Just seven days to get my thoughts straight.'

'Oh, Charles, I can't. Do you know what this uncertainty means to me?'

'I'm sorry, Christine. Sorrier than you can imagine. But just this tiny bit longer. Just seven days and everything will be fine, everything will be as it always has been. Can you wait that long?'

Christine nodded, biting her lip. It was unsatisfactory and left her anguish quite unaltered, but she sensed that her best chance still lay in waiting. Hartmann's sense of duty could then be relied on to force the issue to its conclusion; he was not the sort of man to ask for more time or try to escape from his commitment.

226

He left the room, and Christine, against all her normal practice, poured herself a glass of wine. Hartmann's eloquence had stopped him from having to make a confession, it was true, but she was glad he had said nothing that would have been hard for her to live with afterwards. She might yet emerge triumphant if she could find the courage necessary to keep her resolve stuck fast for just a few more days.

The damp bracken flattened out beneath Hartmann's feet as he strode through the woods. He scrambled down the brick wall of the dyke and out to the beach beyond, where the sea had retreated out of sight. In the pines on the headland a slow wind was gathering.

Hartmann felt his head throb and flare with different emotions, none of them of his own making. It was as if his mind had been opened up to other people and he had no way of shutting off their feelings as they pulsated in the empty space of his brain. He thought of the box full of letters he had come across in the attic and of the desires he had failed to read in them. He thought of Roussel, and the premonition he had felt, but failed to understand, as they stood surveying the Manor together. He thought of the slow anguish of Christine in the face of his impotence and the rumours that had reached her. Most of all he thought of Anne, and here his imagination stalled. He felt the passion of her love for him and he felt her anguish so surely that he thought it was his own.

He had taken apart his feeling for her bit by bit and told himself that he could see no wrong in it. He wanted only to be kind to her, to let her enjoy herself away from the drudgery of the hotel; there was nothing evil or base in his motive. Even when he admitted that he was only trying to justify his physical longing for her in neutral terms, still he could see no harm in it. There was something wrong, he had persuaded himself, in a society that could think of such generous feelings as unacceptable. Equally, he had thought, something was limited in his own understanding of the world when he could not find the grounds of argument on which to explain away the paradox of his good intention and the guilt he felt about it. He blamed his narrow intellect, his cramped imagination, and reassured himself that sooner or later these and other complications would be unravelled.

He kicked his feet in the sand. Above him a sea-gull squawked and bent slowly on the wind.

There was only his feeling for Anne with which he could comfort himself. There was no atom in him which did not wish for her happiness and release. But all this fine feeling was of no use when confronted by the simple paradox of her dilemma: she could not be properly loved until she had disclosed the full story of her life; but by choosing him, at that moment in his own life, as the recipient of her trust, she had set in motion a slow but inevitable rejection. Its pattern would duplicate in her the effects of that first abandonment which had so far shaped her existence, and thus ensure that evil would be triumphant, repeating itself as naturally as if by breeding.

Hartmann stopped walking and for a moment was able to shut off the thoughts that chased each other across his head. For a moment he could see these things clearly, in perspective, and he felt calmer; but no sooner had he repossessed himself than a switch seemed to be thrown and he became once more charged with emotion which seemed to belong to other people but which he experienced as his own.

7

THE WEATHER LIFTED a little, and by the following Wednesday when Anne again prepared herself for her weekly visit to the Manor the air had a dense chill and the clouds were high and static in a set grey sky.

At the hotel one of the chambermaids was off sick, and Anne had spent an hour cleaning bedrooms before returning to her normal kitchen routine. She had discovered a spare set of false teeth in the room used by the bullet-headed Marseillais, possessor of the explosive early-morning cough which caused the dust to tumble in the passageways.

'Your afternoon off, isn't it?' said Pierre, as the cutlery and glasses changed position soundlessly beneath the flutter of his hand. 'God bless M. Blum and his forty-hour week!'

Pierre was unable to pursue his remarks, but smiled at Anne as she was called to the kitchen by Bruno, who fixed her with his good eye and ordered her to begin work on preparing the potatoes.

'My God, what weather,' Bruno said, taking a large knife from the dangerous display on the wall and handing it to her. 'Who would want to live in this lifeless town?'

Anne began to work. 'Never mind,' went on Bruno, taking up his newspaper again from the table. 'We'll all be dead before long. If the Germans don't get us, we'll kill each other. Civil war, that's what it says here.' He pointed at an item in the paper.

Anne had grown to like the people at the Lion d'Or. She ignored most of Bruno's direst statements, and he didn't seem to mind. Pierre was always kind to her, and she had even come to see the good side of Roland. Because her life had been so dependent on it, the kindness of people she was thrown together with was important.

The kindness of Hartmann was something of a different

order, something which in her mind approached the miraculous. It still seemed wonderful to her that a man of his age and standing should have taken her side so passionately. He had understood what she felt more completely than anyone she had known. She didn't believe that he used her, or lied to her so that he could make love to her; she thought that his defence of her was more important to him than his physical love of her. Sometimes she saw his eyes look troubled when she told him some episode of her childhood. He looked as though two emotions were conflicting in him. She thought the battle was between his indignation and his recognition that he was powerless to change the past.

She found her own confidence growing. The misgivings and the shyness she had felt when he had first made love to her were less acute. She wished that he would visit her more often than once or twice a week. When she took off her clothes and saw his eyes on her she no longer rushed to hide; what had once seemed almost paternal in his embrace had shifted imperceptibly into being something desirable. It was not just that he took the world momentarily away; in their closer moments his dependability seemed also to banish the past.

Just after two o'clock she arrived at the Manor. She leaned her bicycle against the side of the house and went in through the scullery door. It was the maid's afternoon off, and Christine had deliberately absented herself, going to stay with her cousin Marie-Thérèse for two or three days. Anne took the cleaning things from their normal place and began to work. After half an hour or so the front door opened and Hartmann came into the hall, throwing his coat over one of the battered chairs that stood beside the piano.

Anne looked up from her work. 'Good afternoon, monsieur.'

'It's all right. My wife's away.'

He took her by the hand into the dining-room.

'The cuff-links,' he said, and lifted his hand.

'Yes. They look nice. What have you been doing?'

'Oh, working.' He moved about the room, trailing his hand along the marble tops. 'And you?'

'Me? You know what I do.'

He looked at her. A button on her shirt had come loose and he could see one or two of the dark freckles at the top of her chest. Her hair was caught at the point of tumbling and held back, not quite successfully, from her neck and face. The earlier flush was gone from her cheeks, which now were the colour of milk, though seeming paler against the black of her lashes and the deep brown of her eyes.

Hartmann turned away and rested his elbow on the mantelpiece. He caught his reflection in the looking-glass and at once turned back into the room, this time gazing towards the window.

He heard Anne's tread behind him and felt her lips against his ear.

'How long is Christine away?'

He swallowed, his throat constricted by desire. 'Three days.'

'And there's no one else here?'

He could feel the touch of her hair against his face and her breasts pressing against the crook of his arm. He shook his head.

'I want to . . .' she began, then stopped. She didn't know the right words. She wanted him to love her and make her life whole again, but how was she to say that?

She tried. 'If you like . . . you can . . .'

While she gave way to the justness of instinct, Hartmann fought against it with all the strength of will and intellect he had.

He felt her hand tugging gently at his sleeve and he turned at last to face her. 'Anne . . . oh, Anne.' With a moan, he lowered his face to her shoulder and kissed the skin at the base of her neck, inhaling the smell of her and feeling the softness of her hair trail across his cheek.

She clung to him, frightened by his response.

He pushed her away. 'No,' he said. 'Not now, not ever again.'

She looked at him, feeling a sudden panic. She hadn't meant to precipitate anything so final.

His voice shook. 'There's nothing I want more in the

world. Nothing at all. I don't mind not having children, I don't mind living forever with a woman I barely love, I don't mind if I die in the coming war – anything if I could continue to make love to you.'

'I . . . I don't understand.'

'I don't understand myself.' Hartmann placed both hands on top of his head, as if to hold it together. 'But I know one thing for certain – that if we were to continue it would cause more unhappiness. I believe that with all my heart, and that is my reason for saying no.'

Anne watched aghast.

'Good God, I must be mad,' he said, striding over to the window. 'But I know, I know.'

Even in her state of shock Anne saw clearly that Hartmann was on the verge of making some terrible decision. There was only a moment for her to plead her case, and she had had no rehearsal. All her life she felt she had suffered from the effects of something over which she had no control, but here, if only for a few seconds, she had the chance to influence her own destiny.

'How can you be sure?' she said. 'I wouldn't mind if you stayed here with Christine . . . I wouldn't ask for anything. It's just that I can't . . . I can't live my life any more without you.'

He turned around from the window and she threw herself towards him. As he took her in his arms she felt something neutral in his embrace as if it had become that of a protector, not a lover, and she realised with a rush that something she had thought a few moments before was imperishable was now lost.

'My darling girl,' he murmured, as he stroked her hair. He felt like a conductor of pain.

She pulled back from him. 'You mustn't leave me, you mustn't. You can't imagine how much . . . Oh God, how can I tell you what you've meant to me? You seemed so perfect in everything you did. And I was so frightened of making a fool of myself. You were the most perfect man I'd ever met. I thought you were flawless. So kind, so clever, so handsome. I – oh, but you must have *known* . . .'

'You're wrong. I'm none of those things. I've no illusions about myself and that's why I know you'd be better off without me.'

He sounded cold and disgusted with himself. Anne hated the deadness of his tone: it was as if there were some stranger within him. 'But you are, you are,' she said, looking up into his face. 'You're kind, the kindest person I've ever met. You're tolerant, and you don't care if people are servants or whatever. And you're so clever – well, I think so, I think you're brilliant. And everything you do is so right, so perfect.'

'Oh yes. Perfect.' Hartmann laughed. 'I'm sorry, Anne. Oh God, I'm so sorry.'

She saw that he was using self-disgust to harden his resolve and that in this mood he might reject her not just in that instant but for all time. The panic this instilled made her begin to sob. She fought against the tears, thinking she would less easily be able to explain if she were incoherent; but she was overcome.

'Oh God,' she wailed, 'this is worse than anything, worse than anything I've ever known.'

She began to tremble through the length of her body. 'I can't bear it,' she sobbed. 'I can't bear it happening again. No, oh God, *no!*'

Hartmann said nothing. She sat down at the table and laid her face on her arms. The words that came out were muffled, and punctuated by wails. Suddenly she swung round, pushing back the chair and collapsed to her knees. She clung to Hartmann's legs, speechless with sobbing.

He lifted her up and once more took her in his arms. She grew calmer for a moment and he said, 'I will think of you every day for the rest of my life.'

'I don't want you to . . .' she sobbed, '*think* of me. I want you to . . . *be* with – oh,' and the words died away in another convulsion.

Hartmann began to guide her out into the hall. When she looked up and thought she might never see these walls again, she imagined for a moment that she loved the house as much as she loved him.

She felt herself being propelled towards the door, and

screamed. 'You can't do this to me, you can't *do* this!' Her resolution faltered. 'You couldn't . . . Oh please, oh my darling, please . . .'

Hartmann's face was ugly with the effort of self-control. Anne hated the sight of it; she wanted that gentle humour back; she wanted back his strength which was to have redeemed her life.

He said, 'You must go.'

'*No!*' She began to scream again. 'I won't go. You're going to kill me, you're a murderer. Oh my darling, oh my love, don't make me, please, please . . .'

She was on her knees again. As he took her by the elbows to lift her to her feet she propelled herself once more into his arms.

He slapped her face hard and shouted at her. 'You must go at once. Go *now!*'

Stunned, she fell silent and stopped crying.

Hartmann shouted at her again. 'Get out of here at once. Go *now!*'

To her disbelief, Anne felt her fingers on the handle of the door, found that it turned under her pressure. She took a pace outside and then, struck by what she had done, stopped and looked back. She saw him. He was beautiful to her eyes, but she heard him shout again, and found that she had begun to walk away.

He turned and flung his arms around a wooden pillar in the hall, sobbing tearlessly.

8

THAT NIGHT ANNE was serving dinner at the Lion d'Or. She told herself, as she asked the diners, 'Have you chosen?', 'What would you like for dessert?' and all the other questions it was her job to put, that at least this was the last time she would be doing it. She would leave tomorrow. Moving on had worked before: it would work again.

After dinner she went to work for an hour in the bar, which was abnormally busy. The bad weather had kept ashore many of the fishermen from the coastal villages, and some of them had come into town. Anne gave them drinks and took their money with measured politeness, riding the lewd remarks, unaware of her surroundings. One fisherman offered her a drink and she accepted, even though it was strictly against the rules. What did it matter now, anyway? It seemed to have no effect on her, so she drank another, to the delight of the men at the bar.

Mattlin appeared at his usual time and elbowed his way through the press. He smiled at Anne in his abstracted way, suggesting he had better things he should be doing. Anne smiled back as she gave him his drink.

When her shift was ending, Mattlin asked her if she wanted to go with him for a drink. She didn't, but she was stunned by what had happened and befuddled by the three glasses of wine she had already had. It was kind of anyone to want her company, she thought; so she agreed. As she took her coat from a hook behind the bar she cast one last look around the room, at the earnest talkers and drinkers and the one or two foolhardy diners who had tackled Bruno's dish of the day at the far end of the room where the lamps gave a splashed effect on the brown wallpaper behind them.

Mattlin took her to a bar near the station, the same one she had been to with Hartmann after their weekend away.

He ordered a bottle of wine and a waitress lit the candle in their raised wooden stall where no one else could see them. Mattlin smoked and waved his hands around. Anne watched the shapes the glowing end of the cigarette made in the air. She was aware dimly that she was smiling in a vacant way and that Mattlin was becoming increasingly excited. He poured her more wine and she raised the glass again to her lips.

He grinned. 'You seem very relaxed tonight, Anne.'

'Oh yes, oh yes. Very relaxed.'

He spoke of a project he was working on and asked her about her work, but she answered only in the briefest sentences, still with the same dazed smile. He ordered another bottle of wine and she, to his delighted surprise, made no resistance when he filled her glass again. When he had taken her to a café or a bar before she had never drunk more than one glass.

He saw her put her head forward into her hands and took her by the wrist. 'Would you like to go now?' he said.

Anne nodded, and as she tried to extricate herself from the stall, she stumbled. Mattlin caught her arm and stopped her from falling.

'Shall I walk you home?'

She nodded, and he took her arm, guiding her along the back streets towards the church.

At the street door in the rue des Acacias, Anne fumbled for her key and Mattlin opened the lock for her. He guided her across the courtyard and to the narrow black door. He said, 'I'd better help you upstairs,' and she made no protest.

She said, 'I want to sleep', and moved over the polished wooden hallway towards the bedroom. Mattlin followed and took her in his arms. She wanted to cry, but no tears came, so she clung to him. He was someone; she was not alone.

He pressed his face into hers and parted her lips with his tongue. She pulled her head away, but she did not let go of his arms because she didn't want to be on her own.

He began to run his hands over her body, squeezing her breasts, then pushing her towards the bed. She was overtaken by a fatigue so complete that even her will to resist was affected.

Again she felt his tongue, huge and hard, sticking into the corners of her mouth, crushing her own fluttering and retreating tongue with its muscular probing. She felt his weight on top of her and his right shoulder jarred into her chin as he tore off his jacket. His breath seemed to blow hotly through her head; so close were his lips that his whisper sounded like a shout and when he began to tell her the things he was doing and what further things he intended to do, it sounded like a threat.

He lifted himself from her to kneel on the bed and fumble with the buttons on his trousers. The sight of this urgency filled her only with indifference. When she felt him inside her she was reminded for an instant of the night at Merlaut when she had experienced this frightening but wonderful sensation for the first time. Then she had felt transfixed and defenceless but also powerful and renewed. Now she felt, more than anything else, exhausted.

Although she heard Mattlin grunting with the effort of self-restraint, it didn't take him long to finish. He eased himself off her and felt in his abandoned jacket pocket for a cigarette. He lay back puffing the smoke to the ceiling.

'I hope that was all right,' he said.

Anne rolled over on her side and closed her eyes.

When he had finished his cigarette, he took her elbow and tried to rouse her. Anne, half-asleep, feigned deeper sleep. He spoke to her kindly and asked if he could fetch her anything. He sounded anxious when she didn't reply.

He stumbled about the room, picking up pieces of discarded clothing. When he was dressed again he leaned over the bed and listened to her breathing with his ear against her face. He kissed her on the forehead.

She heard his footsteps going down the stairs and echoing as he crossed the courtyard. Without undressing or opening her eyes, she pulled the covers over her.

9

EARLIER IN THE evening Christine had telephoned to say she would be back the next day. She and Marie-Thérèse had quarrelled, though Christine didn't sound too upset. Hartmann said he would tell Marie to prepare lunch for two.

He couldn't eat the dinner she had left him, but took a bottle of wine into his study where he tried to read. The sentences seemed to dance meaninglessly in front of his eyes, however many times he looked at them. He walked around the room and sorted out some papers into different files, but there was nothing really left to do. He had prepared all he needed for the insurance case arising from the negligence at the marsh reclamation works and none of the other cases he was working on needed attention. Marie came to ask him if there was anything else he wanted, and he told her she could go to bed.

He thought of driving into town for a drink at one of the small bars up by the station, but since he didn't want to talk to anyone it seemed pointless. Normally he liked being on his own, but on this occasion he found his thoughts exhausting company. For minutes at a time he was quite calm, and then it was as if a sluice had been opened and his mind was filled again with anguish. He didn't know if it was his own or someone else's.

At about eleven he turned off the lights downstairs and went up to bed. He fastened the shutters tight, shivering in the cold blast that drove in between the insubstantial flaps of wood. He climbed into the wide expanse of unwarmed bedclothes and closed his eyes in the darkness. He thought of the dawn at Merlaut when he sat beneath the apple tree before returning to find Anne's arm childishly reach out to him. When briefly he had been able to step aside from the sensuous delight of the evening's events his thoughts had turned to the book of essays, by Montaigne, that he had seen in Anne's rooms. At Merlaut he knew he had gone against one of Montaigne's precepts: I desist. Now by banishing Anne was he following more closely the philosopher's advice? He was desisting in a way; but too brutally and far too late.

After an hour or so he got out of bed and took his dressing-gown from the chair. The floorboards on the landing creaked comfortably beneath his bare feet, and as he descended the stairs he felt the risen banister smooth against his palm. Running his fingers through his hair in some automatic vanity he crossed the cold marble floor of the hall to the piano, on top of which he found a box of cigarettes and some matches. He began to smoke as he walked about the silent house, leaving a thin grey trail behind him. In the dining-room he found his feet lifted by the sprung parquet floor, and he thought of how his father used to sit at the head of the table on one of his rare visits home and of the cowed anxious looks his mother used to give him as she supervised the dinner.

He pulled back the shutters and sat in the window seat gazing out towards the lake. He placed the flat of his right hand against his forehead and leaned his elbow on the window sill. Twice, when Christine had been away, he had slept with Anne. In the course of the night he had been woken by her restlessness and had wondered if the past would ever leave her, even when she slept.

He had loved her then, he was certain, when he had put out his arm to still her troubled movements and willed a sense of peace into her heart. What strange connections in his mind had then corroded that pure feeling?

The energy that had driven him when he had first made love to her at Merlaut had been diverted. Instead of gusting, as it should have done, fitfully and playfully in his dealing with her, it had precipitated a long inward storm of compassion. His obsessed identification with her plight had prevented him from seeing her as someone opposite, discrete, and satisfactorily herself.

It was not through cruelty that he had turned her away, he thought now, as he tried to forgive himself for what he

239

had done, but through an excess of sympathy. The dark-eyed waitress he had longed for when she first stood beside him in the attic of his house, the lover whose name had erased the memory of all others when he whispered it in her ear – Anne, whose every action towards him had been illuminated by the gentlest trust and hope, had gone from his mind. In the slow rage of his imagination, he had subsumed her.

These thoughts were not all clear in Hartmann's mind. Often he saw only a man's hand slip itself around the butt of a revolver. He began to feel rage towards Anne's father. He too could have desisted. What consequences he had unleashed; what chain of despair and loneliness that would contaminate the lives of so many people for decades yet to come.

When Anne had come that day to the Manor and he had stroked her hair, he had felt as though the pain passed through his hand, as though he were a medium of some greater evil. When she had said, 'This is worse than anything I have ever known,' all his frantic imaginings had been confirmed; they were the words he had most dreaded to hear.

Hartmann clasped his hands tight on the window-ledge as he looked out into the darkness. He felt angry, and this anger was better than the aimless anguish he had felt before, but it depended on his being able to hold in his mind the picture of the murder and on his being sure that the consequences followed so surely on the events.

At other moments he felt that every action in the world was alone and complete in itself without reference to others, and then he was filled with a sorrow he could not bear.

Anne did not awake till noon the next day. She washed and changed her clothes and began to pack her suitcases, placing in them the picture of the Parisian roofs, the coffee pot, the doll, and throwing her clothes on top. The first train she could take was at three o'clock, and this would give her time to prepare for the journey. She wrote letters to Mlle Calmette, to Pierre and to her friend Mathilde, promising the last two she would write again from Paris. She had just enough money from her wages and from what she had earned by sewing for

Mlle Calmette to pay for lodgings for a day or two in Paris until she could find a job.

She tried to put the episode with Mattlin out of her mind. It troubled her that she had done the same thing with him as with Hartmann; that the most joyous thing to her could also be the most regrettable. Her sense of repulsion, however, was not as great as her sadness. Because she had no respect for Mattlin she determined not to waste her thoughts on him.

She bumped the heavy cases down the scrubbed stairs and out into the courtyard, then looked back for a moment at the window of her sitting-room, where she had sat and watched the sun on the old walls below. 'Goodbye, Zozo,' she called out to the empty space as she moved towards the street.

She hoped she would see no one she knew as she made her way along the back streets towards the station. Luckily it was cold, and such people as were out had their chins buried in their coats and their gaze on the pavements in front of them. Down a diagonal road Anne saw the sweep of the Place de la Victoire and she remembered that she had prom-ised the Patron to look at the war memorial and think about the men who had died. She glanced towards the station, where she could see the clock: twenty to three. She dragged her cases down into the square and went over to the obelisk with its large stone slab whose inscription bore witness to the town's unwilling sacrifice. What was it the Patron had said? That they would be only names for her? And so they were – sixty or so, with initials, some bizarre but mostly local, homely names with two or three sets of people with the same surname. She wondered what their families must have thought. She tried to put a face and a laugh to some of them, to imagine what they had been like to those who knew them, but it was impossible. At least their names remained; against the gore and squalor of their deaths there was this tiny counterweight of remembrance.

She bought her ticket and sat down in the station waiting-room. She had not been able to bring the gramophone with her because it was too much to carry; she might send for it later. Or perhaps, she thought, as she began unconsciously

241

to rub the swollen palm of her right hand against the rough waistband of her skirt, she might not.

Hartmann sat at the desk in his study. He had told Christine at lunchtime that Anne would not be returning, and she had tactfully concealed her elation beneath some neutral talk about replacing her.

Hartmann knew what Anne was doing. He knew that she would move swiftly to escape and start again, just as she had done before. He knew how hard she would be fighting in her mind. She was saying to herself that it had not been so very wonderful in any case; that most of her time had been taken up in frustration and in waiting. He could feel the energy of her mental processes and wished that she would drain him of his resources and use them too. He willed her to succeed, sitting with his hands folded staring straight ahead in his reverie.

He recalled the time he had first watched her in the bar at the hotel and how she used to swing her long black-stock-inged leg backwards and forwards as her shoe grazed the floor in time to an imaginary dance beat. And then the flush of colour in her cheeks, and those long-lashed eyes that had begun their slow undermining of his self-control. He remembered how he had wondered what her life might be like; and then how, some time after that night at Merlaut, he had stroked her hair as she lay troubled in her sleep and how he had tried to bring calm to her through the gentle touch of his fingers. Then he thought of the explosion of a revolver shot, echoing in a shocked silence underground, and the cry of a small girl running alone into a field.

He looked out of the window, across the lake, with his head in his hands. In his mind he saw a girl, sitting in a railway carriage with two heavy suitcases on the rack opposite her. He saw her hair, her face, her eyes and all her movements. He believed that now his long effort of imagination was over, that he knew truthfully what she was feeling, and so, when he lowered his hands from his face, he found at last that tears were streaming from his eyes.

10

ANNE WATCHED FROM the window as the train chugged
through the pallid countryside towards Paris, blowing clouds
of smoke into the November afternoon. She thought of the
landscape of her childhood and the wooded slopes around
the house where she was born. They seemed as alien to her
now as these anonymous fields through which she passed.
Since she felt she belonged to no part of it, she could make
no sense of this material world, whether it was in the shape
of natural phenomena, like woods and rivers, or in the guise
of man-made things like houses, furniture and glass. Without
the greeting of personal affection or association they were
no more than collections of arbitrarily linked atoms that
wriggled and chased each other into shapes that men had
named. Although Anne didn't phrase her thoughts in such
words, she felt her separation from the world. The fact that
many of the patterns formed by random matter seemed quite
beautiful made no difference; try as she might, she could
dredge no meaning from the fertile hedgerows, no comfort
from the pointless loveliness of the swelling woods and hills.

She pictured her arrival in Paris. It would be crucial to find
work, since she had only enough money to last for three or
four days. If Delphine still worked in the old café near the
Gare Montparnasse then perhaps she would be able to help.

Anne still had no doubt that somehow she would find
either the resilience or the release from feeling and pain that
would be necessary for her to endure what was going through
her mind. After all, she had had to confront the loss of
everything she most valued once before, and in a far more
hurtful way than this. There was no reason why this time
she should not succeed again. If the pain became intolerable
then presumably her body would allow her to lose conscious-
ness. Only her body showed no signs of doing so.

She began to cry. There was no one else in the carriage to see the tears that dripped onto the front of her dress or to hear the sobbing that soon accompanied them. After a time she lay down on the floor of the compartment, the better to clasp herself in comfort. Then all thoughts of how she might survive were lost, because she had no time for anything other than trying to breathe. The sounds of her sobbing eventually frightened her, so she hoisted herself back onto the seat. Now perhaps time would start to help, she thought. But time only brought the train juddering exactly on schedule into the Gare Montparnasse: the required number of hours and minutes had passed. Anne took her cases from the rack and went out into the street. She walked to the house in which she had once had a room, and left the heavy cases in the hall.

Free from their weight at last, she began to walk round the streets, not knowing where she went. Night had fallen and she tried to find somewhere to stay. After an hour or so she found a small hotel in the Pigalle district run by a man with a yellowish skin and a thin moustache. He showed her a room with greasy curtains and a narrow bed for which he asked what seemed to her an appalling price. Too tired to argue, she paid it and lay down dazed on the bed.

That night she had no dreams at all, though she was troubled by a series of waking images. The landscape of her youth took on a greater significance than it can really have had; and against it appeared half-remembered buildings, places of authority and fear that seem to link and merge. Dead people lived, and there was a chance of having her life over again, making this time different choices; there was an odd certainty that just out of reach existed a way of explaining all these inconsistencies – the ache of love gone and opportunities missed, the contradictory landscapes and disconnected palaces.

The next morning Anne thought for the first time that she knew where this place was to be found.

First she went to seek Delphine, but the café proprietor said she had vanished some weeks ago leaving no address. Anne nodded and stepped out again into the street, knowing that now she was quite alone.

For three days she walked round Paris, sleeping two nights in a park after her money had run out. In every bar she saw a telephone and she thought of the instrument standing on the hall table in the Manor. Hartmann had shouted at her to go away; he wouldn't want to hear from her now.

He had never told her the address of his flat, but she knew it was in the seventh arrondissement near where the rue de Sèvres met the rue de Babylone. She walked towards it from the river.

Now she was tired and her body was weak through lack of food. When defeat first creeps into the mind it is not at all unwelcome. There is a strange pleasure in giving up, and although Anne instinctively resisted it she was aware of its sweetness, just as a runner is not really ashamed but pleased when he hangs his head and rests.

She trailed her hand along the sides of the big grey buildings, marvelling at their inconsequence. This she scarcely minded; but more difficult for her to bear was the fact that she could see in human beings nothing more than she saw in the physical world. There was no reason and no trust in them. If houses were wild atoms tamed by man, then people themselves were just unbiddable, skin and flesh and hair — spirals of random matter.

And yet there had once seemed a reason and a meaning, when she had played with her father in the fields, and once again when she had stood on the floor of the granary in Merlaut looking into Hartmann's wise and comforting eyes.

In the rue de Babylone she gazed up at a large grey block with wrought iron balconies and wondered if that was where he had lived, if it was there within the mirrored walls that the suppers after the opera had been taken with laughing and drinking. She looked away back to the pavement and realised that she no longer cared.

As she walked slowly down the street, her trailing hand encountered iron railings and she stopped to peer through them. On the other side was a large, well-ordered garden. What held her attention was not its size or splendour or the neatness of the tended paths, but a solitary apple tree. Something low in her memory was stirred by it. She thought of the tree at the foot of the garden at Merlaut. She wanted to touch its bark and lie beneath its branches; there again she might find peace. She climbed the gate in a side street, feverish with fatigue and desperation. She tore her dress and the skin on her hands, but noticed nothing in her desire to be by the tree. The sound of her landing on the gravel path provoked a distant barking which was abruptly silenced. The street behind her was empty.

She went silently over the grass, pausing only when she stumbled on a pair of shears and a sturdy garden knife the careless gardener must have left out in the twilight. She slipped the knife into the pocket of her dress and lay down on the cool grass beneath the apple tree.

Courage, she heard that gruff and slightly tipsy voice telling her yet again; *it is the only thing that counts*. But what if courage does no good? What, she thought, if my life will never emerge by one final act of bravery on to a new and brighter course? What if all our lives are just a circle where at a certain point you cross an unseen trip-wire that sets spinning the same process again? One act of will, of self-restraint might break the circuit, but neither her father nor her mother had shown it.

Anne felt in her pocket for the knife. Yes, it did take courage. The blade was lifted. Her father's hand was holding it – just flesh and hair and veins and sinew in their determined course – but driven by evil into a blow repeated. Before she could say 'forgive', or 'me' or 'him', the knife descended; but this time it was her hand that held it, plunging it deep and viciously into the fleshy moss at the root of the tree.

She gasped at what she had done. It was not what she had intended. She began to mutter rapid and distracted prayers, then stopped on hearing her voice in the quietness of the garden. She stood up and rubbed the grass and twigs from her skirt. She was terrified by what she had done, or failed to do. To be alive was now truly to be alone.

She heard a dog barking from nearer the house, and this time it was not silenced. There was the sound of footsteps and a man's cry. Anne, startled from her reverie, flew across the grass towards the tall iron gates and began to tear and claw her way up them. A male voice shouted at her to stop and the sound of running footsteps came closer. In her panic and light-headedness she recognised no obstacle to freedom: as the security guard arrived at the gate to resume the position he should never have left, she was already dropping on to the other side. He reached through the bars of the gate and grabbed her arm, but she pulled herself away. As she ran down the street she heard him fumbling with the keys. The pavement rang with the sound of her slapping feet and she felt a strength fill her limbs as if she could have run across the whole of Paris, all the way south to the Cantal, over the mountains and down into Spain.

After a time she rested in a backstreet in the Latin quarter. There were enough unusual-looking people for the sight of one breathless and dishevelled girl to pass without comment. Two or three men even glanced at her admiringly as she panted in the doorway of a furniture shop. There was music coming from a café a few doors down, and she went to peer in through the window. A fat, friendly-looking man with a beard cleared a space on the steaming pane with his hand and gestured her in. She shook her head and smiled, but he came out and took her arm firmly. He bought her some soup and an omelette and gave her two glasses of wine from the bottle on his table. He asked if she had run away from home. She shook her head, her mouth too full to allow her to speak. He watched her as she ate and when he found he could prise no information from her began to tell her instead about a scheme he had for a new kind of motor car.

Anne nodded and smiled at his story. When she had finished eating, the man, who introduced himself as Georges, gave her some money so she could take a taxi to the house near the Gare Montparnasse where she had left her suitcases. She told him she had friends there; he looked at her sceptically, but pressed more coins into her hand. He made her promise to meet him in the same café the following evening. Anne thanked him and shook his hand.

When the taxi had dropped her off she found she still had

a little money left. She showed it to the landlady of the house who took her upstairs to a box-room which, she said, was all the money would buy. Anne unpacked some clothes and stole along to the bathroom. When she had scrubbed the stains from around the rim she found to her amazement that the water was hot. Carefully bolting the door, she undressed and sank into the water. Clouds of grime floated from her legs with puffs of dried blood where she had scraped them on the railings.

Back in the bedroom she found that she was crying, tears that were not squeezed or choked from her but which ran in a hot profusion. In bed she hugged the bolster to herself and for the first time since she had been in Paris slept long and without dreaming.

The next day she looked in the newspapers and the shop windows for work. Twice she offered herself as a shop assistant only to find the position had already been taken. Vacancies were few, and the wages on offer even smaller than those she had been paid at the Lion d'Or.

Anne, however, didn't feel discouraged. She walked all morning, and although she had little idea of where she was going, she felt a lightness and vigour in her movements. Her wanderings eventually brought her to the Avenue Foch which she remembered was spoken of in hushed tones by Parisians. The people who lived there were so rich they didn't have to work; they drove to the seaside at weekends and had parties every evening. Feeling she might be arrested even for being there, Anne hurried across into the Avenue de la Grande Armée, a broad thoroughfare which began with a pompous flourish at the Arc de Triomphe but whose massive grey houses acquired an air of the suburban as the road trailed down towards Neuilly.

When she had walked a little way she saw a street called the rue des Acacias. At first she was angry that even in Paris there seemed to be no escape from the sadness of Janvilliers; but then she smiled as she walked slowly down it, past the tranquil open food shops with their displays of vegetables and shellfish, the stationers and huddled cafés. In the window of one she saw a sign advertising vacancies for bar staff. It was not what she wanted to do, but there could certainly be no question about her suitability or experience. Before she committed herself, she decided to walk once more up and down the narrow sloping street.

Through one of the ground-floor windows she saw a telephone, and she thought of the instrument that waited silently on the table in the hall at the Manor. She imagined Christine answering it. Then she imagined Hartmann doing so. It wasn't difficult to resist the temptation.

The unexpected sensation of being alive lent her a precarious self-confidence. She turned over her hand to feel the rain that was drifting in from the wide spaces of the Avenue de la Grande Armée. It didn't trouble her; and in the breeze that filtered down the street, blowing the rain beneath the awnings, causing the shoppers to hurry for the doorways, there was a lightness that could be taken for a blessing. She turned her face to it, the pale cheeks with their handful of freckles, the long-lashed eyes, and felt on her skin the touch of the world in its renewed strangeness.

She found herself once more at the door of the café that was advertising vacancies. Two small lines of determination ran diagonally from the corners of her mouth as she pushed at the door. A couple who were sitting at the window looked up without interest.

A wireless was playing loudly. Behind the bar a bald man wearing glasses sat with a proprietorial air, reading a newspaper.

Anne went and stood in front of him, playing with the handle of her bag.

The man continued reading. She coughed and shifted from foot to foot. At last he put down his paper and peeled the glasses from his nose.

He looked her up and down, appraising her from the dusty shoes to the expression of guarded hope in her eyes. 'Can I help?' he said.

Also available in Vintage

Sebastian Faulks

BIRDSONG

'A brilliant, harrowing tale of love and war'
Phil Hogan, *Observer*

'An amazing book - among the most stirringly erotic
I have read for years...I have read it and re-read it and
can think of no other novel for many, many years
that has so moved me or stimulated in me so much
reflection on the human spirit'
Quentin Crewe, *Daily Mail*

'This book is so powerful that as I finished it I turned
to the front to start again'
Andrew James, *Sunday Express*

'Devastating ... a considerable addition to the fin-de-
siècle flowering of first world war literature. Read it'
Penelope Lively, *Spectator*

'This is literature at its very best: a book with the
power to reveal the unimagined, so that one's life is
set in a changed context. I urge you to read it'
Nigel Watts, *Time Out*

VINTAGE

Sebastian Faulks

A FOOL'S ALPHABET

The events of Pietro Russell's life are told in 26 chapters. From A-Z each chapter is set in a different place and reveals a fragment of his story. As his memories flicker back and forth through time in his search for a resolution to the conflicts of his life, his story gradually unfolds.

'The uniqueness of this lovely heart-warming novel is the way it plays with the arbitrariness of significance whilst telling the story of an uprooted life lived as a journey towards love and belonging'
Observer

'Faulks has written an ambitious and beautifully crafted novel'
The Times

'Sebastian Faulks's third and most magnificent novel is a 'feel-good' experience from cover to cover'
Daily Mail

'He is the best novelist of his generation'
Allan Massie, *Scotsman*

VINTAGE